I0788710

THE KING'S CONJURER

THE HENCHMEN CHRONICLES

BOOK FOUR

CRAIG HALLORAN

The King's Conjurer

The Henchmen Chronicles Book #4

By Craig Halloran

Copyright © 2018 by Craig Halloran

Paperback Edition

TWO-TEN BOOK PRESS

PO Box 4215, Charleston, WV 25364

ISBN eBook: 978-1-946218-47-6

ISBN Paperback: 978-1-793081-40-7

www.craighalloran.com

Publisher's Note

This book is a work of fiction. Names, characters, places, and incidents either are the product of the author's imagination or are used fictitiously, and any resemblance to actual persons, living or dead, events, or locales is entirely coincidental.

❧ Created with Vellum

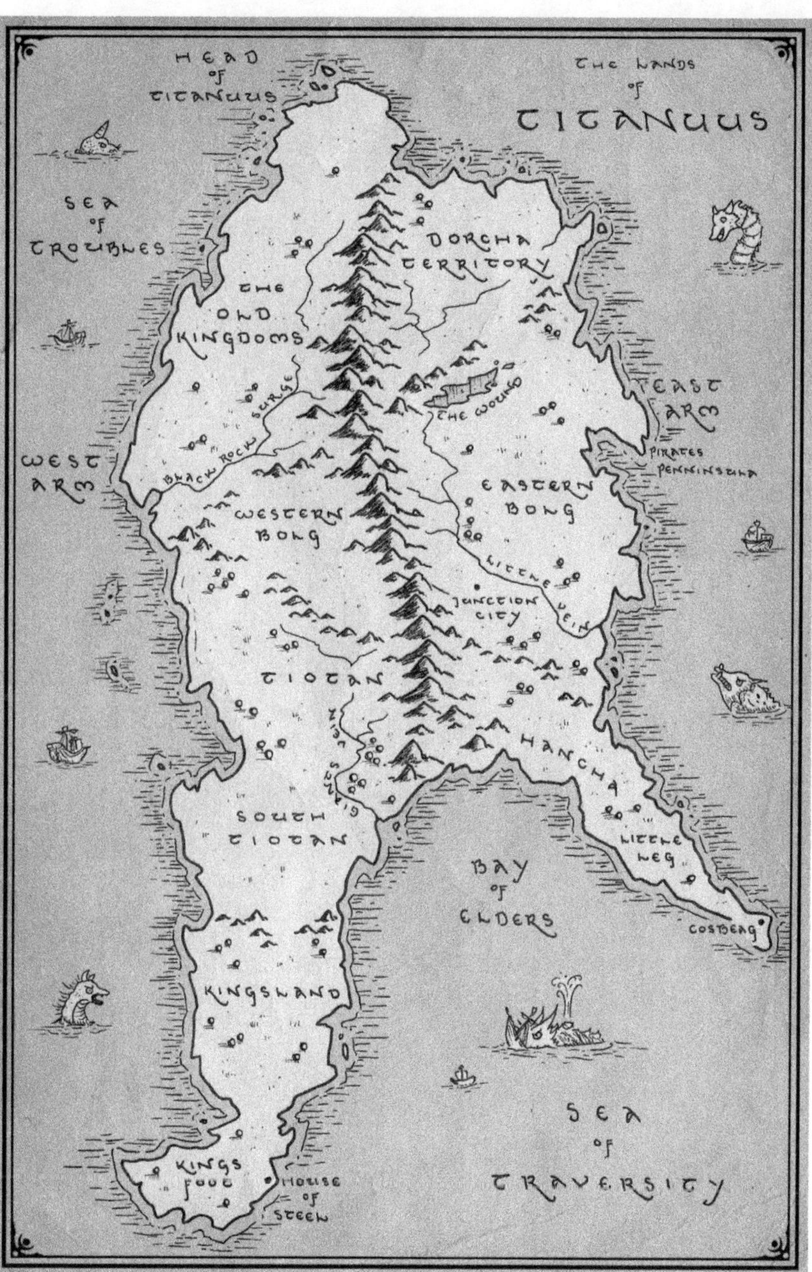

HEAD OF TITANUUS
THE LANDS OF TITANUUS
SEA OF TROUBLES
DORCHA TERRITORY
THE OLD KINGDOMS
SURGE
BLACK ROCK
THE WOUND
EAST ARM
PIRATES PENNINSULA
WEST ARM
WESTERN BOG
EASTERN BONG
LITTLE VEIN
JUNCTION CITY
TIOTAN
GIANTS VEIN
HANCHA
SOUTH TIOTAN
LITTLE LEG
BAY OF ELDERS
COSBEAG
KINGSLAND
KINGS FOOL
HOUSE OF STEEL
SEA OF TRAVERSITY

1

AT MIDDAY, THE SUN WAS SHINING BEHIND THE CLOUDS ON A BRISK day that kept the leaves rustling in the wind. He stood on the mound and dug his toe into the dirt. Ninety feet away, the smoky-eyed Tark stood over a flat piece of limestone that represented home plate. All the bases were made from slabs of limestone that formed an imperfect baseball diamond. He held the autographed baseball of Buddy Parker—his former teammate, now perished—behind his back. He ran his fingers over the red laces. He looked out from underneath the bill of his baseball cap.

"You aren't going to hit this," he said to Tark.

Tark held a club whittled down into a crude baseball bat. He wiggled it in the air, took a couple of test swings, and said, "We'll see about that. As you say, 'Bring the heat.'"

"Bring something," Horace said in a grumpy voice. The bearded big belly squatted behind home plate. He wore a full helmet and leather chest-plate armor. His beard spilled out from underneath his helmet and over his chest. He had a catcher's mitt too. His voice rang hollowly inside the helmet when he spoke. "I'm getting hungry. We've been at this silly game long enough."

Narrowing his eyes, the strapping athlete Tark said, "I like it."

Six more Henchmen were on the field. Vern, Bearclaw, and Dominga were in the outfield. Sticks stood on first base, Apollo manned second base, and Prospero stood over third. Shades played shortstop, between second and third base. All of them wore thick leather gloves, for Abraham had shown the picture of himself on a baseball card to a leather worker who in turn made the gloves.

"Now remember," he said, "three strikes, and you're out. Someone else will bat after that. We'll rotate you in the field."

"So all I have to do is hit that little white ball? And run around those bases. And I win?" Tark asked. He showed a big white smile. "This will be easy."

"One thing is for sure. It will be interesting," Solomon said. The towering troglin stood behind Horace in the umpire position. He looked at Abraham and said, "You better not hit me with a wild pitch."

"I won't. Besides, how bad could it hurt? You're a troglin."

"An old troglin." Solomon flipped up his thumbs and said, "Play ball!"

Abraham took a breath. His haphazard Field of Dreams was far from perfect, but it kept his mind off other things.

Standing in the fields at a distance were the rest of the Henchmen and his retainers. Iris the mystic was there, along with the young brothers, Skitts and Zann. The three dusky-skinned beauties, Sophia dressed in black, Selma wearing red, and Bridget draped in white, were present. They stood out like gorgeous flowers among the weeds.

Lewis, Leodor, and Clarice were not present. They'd been retained at the House of Steel by the order of King Hector. Abraham couldn't have been more relieved after the bombshell Queen Clarann had dropped on him: that Ruger was Clarice's father. He and the queen had talked briefly, but he made himself scarce after that. She hadn't called on him since.

"Are you going to throw that thing or not?" Horace shouted. "My knees are aching."

"All right. All right. Here it comes." Abraham wound up the pitch and let the ball fly.

The baseball slipped right underneath Tark's powerful swing. *Swish.* He spun around, off balance.

Solomon made the call, showing the strike signal. "Strike!"

Horace threw the ball back to Abraham.

He caught the ball in his homemade mitt and smiled. "You know, Solomon, I didn't take a hippie for a baseball fan."

"Hippies like baseball too. Heck, I played in Little League for years. The old man wanted me to even though I hated it—of course, every boy did it back then—not because I didn't like it. I just sucked at it. I was more fit for watching it on television." Solomon shrugged. "But I was pretty good at ping-pong."

Tark took his place back over the plate. "Let's try that again."

"My pleasure." Abraham looked over at Sticks, who was hovering over first base with her usual straight face. He couldn't tell whether she was bored or not. He winked at her and said, "Having fun?"

Sticks shrugged.

"I must say, this is far from stimulating," Shades said as he tossed his glove up and down in the air. "And I don't see the need for this leather gauntlet. It's a clumsy device."

"You'll understand soon enough." Abraham ground his feet into the mound. Ruger's body was the makeup of a perfect athlete. Generally speaking, the man could do it all. He could pitch too, but not like the real Abraham Jenkins. Abraham had a gift. It was how his shoulder, arm, hand, and fingers were made. Whenever he would wind up and throw, the ball would whistle out of his hand.

Only God could make an arm better. But at least Ruger was accurate.

He eyeballed Tark. *I'll take some heat off so he can get a good crack at it.* He wound up and threw the moderately fast pitch straight down the line.

Tark unleashed a mighty swing.

Crack!

The ball skipped across the dirt field right between first and second.

"Run!" Solomon yelled at Tark.

Tark sprinted toward first base.

"Drop the bat!" Solomon hollered.

Tark arrived at first base as fast as a jackrabbit with the baseball bat in hand. He handed it to Sticks. She chucked it aside.

"Keep running!" Solomon hollered.

"Will somebody get the ball?" Abraham yelled as the ball skipped toward right field, where Vern was standing. "Vern, get the ball!"

"You get it!" Vern said.

Tark rounded second base and sprinted toward third.

Cudgel ran over from center field and snatched up the ball, which came to a stop at a knee-high outfield wall made from large stones.

"Throw it home!" Abraham yelled. "Throw it home!"

"Where's home?" Cudgel shrugged.

"To Horace! Throw it to Hor—"

Cudgel chucked the baseball three hundred feet toward Horace, hovering over home plate.

Tark sped past third base toward home plate. Solomon kept waving him in.

Abraham watched the ball sail over his head. *Nice throw.*

The baseball dropped right into Horace's mitt.

"Tag him! You have to tag him!" Abraham shouted at Horace.

Horace tossed down his glove, and the ball rolled out of his mitt and across the dirt. He stepped in front of home plate and braced himself for Tark's charge. Horace tackled Tark and pinned him to the ground.

"I did it, Captain. I tackled him!" He nodded with excitement as he sat on Tark's back. "I like this game."

Tark stretched out his fingertips and touched home plate.

Solomon loomed over home plate, stretched out his arms, and swiped them through the air. "Safe!"

Abraham slapped his forehead and ran his fingers down his face. "Good grief."

2

––––––––

SINCE THE HENCHMEN HAD RETURNED TO KINGSLAND IN TRIUMPH from their invasion of Hancha, where they'd killed Arcayis, life had become somewhat normal. By King Hector's order, they weren't allowed to travel away from Kingsland but otherwise were given full liberty. For all intents and purposes, life had been normal for Abraham. Aside from creating a baseball field, he and the Henchmen managed the Stronghold and its fields and conducted training.

Several weeks passed without interruption from the House of Steel. Lewis and Leodor never showed up. Ruger's alleged daughter, Clarice, didn't show up either. He tried not to think about her or Queen Clarann. Whatever had happened between Ruger and the queen was their business. The last thing he wanted now was to be drawn into any sordid affairs.

Outside of the Stronghold, Ruger labored in the heat of the day, rebuilding the barn that had burned down, courtesy of Leodor. He was on the top pitch of the roof, hammering in shingles, with Prospero and Apollo helping him. Prospero hummed a cheery

tune that carried an Irish-sounding jingle while Apollo sang the
words:

> "Her name was Sherry, and she said we should marry.
> And I said, 'I'll have to ask my horse first.'
> She said to let me know what the horse says,
> And good luck finding her after that.
> 'I need a fit man that is smart as a beast
> And not a man that can't think for himself.'
> I chuckled and giggled, and I tickled her rump
> And said with delight, 'I'd rather marry a horse
> Than a stubborn old goat.'"

Abraham mopped his sweat from his brow with a navy-blue handkerchief as he laughed. "That's not half bad, Apollo. Has anyone
ever told you that you have a voice like Tom Petty?"

"No." Apollo clawed at his scraggly beard. He and Prospero, no
matter what time of day, always maintained their haggard and
older appearance. "Who is Tom Petty?"

"A famous bard back in my world. I think you'd like his music."

Apollo lined a nail over a shingle he put in place, and Prospero
drove it halfway in with a single hammer strike. He pulled his
fingers away and readied another shingle and nail. "Was this Petty
man a knight in your world?"

"No, nothing of the sort. Just an entertainer."

"They make a big deal about entertainers in your world."
Apollo tacked on another shingle.

Across the courtyard, Sophia and Selma were sitting within the
top window of his bedroom in the Stronghold, eyeballing him.

They used their slender hands to fan the sweat glistening on their necks. Abraham swallowed.

Prospero hit Apollo on the hand with his hammer.

"Ow!" Apollo rubbed his hand and said, "Pay attention to what you are doing and stop gawking. Those are the Captain's concubines. You should know better."

Prospero grunted.

"Actually, they aren't my concubines. They are holdovers from the, well, last guy that was in charge." Abraham watched as the gorgeous women waved at him. He waved back. He still hadn't worked up the nerve to sleep with them, though he badly wanted to.

They were all a man could hope for. He'd ended up sleeping in a separate room with Sticks even though she made it perfectly clear she was all right with him sleeping with the trio of beauties.

"You know, you can talk to them," Abraham said. "They might be waving at you, not me. Those ladies aren't spoken for."

Apollo and Prospero exchanged a look. Apollo looked at him and said, "We can't do that, Captain. We are married."

Abraham tilted his head and gave them a funny look. "What do you mean, *married*?"

Apollo set his hammer down and asked, "Don't you have wives in your world? Like the king and the queen. We are married. Married to our women."

"What women?"

"Our wives?" Apollo shook his head and said, "You were at the wedding. A double wedding. We married twins, but Prospero and I are cousins. Many think we are brothers, but there is a distinction in our family line that carries."

"Well, why are you here?" he asked with incredulity. "You should be with your family. Your children. Do you have children?"

"Aye, we both do," Apollo said as Prospero nodded. "But they are grown now. They live in the foot of Kingsland. They are fine."

"I think you should go see them."

"No. They understand. When we go back, if we make it back, we'll be staying." Apollo clenched his leathery hand, which showed thick calluses on the palm. "The king comes first. It's our sworn duty."

"You are good men—faithful to the king and your wives. I appreciate it."

"It's an honor to serve whether it's good or bad."

Apollo and Prospero got back to work. Shingles were laid down, and the hammer drove in more nails.

Abraham resumed his work. He had never been much of a handyman back home, but Ruger seemed to take to it with vigor. Once they finished up the rooftop, he let the hirelings cover it with an inky tarlike coating that waterproofed the roof. He watched from below while he sucked on a flask of water. By the end of the day, the barn would be finished.

Sticks walked out of the Stronghold's open door. She had a small basket of rolls in her hands. "Why don't you eat something? I helped out with these."

"Sure." He grabbed a roll and ate. "Mmm… that's good. And you stuffed the sausage and cheese in them. You girls are getting there."

Sticks looked up at the women perched in the master bedroom's window. Their shapely legs dangled over the sill. Sophia and Selma looked at Sticks, whispered to one another, and giggled.

"Don't you think it's time to cut them loose?" Sticks asked. "They don't cook, and you aren't sleeping with them, so why keep them around? They don't do anything."

"I thought I'd make them Henchmen," he said. "They only need a little work. Perhaps you can train them."

Sticks made a dry "ha ha" and headed back toward the front door. "Enjoy your sausage roll."

"I am," he said with a smile. Then a sharp pain split him

between the eyes. He hadn't had a migraine in weeks. This one hit him like a freight train, and he dropped to a knee. "Uh, Sticks."

Sophia and Selma screamed his name.

The ground began to twist. A sun ring burst in front of his eyes. A portal opened before him. Two men approached from the darkness of the portal's tunnel.

Sticks appeared in front of him. Her warm hands cupped his face. "Ruger! Ruger! Stay with me!" Her eyes widened. "Ruger, stay awake! Stay awake…" Her voice trailed off.

Abraham descended into darkness.

3

—————

BACK HOME

ABRAHAM WOKE WITH A NAGGING HEADACHE. HE CRACKED HIS
eyelids open. A small fire was burning inside a stone fireplace.
Nothing was between him and the low-burning fire except a
wooden coffee table with deer antlers for table legs. He blinked
and rubbed his temples. A heavy quilt covered his body.

Where am I now?

He shifted inside the sofa. His body sank deeper into the foam
cushions. A musty smell mingled in the air with the burning wood.
Aside from the fire, the room was dim. He was inside a log cabin
with an open ceiling. Cobwebs were spun in the corners. The
building groaned against the wind whistling outside.

Abraham sat up and took a closer look around the room. The
dreary log cabin couldn't be any bigger than a thousand square
feet. It appeared to have been abandoned years before. Closed
curtains hung in windows. A wrought-iron chandelier hung over a
small dining table. A midsize bed stood with a chest of drawers
and a few other modern furnishings. The cabin had *woodsman*
written all over it. The deer heads mounted on the walls were
testament to that.

"Oh no," he said quietly. The hairs on his neck stood on end.

Clearly, he was back home. Or somewhere like that. He envisioned Dr. Jack Lassiter, the psychiatrist he'd encountered before. The curly-haired man reminded him a lot of Gene Hackman. The doctor was a devoted hunter, and this cabin looked like something Dr. Jack would thrive in.

Abraham sat up. "Whoa." His arms and legs were free. No straitjacket or shackles bound him either. He rubbed the back of his head. "Ruger, did you get this place all to yourself? Did you escape that hospital? Good for you."

Outside the front door, wooden boards groaned underneath the sound of footsteps.

Abraham moved to the fireplace and grabbed the metal poker leaning against the mantel. The front door swung open with a groan. The chill night air swept through the room. A shapely woman backed her way into the cabin. Her brunette hair was braided into a single tail. She wore a heavy cotton sweater, tight jeans, and work boots. Her arms were loaded with snow-covered logs. She shut the door with her toe and turned. Her jaw dropped. The wood she carried fell on the floor with a clatter. "Ruger. You're awake."

"Mandi?" Abraham said. His heart swelled. "What are you doing here? What is going on?"

A smile broke out over Mandi's face. She hopped over the logs and rushed into his arms. "Abraham! It's you, isn't it? I knew you would come back. I had faith."

He wrapped his bearish arms around her and said, "Of course it's me. Who else would I…? Wait a minute." He pushed her back gently and looked into her pretty eyes. "You called me Ruger. Why'd you do that?"

"I'll explain in a minute." She rose up on her tiptoes and kissed him fully on the lips. She wouldn't be denied. Her long fingers pulled his long hair. She walked him backward toward the bed and pushed herself down on top of him. She sank her face and soft lips into his neck.

He pulled away.

She straddled him and pulled off her sweater. Her full breasts jiggled inside her black bra as she tore at the buttons on his flannel shirt. Her athletic thighs clenched his own.

With his heart racing, the captivated man mumbled, "Resistance is futile." He turned himself over to her, and she turned herself over to him. They made love until the logs in the fireplace dimmed.

They lay underneath the covers. Mandi lay on his side with her gentle fingers touching his chest.

"Uh, I hate to spoil the wonderful moment," he said, "but what is going on?"

She kissed his neck, sat up in the bed, and said, "I don't even know where to start." She shivered. "We need to keep the fire burning. It's going to get cold if we don't. Not that I can't keep you warm all night."

"I believe that." He pulled her back as she tried to get out of bed. "I'll take care of it. You talk."

"So much for pillow talk, huh?" she replied with a playful smile.

He slipped on his boxers, grabbed the wood logs near the front door, and placed a couple of them in the fire. "Hope this wood is dry."

"It is. There's a shed filled with it." She started dressing. "I'm sorry, Abraham."

"For what?"

"You know. Jumping your bones."

He looked at her with a big smile and said, "Apology accepted."

"Well, aren't you the spry and cheerful one. I like it."

He dusted the grit of the snow and wood from his hands and said, "I've been through a lot. Let's just say it changed me." He replaced the screen in front of the fireplace. "It loosened me up, in a way."

She stood up in her bra and panties, arched her back, and stretched. "Listen to me, apologizing for having sex with a man. Me."

"I see your point. So why are you making an apology?"

"I just told myself that if I ever got you back again, I wouldn't hold back." She pulled her sweater down over her shoulders. "I believe you, Abraham, and I wanted you to know that. I am here for you."

He crossed the room and clasped her hands in his. "It means a lot. I swear, this Titanuus place is the real thing."

"Oh, I don't have any doubt about that. I did before, but given all that has happened, I'm more than convinced. Ruger took care of that."

"Ruger?" He gave her a serious look. "That's right. You called me that when you came in. He didn't hurt you, did he?"

"No, no, he's a perfect gentleman. Perhaps too perfect." She made a sheepish look.

"Did you and he, you know…?"

"No, but it wasn't from a lack of me trying." She pulled him over to the couch. "You better sit down."

4

SHE SET A PROTEIN SHAKE IN A CARTON ON THE COFFEE TABLE. "I'D make coffee, but I don't have the means. This place doesn't run electric. It's off the grid, so to speak. It's our family cabin, dating back a few generations." She sat down.

"So where are we?"

"Down by the Greenbrier River in Summers County."

"Back in West Virginia, huh?"

"Yeah." She leaned forward with her elbows on her knees and stared into the warm fire. "Where to start? Where to start?"

"How about from the last time you saw me? Back in the hospital. With Nurse Nancy."

"Oh yeah. That seems like it was ages ago even though it's only been several weeks. Anyway, I did what you said. I tried to look up Eugene Drisk. I'll tell you more about that later. But he exists. Saw his name in an article in a Pittsburgh paper." She rubbed her hands on her thighs. "So, you went into a coma. I came to visit a few days after. Then, *poof*, you were gone. That nasty Nurse Nancy in the Hello Kitty scrubs treated me like a red-haired stepchild."

"Really, I can't imagine," he quipped. "That little Billy Goat Gruff."

"You can say that again. I almost put a fist through her pudgy face. But I wasn't direct family, and Luther Vancross wasn't either. Given the Health Information Portability and Accountability Act, we had as much of a chance in finding out where you were as breaking into Fort Knox. It's asinine."

He patted her knee. "What did you do?"

"What any gorgeous and sexy woman like me would do." She crossed her legs and put her warm hand on his. "I used my powers of seduction. Do you remember Colonel Drew Dexter?"

Abraham looked up in the corner of his eye socket and said, "Oh, you mean Mr. Moustache."

"Yeah, him. If you remember, he took a shine to me and had been calling on me. Pretty regular. When I mentioned you and what was going on in the hospital, he would change the subject." She looked into Abraham's eyes. "But I saw that shift. That flicker in those hazel eyes. I knew that he knew something. Believe me, I know. That douchebag I married has been cheating on me for years. He never fooled me. My attorney got it out of him on paper."

"Sorry to hear about that," he said.

"Don't be. I was a faithful and dutiful wife. I don't have anything to be ashamed of. It's the kids that I worry about. But they are mostly grown, and given the screwed-up nature of this world, they understand."

Abraham studied her face, not a wrinkle of worry on it. She was like Sticks in that manner, but far prettier. But her eyes were tired. Puffiness and a slight red rim showed before her eyelids.

"Keep going," he said.

"Just so you know, I didn't sleep with Colonel Drew. He kept coming around. I continued to warm up to him. I'd get close and pull away. We kissed, but that was all. But I finally knew that I broke him when he said, 'I know things. But I can't say because of my top-secret clearance. I'll see what I can find out.'"

His belly moaned. He reached for the protein shake. "And?"

"And that's when it really got weird." She moved away and grabbed a red Playmate cooler sitting on the floor near the dining table. "I have some snacks."

"Snacks?" He arched a brow, and his mouth started to water. "I could go for some snacks. Titanuus is severely lacking in the snack department. Tell me, you have some Dilly Bars?"

"No." She set the cooler down on the coffee table. "Sorry, didn't make it by Dairy Queen when we fled. But"—she opened the cooler—"I have plenty of protein bars and Little Debbie snack cakes."

He snatched the box of Oatmeal Creme Pies out of her hands. "I love these things!" He tore the box open and ripped away the clear plastic wrappers. He stuffed three in his mouth at once and chewed with joy.

"I guess I can say goodbye to those washboard abs," she replied.

"Huh?" He lifted up his shirt. His belly was long gone and replaced by a rock-hard stomach. "Oh. Well, that's what happens when they starve you, I guess."

"I don't think you've gotten a good look at yourself. You are you but built like a chimney stack."

He flexed his big forearm. It was knotted with muscle as in his playing days. He swallowed. "Man, those are delicious. The food in Titanuus—it's good, but it's not this good."

"Clearly. Can I continue, or do you want to finish the box first."

He grabbed two more Oatmeal Creme Pies. "I'm good. Go on."

She unwrapped a protein bar. "I really put a spell on Drew. He was smitten by me. After staying clammed up, he showed up at Woody's Grill late in the evening. I was closing, along with Herb and my mom, Martha. As usual, Mom had to try to feed him, but he was in a hurry. He didn't even crack a smile when Herb joked about the UFOs. He whispered to me that he knew where you were. It was top secret, but he managed to use his connections and get me clearance."

Abraham stopped chewing and asked, "What happened then?"

She shivered and said, "He took me there."

"Where?"

"Facility 117."

5

———

ABRAHAM SQUINTED. HE COULD SEE IN THE RECESSES OF HIS MIND A bronze nameplate on a building marked Facility 117. "It's a cement building with grooves running vertical from top to bottom. About ten stories tall. A high chain-link fence all around it."

"That's it." She rubbed her arms. She got up and put another log on the fire. "Sorry, but the place gave me the chills." She rubbed her hands in front of the flames. "Drew drove me up there in a black Humvee. That was the first thing I thought was odd because there weren't any markings of the Army on it, but there was some special gear inside. He took me up a gravel road that winded through the hills near the East River Mountain Tunnel. I never would have imagined that a huge building was up there in the middle of nowhere."

"Yeah, me either."

"Drew said it was an old military hospital that was built after World War II. I didn't think much of it. We checked in at security and went inside." She took her spot back on the couch. "There weren't a lot of people around that I could see. There were the four guards at the front gate and two waiting behind the security desk.

All of them wore the same security uniform. They weren't military. I gave them a big smile. They didn't crack a grin, but they went all TSA on me when they searched me."

Mandi started taking the braid out of her hair. "Once I passed through the scanner, I had chill bumps all over. I felt like I might be going in but not coming back. There was this weird humming, like a generator running, but more natural."

Abraham felt a sinking feeling in his stomach. "You shouldn't have gone there. Not over me, anyway."

"Well, it's too late for that. Besides, I'm nosy. All of the women in my family are. I have a cousin, Tori, up in West Virginia. You'd be amazed at what her big nose got her into several years ago." She reached over and locked her fingers with his. "Anyway, I was worried about you and needed to see that you were all right. Up the elevator we went to the fifth floor. We met Dr. Jack Lassiter."

"Yeah, I know him."

"You do?"

"Another long story, but keep going," he said as he gave her hand a firm squeeze. "I'm listening."

"Thanks, Dr. Crane." She giggled. "Dr. Jack, as he preferred to be called, was very polite. He explained your condition by using a bunch of medical terminology that lost my attention. Sorry, but I really hated biology and other complicated college courses like that. So I dropped them. Finally, after some flirting and pleading, they took me to your hospital room. It was a quiet place with only one nurse on call. You were shackled to the bed but sleeping as sound as a baby. You had cuts and bruises all over you. That made me mad, and I let them have it.

"Dr. Jack went on to explain that you were only being protected from yourself. He talked more about the delirium and schizophrenia that you were dealing with. As truthful as he sounded, I didn't believe a word of it. Dr. Jack was likeable but more of a wolf in sheep's clothing. While you were sleeping, Drew and Jack started talking. I don't know why, but I whispered in your ear who I was and who you were. I even mentioned Titanuus and said the name Ruger Slade." She looked up and shook her head. "It was all a bunch of senseless babble. The kind of babble that Drew and Jack didn't like.

"'Let's not irritate him,' Jack had said. 'He's prone to violence when he wakes. But he is doing fine. You can see the IVs and monitors. I promise, he's getting the best care he can get.' Well, I insisted on giving you a kiss before he hauled me a way. When I did, I placed that picture you gave him in his hand. You know, the crest of the lion's head with the wings." Her eyes searched Abraham's. "You swallowed the note up in that big palm. They didn't see a thing. I knew something was brewing."

"Wow," he said in a low voice.

"After that, I didn't overdo it. I said what any naïve woman would say. 'Let me know if he wakes up. Keep me posted.' You know." She shrugged. "Jack said he'd have me over again. He hoped that my presence might be helpful and perhaps, if you woke up and behaved, I could visit again. But he was very specific when he said, 'Don't tell anyone about this place.' I agreed, and Drew and I left. I was careful to thank him all over."

Abraham scratched the scruffy hairs on his chin. "I don't know what to say, Mandi. I can't believe that you did all of that for me. I don't understand why."

"A man should never ask why a woman loves him. He should only accept it."

He nodded, reached into the cooler, and grabbed a canister of cashews. "Mmm, Planters. The best. No peanuts in Titanuus either."

"You really speak like you are fond of that place. Is it better than here?"

"Sort of," he said. He stuffed in a handful of salty cashews. "Then what happened?"

She leaned back into the sofa and said, "Everything pretty much went back to normal. I tried to not overthink it and checked in with Drew from time to time. We went to the movies… twice."

"I see, and…?"

"He only got to second base."

"No, not that part."

"Oh, well then. Per the routine, me, Mom, and Herb were closing the Grill. You showed up, drenched by rain, wearing hospital garb. Except it wasn't you—it was Ruger. I knew it when he said, 'Take me home to Titanuus.' We've been on the run ever since."

6

ABRAHAM COMBED HIS FINGERS THROUGH HIS HAIR. "MAN, THAT'S A whale of a story."

"What do you mean? It's no bigger than yours."

"I know that. It's just…" He gave her a blank stare. "I'm not crazy, am I? All of this? Me… you?"

"Don't start riding the crazy train now," she said with a huff. She got up and paced around the sofa, making the boards creak underneath her feet. "Because if you're crazy, then I'm crazy too."

"So, you really do believe this?"

"Well, the Titanuus story is a tough sell, but Ruger did a fair job convincing me of that."

"You talked with him? He can speak?"

"Turns out he's a pretty sharp fella. He picked up our lingo while he was in the facility. It seems that Dr. Jack spent a lot of time with him. He learned enough about how everything works and managed his escape." She stopped in front of the fire. "He called it playing possum."

Of course Ruger would be able to figure out the language the same way that Abraham had quickly picked up the words of

Titanuus. *Man, this all better not be a part of my imagination. I can't be crazy.* "Tell me more about being on the run."

"I don't know how Ruger slipped from the facility, but I knew that they'd be looking for him and eventually come to me. I decided to skedaddle. Ruger was reluctant. All he wanted to do was get back to Titanuus. I didn't know the way, but I let him know that you were working on it on your end. He's working on it on his end. So we headed down the road. I told Herb and Martha not to say a word about it, that I'd be back to keep up appearances. But we've been staying here for the past few days."

Abraham dusted the salt off his hands and said, "Tell me more about Ruger. What is he like?"

"Determined. There is a restlessness in his eyes," she said, "but he's confident and in complete control." She sat back down beside Abraham. Her fireplace-warmed thigh rubbed against his. "I can see who is who by the eyes. And tell by your mannerisms. That's how I knew it was you. The funny thing is that I feel as safe with you as I do him."

"He made you feel safe?"

"Yeah. It was like being with the perfect gentleman but one that could really kick ass if need be. He can do things, or at least he can do things with that body that I never imagined."

"I thought you said you didn't sleep with him?"

She pushed his shoulder. "That's not what I mean. Something tells me that he wouldn't have me anyway. Like I said, he's a straight shooter."

"Well, I think I can understand why he would resist. In his world, he was the Guardian Commander. They were knights who lived by the highest standards. A code." He rubbed her thigh. "Don't feel bad. He's already committed."

"He has a wife? Have you been sleeping with his wife?" She looked appalled.

"Well, you have to keep up appearances."

She playfully shoved him. "You pig."

"I'm only kidding. He's not married, but it's still complicated. As it turns out, he has an illegitimate daughter with Queen Clarann." Abraham gave a quick account of the who's who and what's what, bringing Mandi up to speed on the Henchmen and King Hector's family. "Needless to say, that puts me in a fine predicament as well. It's one more complicated thing after the other."

Mandi buried her pretty face in her hands and moaned. "This is better than anything that I could have imagined." She looked at him. "So what are you going to do? What are we going to do?"

"Somebody has to know something, and my guess is that it's Eugene Drisk. You said that you saw something about him? What did you see?"

"I did what you asked, including taking flowers to Jan and Jake at the cemetery. It's a very pretty place and well taken care of. There were some fresh flowers still there."

Abraham's throat tightened. He hadn't given them a thought since he'd arrived back home. He'd been too wrapped up in himself. He wiped his eyes. "Thanks."

"It's okay." She squeezed his hand. "They would understand what you are going through. I'm sure of it."

"I feel guilty for not feeling guilty. I'm so used to carrying all of that guilt. Now, I carry other problems. My own."

"You can't feel guilty. That plane accident wasn't your fault. They are in Heaven, right? They are better off."

He nodded. "I know." Then he sobbed.

Mandi wrapped him up in a hug and stroked his hair. "It's okay, Abraham. You're allowed to let go."

He took a breath and broke off the embrace. "Not yet. I'm not ready. Tell me more about Eugene Drisk."

"I found microfiche of the old newspapers that talked about his appearance. He vanished without a trace. Anyway, I have another cousin in Washington, DC, named Sid. She used to be in the FBI. I asked her to look into it. She's really cool and has a bounty-hunter business. Anyway, she set me up with a man that writes a magazine called *Nightfall DC*. I think his name is Russ. Believe it or not, he had an article mentioning Eugene Drisk. The lost man suddenly reappeared, along with a few other sightings, only to disappear again."

"Do you have a copy of it?" he asked.

"No, it was on the web when I looked. I'd try now, but I don't want to use my phone. I've been keeping it off. For protection."

"Good thinking. But I'm not so sure that keeping your phone off will eliminate any tracking. Did you bring it with you?"

"Well, yeah. In case of emergencies. But I've been careful. And if they would have found us, they would have done so by now." She winked at him. "See, I'm careful. Besides, I don't think you can get a signal down in this river valley."

"I hope you're right." He sank into the couch and stared into the fire. "Would it be bad if I told you that I'd rather live in Titanuus?"

"No." Mandi snuggled her cheek against his shoulder. "Not as long as I can go."

"Mandi, you're something."

"I know."

Abraham's ears caught the sound of tires rolling over a gravel road. He sat up straight.

"What is it?" she asked.

"Someone is coming." He moved to the front-window curtains and peeked through.

Bright halogen headlights shined at the dingy windows.

"Devil's donuts. I think they found us."

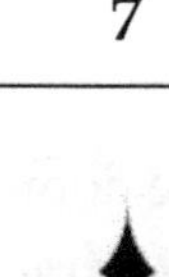

7

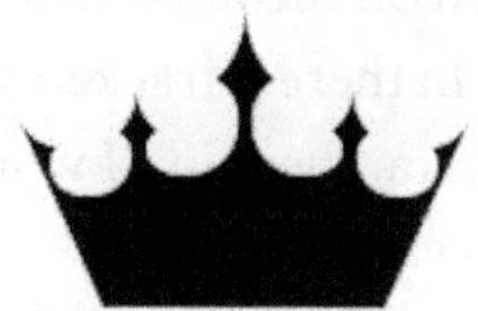

MANDI LOOKED THROUGH THE OTHER SIDE OF THE WINDOW AND said, "That's Drew. He's got a ball cap on, but it's him."

A man with rugged good looks, a black ball cap, and a caterpillar moustache exited a black Humvee.

Colonel Dexter was dressed in blue jeans and an army-green hoodie. A semiautomatic pistol was strapped on his hip. He walked slowly toward the cabin with an air of confidence in his stride.

"Come here," Abraham said as he walked back to the fire. He wrapped his arms around Mandi and kissed her head. "You've been great, but I'm not going to let you endanger yourself over me. But I want you to listen."

With her face buried in his chest, she nodded.

Quickly, he told her everything pertinent that he could remember about Titanuus. He explained about the Crown of Stones and their quest to obtain all the gems. He mentioned the death of Arcayis the Underlord. "Look into a man named Edgar Gravely from Queens. He had palsy, but now in Titanuus, he's a horned halfling that calls himself Big Apple. He doesn't want to leave, and I think he wants to stop us. I've got to track him down next."

"Why are you telling me this?"

"In case I flash back to Titanuus, you need to fill Ruger in if you can. Every bit helps, but most of all, I think Eugene Drisk is the key."

"I'll keep looking," she said.

Drew Dexter knocked on the door and said in his deep voice, "Mandi, I know you are in there. I tracked your phone."

Whispering to Abraham, she said, "I would've sworn they couldn't do that. I'm sorry."

"It's okay. Just ask him what he wants."

She nodded. "What do you want, Drew? Why are you stalking me?"

"I'm not stalking you. I'm worried. So are Herb and Martha. You are running around with a schizophrenic, you know."

"What I do in my personal time is my business, not yours," she halfway yelled. "Just go away, or I'll have *you* charged with stalking."

Abraham heard the porch boards groan when Drew moved toward the window. The hairs on his neck stood on end, and the tips of his fingers tingled. *He's not alone. I can feel it in my bones.* He rolled his hand, motioning for her to keep talking.

With her hands jammed in her back pockets, she said, "Uh, why don't you go away, Drew! I need some time to think."

"Is Abraham in there with you? I need to know that you are all right. How do I know that you are safe?"

"Don't I sound safe?" she fired back and shrugged at Abraham.

He whispered in her ear. "If anything happens, let them think I'm Ruger and not Abraham. Okay?"

Mandi nodded. "Just so you know, after this, I'm not going on any more dates with you. And I don't like your moustache either! It's creepy!"

Abraham peeked through the window curtains in the back of the cabin. The wind swayed the trees, and snow swirled off the roof. He crept back over to the front door. The floorboards groaned.

Drew called out from the other side of the door. "Mandi! Are you okay? Is he armed?"

"No! He's sleeping."

Abraham shrugged at her.

She shrugged back.

He tiptoed back to the couch and lay down.

"Don't lie to me," Drew said. "This is a potentially dangerous situation, and we can't afford to play any games."

"I'm not playing games. Fine! I'll let you in, but don't do anything stupid. And you better be alone," she said.

"I'm alone," Drew replied.

"You better be," she said.

Abraham heard her footsteps walking over to the door. The door opened. A heavier person walked inside, bringing cold air with him. The door closed.

"Will you put that gun away?" Mandi said. "He's asleep or catatonic. I don't know. He went blank yesterday and hasn't moved since."

Abraham let his body relax, but he could hear everything around him. Colonel Drew's footsteps were a dead giveaway to his location. The man bumped into the coffee table as well, and the legs scraped over the floor.

"I said put the gun away," she repeated.

"No can do," Drew said. "This old fox caught the guards in the facility with their pants down more than once using this act. He's not going to fool me." Drew spoke louder. "And just so you know… Try anything clever, Mr. Jenkins, I have over two dozen men outside, waiting on you."

"You liar," Mandi said.

"Ah, come on, you knew that I was lying. Here, take these flexi-cuffs and bind his wrists and ankles together."

"What?" she said. "I'm not doing that. Look, he hasn't broken any laws. The only thing he is guilty of is being in a coma."

"No, he's guilty of being crazy. He's a danger to society. There are a whole bunch of people running around with these delusional fantasies. Dr. Jack is trying to cure them." Drew cleared his throat. "Trust the process."

"You trust the process. I'm not binding up my friend."

"Listen, Mandi, you are already looking at criminal charges: aiding and abetting a fugitive as well as a psychopath. This is the moment where you need to earn our trust and help out."

"Well, I'm not doing it."

"Fine, I'll just shoot him," Drew said.

"Nooo," she pleaded.

"Relax. It's a tranquilizer gun. But it has enough juice to take down an elephant… or two. This Abraham is really something, I've seen the video. Really something."

Something buzzed.

"Hold on," Drew said. "I need to take this."

"How'd you get a signal?" she asked.

"I'm Army. We always get a signal," Drew said. "Colonel Dexter here. Yes, we have him in custody. Uh-huh. He's catatonic again. Uh-huh. The area is all secure. Uh-huh. Got it."

Abraham could visualize Drew sliding the phone into his jeans pocket.

"What did he say?" Mandi asked.

"He said don't take any chances. Trank him and bind him with all that I got." Colonel Dexter charged the slide on his gun. "Sweet dreams, Abraham Jenkins, or whoever the hell you are."

8

———

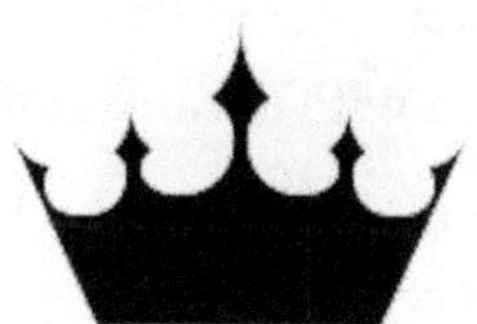

He opened his eyes in time to see the gun sailing out of Drew's hand.

Drew threw a punch at Abraham.

Abraham slid his head aside and sank his fist deep into the colonel's stomach.

Colonel Drew let out a *woof* and sagged to the floor, holding his belly.

"Cuff him," he said to Mandi.

"Gladly." She secured Drew's wrists and ankles with the flexi-cuffs in a matter of seconds.

"You're pretty quick with those things," Abraham said as he hauled the man up onto the couch. "Why do I get the feeling that you've used those things before?"

"I'm a sorority girl. I'm sworn to secrecy, so I'll only kiss but never tell." She winked at him and picked up the gun. "What do you want me to do with this?"

"You mean you don't already know?" he said sarcastically.

"Oh, okay."

She pointed it at Drew, whose eyes turned as big as saucers. She shot him in the chest. Drew's eyes bugged out, rolled up, and showed their whites. He wilted on the sofa like a leaf.

"Nooo!" Abraham grabbed the gun out of her hand. "Are you crazy? I was joking around. You know, the sorority thing?"

"I wasn't joking about that! And you shouldn't have joked about shooting him with the gun."

"I didn't say shoot him with a trank gun. Man, who are you? Mad Mandi?"

"Thanks—not very nice."

"Sorry." He opened Drew's eyelids, and only the whites showed. "I hope his heart can take it, because he's going to be out for a while." He plucked the dart out of Drew's chest and held it out for Mandi. "Care for a souvenir to show your sisters, or would you rather scalp him?"

"Ha ha," she said dryly. "I don't see what the big deal is. He had it coming."

"True, but I wanted to question him. He knows stuff. I need those answers." He went over to peek out the windows. He didn't see anyone else. "We need to move. They'll be expecting us to come out soon."

"How are we going to pull that off?"

Abraham started taking off his shirt. "He's about my size. We'll switch clothes."

"Uh, a little hard to do since I cuffed him," she replied. She searched Drew's belt. "Never mind—he's got a knife and, it appears, plenty of cuffs. Army man is well prepared." She started stripping him down.

Abraham slipped into the man's hoodie and placed the black ball cap on his head. "I've got everything but the moustache."

"Yeah, let's leave that in the seventies, where Ron Burgundy left it," she replied as he fitted Drew into Abraham's clothing and cuffed him up. She clasped the man's face in her hands and stared at his sagging face. "Stay classy."

Abraham picked the man up and slung him like a carpet over his shoulder. "Grab his phone. And the cooler. We can't leave Little Debbie behind."

"Of course not."

Abraham kept his head down, opened the door, and headed outside while holding the gun on Mandi. The icy wind stirred up flecks of snow and chilled his face. With frosty breath, they crossed the headlights, and she got into the passenger side of the Humvee. He loaded Drew through the back doors and hopped into the driver's seat. He closed the door and turned over the engine. The Humvee rumbled to life.

"I haven't driven in a while. You might want to buckle up."

She clicked her seat belt in place and said, "Just don't go catatonic on me again. Please."

"We'll switch the first chance that we get. You might want to pray in the meantime."

"So where are we going?"

"Back toward the facility. At least, that's what I want them to think."

He put the car in drive and backed up. He turned the wheel and headed back up the gravel road. As he sped his way up the hairpin turns that led out of the river valley, they zoomed by several Jeeps pulled alongside the narrow road. He didn't slow or look at any over them.

"I want to see if they follow," he said.

"You're the boss."

"No, I'm the leader of the Henchmen."

They hit the main roads several minutes later. A train of black Jeeps followed them as far as the interstate ramps and then started to splinter off. One Jeep sped past them. Abraham flashed his lights at them, and the Jeep moved on.

He checked the rearview mirror. "It doesn't look like we are taking a full escort back to Facility 117. It's just us."

Mandi leaned her chair back and closed her eyes. "I hope so."

He glanced at her. She was as pretty as an angel, with her hair cascading onto the shoulders of her creamy white sweater. With her full lips barely pursed, she couldn't have been more beautiful.

A few more minutes into the drive, she began to whistle softly through her nose. Abraham turned on the radio. The sad whine of a saxophone played.

"Really? The first song I've heard in months, and they're playing Seger again."

Directions to Facility 117 were already locked into the Humvee's navigation system. He drove down the interstate exit ramp that was a few miles away from the road leading to the facility. He woke up Mandi. Her head was propped up against the window.

Stretching her arms, she asked, "Where are we?"

"Near the facility," he said.

"Now what?"

"We need to ditch the phones and find another car. There's a mini-mart up the road. We can make the swap there."

She yawned. "Okay, but I'm not very keen on ditching my phone."

"It's either that or I ditch you." He shrugged. "Sorry."

"No one ditches me. Besides, we can get a burner phone in the store. I have cash." From her back jeans pocket, she took her phone, in a sparkling pink jewel case. "Let me check and see if I have any messages."

Abraham drove down the road.

"Oh!" she said, excited.

"What?"

"It's from my cousin, Sid. She said they found Eugene Drisk!"

"No way."

Mandi held the phone in front of his face, showing a picture of Eugene Drisk sitting at a bar. "Is that him?"

Abraham nodded. "Way."

9

ABRAHAM WAS RIDING IN THE BACK SEAT OF A SHINY SEA-GREEN Cadillac Coupe DeVille. An older couple sat in the front. Abraham and Mandi had met the couple in the Mini-Mart Gas and Go. The old man driving had recognized Abraham. He was from Pittsburgh, and they were returning there from a trip in Florida.

Miles and Carla were the names of the old couple. They played gospel music, sang along, and hummed as the Cadillac floated over the highway ten miles an hour under the speed limit. The trip with the older couple made for an ideal cover. No one stopped them along the way.

"You know, I never believed a word about you being at fault in that plane accident," Miles said. He had a full head of hair, neatly cut and swept over to one side. He'd look in the rearview mirror when he talked. "You were one of the good guys. Real good. I can't wait to tell my pals that Jenkins the Jet rode in my car."

In the passenger seat, Carla was knitting. "The papers say the most awful things about people." Her cotton top had a blue sheen that seemed to reflect the ocean-blue dashboard and upholstery. "You can't believe hardly any of it. We hardly read it anymore." Her glasses on the rim of her nose, she asked, "So, tell me, how long have the two of you been a couple? Are you engaged?"

"No, we just started a new relationship," Mandi said. She was cozied up to Abraham with her head on his shoulder. "But it's looking more promising by the day."

"That's nice to hear. You know, Abraham," Carla said. "This is a nice place to pop the question. This is where Miles asked me, some twenty-five years ago."

"You mean you haven't been married longer?" Abraham said.

"We were both widowers," Miles fired back. "We met at my wife's funeral. But it's not weird. They were distant cousins, second cousins, I believe. I never thought I'd fall in love again, especially at my wife's funeral. Heh heh. But it happened. The Lord works in mysterious ways." He leaned over and tried to kiss her.

Carla shoved him back. "Will you watch the road, you silly goose? You're gonna wreck us."

Mandi leaned forward. "We can't thank you enough for giving us a lift. When the ol' Hummer broke down, I thought we were screwed."

Carla stopped knitting.

Mandi continued. "Sorry. But we really needed to make the trip, because the wedding is tomorrow and I'm running kind of late. I was supposed to be there yesterday, but we lost our luggage at the airport check-in, and well, it's been a mess ever since."

"I see," Carla said.

Mandi gave a frozen grin and shrugged. Abraham tipped his chin. They were lying about everything, but what else were they supposed to do? They needed to find answers. The hard part had been abandoning Colonel Drew Dexter in the Humvee. Mandi assured Abraham that it wouldn't be long before his people found him. Abraham agreed. He had enough to worry about, let alone one of the bad guys.

"Only thirty miles to the Fort Pitt Tunnel," Miles said cheerfully. "You know, when I was young, I'd sit in the back seat of my parents' car with my girlfriend, and we'd kiss the entire way through. We called it the Love Tunnel." He looked in the mirror and shrugged his brows and winked.

"You never told me that," Carla said.

"Well, you never asked," Miles replied.

"A fine time to bring it up in front of company. You could have prepared me for it," Carla said in a bickering tone. "That's embarrassing."

"Embarrassing. This coming from a woman that made out with me at my wife's funeral."

Carla gasped and stuck him with a needle.

"Ow!" he said. "Take it easy. I'm driving."

As Miles and Carla bickered, Mandi gently took Abraham by the chin and said, "Are you okay? You looked like you saw a ghost."

"No, but my friend, Solomon Paige, the one that looks like Bigfoot, well, he transformed when he passed through the Fort Pitt Tunnel." He shifted in his seat. "Needless to say, it's in the wee hours of the morning, and hardly a car is on the road. Pretty weird that we have old folks driving us too."

"We are night birds," Miles said. He tapped his ear, where a hearing aid sat. "Less traffic on the road. Great for travel, and we sleep a lot in the day. I hate traffic. Carla hates it more."

Abraham and Mandi exchanged a surprised glance.

"Shame on you for eavesdropping, Miles," Carla said as she gave him another poke with her needle. "That's rude. It's rude to them, and worse, it's rude to me 'cause you weren't listening again."

"Sorry, folks. But these hearing aids are great. They take the ringing out of my ears, and I can hear all the sounds of music. All thanks to the VA." Miles grinned in the rearview mirror. "Your time will come. You need them. So, Abraham, do tunnels make you nervous? I only heard part of it."

"I guess you could say that."

"Well, do what I would do if I had a pretty lady in the back seat like that. Make out from start to finish."

"I'm going to throttle you when we get home," Carla said to Miles. Her needles resumed their clicking.

"Thanks for the advice," Abraham said. He pinched his nose as he saw the sign for the Fort Pitt Tunnel, which was only five miles away. His head started splitting.

"Oh no," he muttered.

"What is it?' Mandi asked.

"I'm feeling it again."

"Don't look at it. Just lay down in my lap."

He did so.

"Say, that's a nice move," Miles said. "Ow! Stop doing that."

Mandi ran her fingers through his hair. She gave him a warm smile. "It's going to be all right. You're with me."

He held her hand in his sweaty grip. "I hope you are right."

"I'm a woman. I'm always right." She kissed him full on the lips just as the Fort Pitt Tunnel swallowed them whole.

10

ABRAHAM AND MANDI WALKED THROUGH THE BUSY STREETS OF
Pittsburgh, trying to find a hotel. They parted pleasantly with
Miles and Carla, both of whom gave them a long and loving
embrace.

"The two of you should get married next," Carla said with a
tear in her eye. "I have a good feeling about you. Enjoy the
wedding."

Mandi secured a room with the help of her cousin Sid. With
Sid's direction, she'd acquired paid credit cards and a burner
phone with the cash she had. Now, they were secure in a nice hotel
room that had a nice view of the three rivers.

Abraham took a shower and cleaned himself up while Mandi
went out and purchased new clothing. Inside the steamy bathroom, he wiped the mirror with a towel. Bruises, cuts, and scrapes
decorated his body, but otherwise, he was in pretty good shape.

He nodded. "Not bad. I might not be Ruger, but I still have
something going on."

He threw a terry cloth robe on and sat down on the bed. Dirt
was still underneath his fingernails. The television was on, and a

group of men and an attractive woman were talking about Pirates baseball.

He found the remote on the nightstand and turned it off. "I don't even want to know."

Abraham flopped back on the lone king-size bed and stared at the ceiling. "How long is this going to last?"

A chill went through his bones. The last few times, his encounters back home hadn't lasted very long. This one was going on two days. He expected to be zapped back to Titanuus at any moment. However, no pain was brewing inside his skull. This was, for the first time in as long as he could remember, normal.

He continued talking to himself. "Don't get caught up in it, Abraham. This might be real for now, but it won't stay real." He sat up and looked out the window at a perfect view of PNC Park. "Ah man, I must be dreaming. This is all so twisted."

Seeing the ballpark left an emptiness inside him, a void that could not be filled. He thought of Buddy Parker. His close friend and teammate had never gotten to see the field again. The airplane crash took that all away from the man. It had taken everything away from Abraham too.

"I don't belong here," he mumbled as he shut the curtains. "Why did I even come here?"

He knew why. They needed to find Eugene Drisk. The professor would have answers. He had to know the truth.

The hotel room door opened. Mandi entered, carrying a couple of shopping bags. She'd changed into a new pair of blue jeans and wore a Steelers jersey fit for a woman with the number fifty-eight.

"I don't think Jack Lambert ever looked that good in his jersey," he said.

"Who?" She looked down at her chest. "Oh, this. I just bought it because it was on sale."

"A Lambert jersey on sale, here?" He shook his head. "It must be a knockoff."

"Maybe." She shrugged and tossed the bags on the bed. "So how are you doing?" She caressed his face with her hand, rose up on tiptoe, and kissed his cheek. "You look good, all cleaned up."

He combed his fingers through his beard. "I was gonna shave but thought I might be recognized. So I didn't bother."

"Well, it's pretty scraggly. A trim wouldn't hurt. I can do that if you like."

He shrugged.

"I'll take that as a yes. Have a seat on the bed." She headed to the bathroom. "Are you okay?"

"I don't feel right being back here. You know, lots of memories. I upset a lot of people."

"I think they'd be over it by now." She had a small pair of scissors in her hand. She dragged over a chair from the small desk, placed it in front of him, and sat down. "People will get over it."

"Not in Pittsburgh. They don't forget, trust me. There were some pretty angry people out there."

Mandi started trimming his beard. "I'm sorry for how you feel. It's not fair."

"What's the plan? Any word from your cousin?"

"Yeah. Her contact got a hold of me. Russ. He said that Eugene hangs out at a place called the Yard." She flicked Abraham's hairs into a wastebasket.

"Wait, we're tracking him down at a bar? Don't we have a home address?"

"Yes, I have that too. But it's a high-rise. Decent security. I don't think we could barge in there if we wanted to." She cut off another section of beard. "You're looking even better. I like it."

"Don't take off too much. I don't want to be recognized."

"Do you really think they'll remember?"

"Trust me—they remember. I've signed thousands of autographs in this town."

"True, but there are millions of people."

"Yeah, millions of people with television."

She straddled one of his legs and started cutting some more. Her perfume smelled great.

"We can play this however you want to," she said. "I'm here to help. I thought it would be best to catch him, you know, by surprise."

Abraham had been on plenty of dangerous missions on Titanuus, and he thought this one should be a piece of cake. He didn't want to lose any time either. There was always a chance that he'd zip back to Titanuus. He couldn't let that happen without more answers about how to stay back home. This time, he'd be sure that Eugene Drisk didn't slip through his fingers.

"What are you going to do if I turn back into Ruger?" he asked. "You know it will happen."

"Maybe it won't. But he seems to understand what to do. I guess I'll hope for the best," she said with a no-look smile.

His current situation seemed to be working out too perfectly. Perhaps Dr. Jack had been right. Things worked out the way he wanted because he imagined them. Abraham was living in a fantasy world he had created. It was either that or reality. He worried that he couldn't tell which was which.

"This is crazy," he said.

Mandi lifted his chin and met his eyes with hers. "Hey, now is not the time to doubt. I believe in you. You have to believe in yourself."

He nodded. "Death before failure."

"Huh?"

"It's something that we say. You know, the Henchmen."

"Interesting. Sounds like a really fun place to be." She brushed fingers over his beard. "Think that will do it." She put all her weight on his knee. "Don't you run away yet. Let me ask you something."

"Sure."

She looked deep into his eyes. "Would you rather be stuck here or there?"

Abraham started to say "here," but that would have been a lie. He liked Titanuus and who he'd become. A fresh start might have been just what he needed, and he got off on it.

"Honestly, I think I like it there better."

Mandi frowned as she rose up from his knee. "I guess it's true what they say."

"What's that?"

"The truth hurts." She walked away and shut herself in the bathroom.

11

ABRAHAM AND MANDI WERE SITTING AT A BOOTH IN A LARGE microbrewery restaurant called the Yard. The large sports bar offered plenty of seating and had a very long L-shaped bar front with scores of tall stools. Flat-screen televisions could be clearly seen from any angle. Sporting events filled all the screens. The time was after five o'clock, and the robust restaurant, which smelled like beer and buffalo wings, was filling up fast.

"Come on, Mandi. You can't be mad at me for being honest. Besides, you said you would want to come to Titanuus," Abraham said.

She was giving him the cold shoulder since they'd talked in the hotel. Her words with him were short but not sweet.

"Would you rather that I lied?"

"Yes, Honest Abe. I would have." She sipped on her mug of an amber-colored beer. "Will you drop it? I'll get over it. I always do."

A waitress wearing a zebra-striped apron set down a mixer of appetizers on the table. "Can I get you anything else?" she asked in a perky voice as her stare hung on his eyes.

He lowered the bill on his Steelers cap and said, "No, this will do."

"I'll bring you both your free round in a bit. Just raise your little Pirate flag on the table up if you need me." The waitress vanished into the tables.

He reached over and covered Mandi's palm with his hand. "Do you know that feeling you get when you get back home after a long vacation? You make it back from a long trip, and you are so relieved to be back home and in your bed."

Mandi barely looked at him and nodded.

"Well, when I come back home, I don't get that at all. My bed in Titanuus is more comfortable than my bed here. I know that sounds strange, but it's true. And I'm sorry."

"Just stop apologizing. I understand. I can't help it if I want you to myself. I think if you gave it a chance, we could have a good life here together."

"I'm not in any kind of position to commit to anything now. You know that."

She pulled her hand out from underneath his and said, "Sure."

"Well, what do you want to do? Go to Vegas and get married?"

She shrugged her eyebrows.

"Wow." He slumped back in the booth.

His problems in both worlds continued to mount. Mandi was beginning to complicate things. *Maybe I need to cut her loose. Keep her out of danger. It's the best thing to do in the long run. Especially if I'm nuts.* He glanced over her inviting features. *Besides, she's too hot to be this helpful.*

Mandi kicked his shin.

He sat up straight. "That's fine. Let it out."

"No, you dope. Look. That dude taking a seat at the bar." She had her eyes locked on a man wearing an oversized beige overcoat. "Isn't that Eugene?"

Abraham recognized the shabby man from his encounter in the

East River Mountain Tunnel from what must have been months before. Eugene had thinning hair on his balding head. The remaining locks were stringy. He had a pronounced nose for a small man. He hunched over the bar and raised his hand, and the bartender brought him a mug of dark beer.

"That's him," Abraham said.

Mandi started up out of her seat and said, "I'll feel him out."

"No, stay put. I made it this close, so I'm not going to miss out on the opportunity." He got up and beat another man to the stool beside Eugene.

Eugene's big eyes were glued to the television screen. He stuck his lips out and sucked on his beer. His hand trembled when he drank.

"Do you have any money on the game?" Abraham asked politely.

Without looking at him, Eugene said in a condescending tone, "No. Betting is for fools."

With the crowds whistling and cheering at the television screens, he said, "It looks like you are in the company of fools."

"Yes, well, it's been that way all of my life." Eugene turned his back farther toward Abraham. "It seems this moment is no different."

"You know, I'm a betting man, and I'd be curious to get your take on this game. Just for kicks, who do you like? The Penguins or the Brewers?"

"There are hundreds of people in the room. Why don't you ask them?" Eugene swallowed a couple more gulps of beer. "What are you, one of those vagrants looking a free drink? I say hit the road. They don't take kindly to your ilk here."

"Sorry, old dude, I was just making conversation."

Eugene shuddered inside his overcoat. He clenched a fist, took a deep breath, and sighed. "Mister, will you please leave me be? I'm not bothering you, so don't you bother me."

"I'm not from around here. I only wanted to make conversation. I just thought an elder like you would be more hospitable," Abraham said.

"Oh lord, you're one of those obnoxious Canadians, aren't you? Coming down here to gloat over some ancient Stanley Cup string of victories."

"I'm not Canadian, but you have some respectable knowledge of the sport." He glanced at his booth and found Mandi was gone. He scanned the room but didn't see her anywhere. *Crap.* "Look more like the academic type. Perhaps, back in your day, you played the very dangerous sport of ice hockey."

"Hockey, dangerous? Pah. If you think hockey is dangerous, then you don't know what danger is. Trust me."

"I guess you're right. But hey, I got you to make some conversation, didn't I?" He chuckled and gave Eugene a hearty slap on the back, knocking the older man toward the bar. "Where I come from, we are people's people."

Eugene shrugged in his coat. "Fine! If you are dying for me to ask, I'll ask. Where are you from?"

"Titanuus."

Eugene set his beer down, turned, and faced Abraham. His eyes filled with recognition. He leaned toward Abraham. "I'll be. It's you. Or is it?"

12

———————

"No, it's me, Abraham Jenkins," he answered. "The real one." He laid a heavy hand on Eugene's shoulder and squeezed. "I've come a long way. We need to talk."

"Talk about what? You're back, right? Consider yourself lucky. I was stuck in the hellish place for years." Eugene made a bitter face. "It was one insane mission after the other. More treachery afoot than a pirate's ship. No, you consider yourself lucky that you found a portal. Even in ol' Ruger's body, eventually the place would become insufferable." He hoisted his glass. "Here's to you!"

Abraham gave Eugene a doubting look as he clicked mugs with him. The older scholar hadn't reacted the way he'd expected.

"You really thought Titanuus was that bad?"

"All of the fighting and killing? Me? As you can see, I was never built for that. I'm an academic." Eugene's eyes brightened. "But being so youthful and vibrant wasn't without its benefits." A goofy smile crossed his wizened face. He licked his lips. "So tell me, how are my triplets?"

"They are living like queens in the Stronghold."

Eugene poked him in the chest. "So, I imagine that you've taken full advantage of their erotic abilities."

"No."

Leaning away, Eugene lifted an eyebrow and said, "What happened? Did Ruger become impotent?"

"No, he's fine in that department."

Rubbing his saggy chin, Eugene said, "Oh, I see. You courted with another one of the Henchmen. Sticks, aye?" He tapped on Abraham's ribs with his fist. "Yes, I can see in your eyes that you did. She's a raw gal, isn't she, with a smile like a fish."

"I'd rather not talk about it." Abraham set down his mug. "Look, we need to talk about more serious business."

Mandi cozied up to his side and hooked his arm. "Am I interrupting anything?"

Eugene seized her hand in his and said, "No, not at all, you lovely vision." He winked at Abraham. "It didn't take you long to get back on track, did it?" He gave her hand an awkward smooch. "Well done, young man."

Mandi pulled her hand away and wiped it off with a napkin.

"Eugene, this is Mandi."

The older man nodded and asked, "Does she know?"

"Yes."

Eugene searched her eyes with a penetrating stare. "And you believe your friend, about Titanuus?"

She gave a little shrug and said, "I wouldn't be here if I didn't."

"Fascinating. You found yourself a keeper." Eugene took out a handkerchief and blew his nose. "So, what is the problem? Why did you seek me out? Better yet, how did you find me?" He rose up in his chair and scanned the crowd. "I'm very discreet."

The crowd let out a roar. The Penguins had scored a goal.

"I need to understand what is going on." Abraham leaned toward Eugene and spoke over the riled-up people. "You see, I keep going back and forth between worlds."

"You mean through a portal? You've seen more than one?"

"No, not a portal. I fall asleep or get a bad headache, and I bounce between one world and another. I need to find a way back. And there are others like us back there."

Eugene tucked his handkerchief away and said, "This is very interesting. You really didn't see a portal?"

"He said he didn't," Mandi said.

"No need to be snippy, my raven-haired goddess." Eugene rubbed his jaw and stared at the ceiling. "You know, you really caught me off guard. I thought I was finished with the entire matter. Your appearance is quite distressing."

"Why don't we start at the beginning? These portals—are they some sort of experiment? Were you a part of it?" Abraham asked.

Eugene's head dipped down to his chest, and he sighed. "Well, I guess it won't hurt to tell you who I am. I'm a scientist. I was a tenured one at Carnegie Mellon. A very prestigious position. I was part of a team that did research and experimentation aimed at discovering other dimensions. Purely fantasy, and I thought it was a joke when I was assigned to it, but the work proved to be fascinating. The theory, so to speak, grew on me."

"So you opened a portal? Titanuus *is* real?" he asked.

"Oh yes, it's as real as this place or any other," Eugene admitted. "But the problem is that once the portal opened, we didn't have any control of it. And like those ancient *Stargate* theories that we studied, this portal was different. It moved but seemed to like tunnels."

Abraham leaned back against the bar. Eugene had given him an answer that he needed. He felt a tiny bit of relief. His concerns about being crazy faded.

A waitress walked up to Mandi and handed her a strawberry daiquiri.

Mandi looked puzzled and said, "I didn't order this."

"No, that group of guys in the corner booth did," the waitress said. "Here is one of their numbers."

A bunch of young men with preppy haircuts, wearing Pittsburgh sports regalia, waved at Mandi. One of them winked at her.

"What a bunch of douchebags." She handed the drink back to the waitress and said, "Take it away." She held up the napkin with the number on it so that the young men could see then ripped it up.

"It's mating season in here sometimes, but I can't blame them for showing you attention," Eugene said as he slid out of his chair. "I need to excuse myself. This old bladder doesn't hold up for days like the one in Titanuus did. More like minutes, and the first beer runs through me." He patted Abraham on the shoulder. "Now, don't go anywhere. I'll be right back." He teetered away.

"What do you think?" Mandi said as she watched Eugene head toward the bathrooms.

"Pretty surprising. I thought he'd be a real jerk. I guess he's glad he's back."

"Yeah well, you should be too."

"Come on, you know this won't last," he said as he reached for her.

Mandi backed away and bumped into one of the young men who had sent her a drink. The rest of the group was standing behind him.

With an irritated stare, she said, "Pardon me."

"It's okay, gorgeous. I just wanted to come over here and give you another chance to get to know me. You see, I'm a real nice guy." The young man talking was tall, handsome, and built like a quarterback.

His friends sniggered behind him.

"I'm Colt."

"Listen, junior, I'm with someone. Go find someone else your own age." She turned her back.

Colt hooked her elbow and pulled her back. "I don't think you understand. I'm Colt. Don't you know who Colt is?"

Abraham came to his feet and stepped toe to toe with Colt. They were about the same height. The other young men with Colt were just as big and bigger.

"Back off, Colt," he said. "You're being rude."

Colt flipped Abraham's ballcap off. "Sit down, old man."

"Hey!" someone in the crowd said. "That's Abraham Jenkins!"

13

THE BAR IMMEDIATELY FILLED WITH A CHORUS OF BOOS AND JEERS, and the patrons shouted a bunch of rude comments.

"Killer!"

"Murderer!"

The list went on and on.

"It looks like you aren't a very popular guy around here," Colt said to Abraham. "What are you, some old sports jock?"

"No, that's Jenkins the Jet," said a black young man standing behind Colt. He was built like a chimney stack. "He's the one that killed Buddy Parker and his family in that crazy plane wreck. I know the Parkers."

Abraham grabbed Mandi by the arm and said, "Let's get out of here."

"What about Eugene?" she asked.

"I'll get him. Maybe there's a back door." He started to move away from Colt and his crew.

Colt stepped in his way. "Hey, we aren't finished talking yet. I still don't have the lady's name and number."

"I don't have time for this." Abraham balled up his fist.

Mandi took him by the wrist and said, "Don't you dare. You get Eugene. I can handle this." She stepped between him and Colt. "Okay, big fella. You win. Let's talk."

With trepidation stirring inside him, Abraham picked up his hat and took off to the bathroom. The crowd wasn't kind to him at all. The men, with their fists loaded with bottles of beer, wouldn't budge as he tried to push his way through them. He escaped into the bathroom hallway. A line was at the women's door, and he pushed the door into the men's.

A large stainless-steel trough for a urinal was crowded with men lined up in front of it. Three bathroom stalls were there also.

He peeked underneath the stalls and saw three different pairs of shoes. He had no idea what Eugene was wearing, but the man had said he had to pee. He knocked on each door saying, "Eugene? Eugene?"

"Wait your turn, idiot!" a man shouted from the middle stall.

"Did anyone see an old man in a beige overcoat, about yea high?" Abraham asked. "Devil's donuts, he's not in here?" He hustled out of the bathroom.

Eugene had given him the slip. *I knew he was being too nice.* He hurried down the hallway. Two college-aged goons blocked his way. They were beefier versions of Colt and built like linemen.

He stopped. "Guys, I don't have time for this. It's an emergency."

"Yeah, well, Colt and your lady aren't done talking yet. When he's done, you can go," said the black man who had spoken earlier.

"Are you guys on scholarship?"

"Yeah."

"Interesting. I'm close friends with the athletic director. I could make a call and change that scholarship situation," Abraham said.

The young men exchanged a look and stepped aside.

Abraham squirted between them and hustled over to the bar where Mandi was seated with Colt. "He slipped us."

"What?" She started out of her seat.

Colt hooked her arm. "Hey, where are you going, baby? Huh? We aren't finished talking yet."

"How about a shower, Biff?" She poured Abraham's beer over Colt's head.

Colt gawped.

Together, Abraham and Mandi raced through the spirited crowd and out the front doors.

"What are you idiots looking at?" Colt screamed. "Go get them!"

Outside, Abraham caught a glimpse of Eugene on the other side of the street. He started crossing the adjacent street. "Eugene, stop!"

Eugene looked at him, turned, and broke out into a run.

"Hey, he's moving pretty fast," Mandi said.

"You can say that again."

They ran through the slow city traffic and picked their way to the other side of the road. Small-business buildings made up block after block of the area. They chased after Eugene.

Behind them, Colt hollered after them, "You can run, but you can't hide, Rose!"

"Rose? You told him your name was Rose," Abraham said to Mandi.

"He's stupid. He bought it," she said, racing alongside Abraham with her hair trailing behind her.

Half a block away, Eugene ducked into an alley.

"There he goes," she said. "Man, we didn't even catch up with him?"

They turned into the alley and saw green dumpsters and bags of trash. A few fire escapes were anchored to the buildings on both sides. The alley dead-ended half a block up. Abraham saw no sign of Eugene.

"Oh where, oh where did that tricky fish go?" Abraham muttered.

Several back entrances to business buildings were there, but after business hours, all of them were closed.

"He could have gone into any of these doors," she said.

Security cameras were posted over the doors, and two sedans were parked in the alley.

Abraham got down on his hands and knees and looked underneath the cars. "Not here," he said as he stood up and dusted off his hands.

"Abraham, we have company," she said.

Colt and his crew entered the alley. Six of them were marching behind the young man's lead. Colt stopped twenty feet away and pointed at Abraham. Some of the others smashed their fists into their hands. All their eyes had a starry glow.

Colt said, "Now you're going to get what's coming to you, Ruger Slade."

14

WITH CHILLS RUNNING UP HIS SPINE, ABRAHAM ASKED, "WHAT DID you call me?"

"We know who you are and where you are from. Titanuus," Colt said with a darkening expression. "We are from Titanuus as well. Now trapped in this abominable world." He came closer and leered at Mandi. "But it has its perks."

Abraham stepped in front of the brood of men with his thoughts racing. "Who are you? Where are you from?"

"That's not what you need to be concerned with. Right now, your situation is, well, a lot more terminal, Blade Weaver," Colt said. "But we are otherworlders like you too."

Mandi clung to Abraham's arm and said, "I'm scared."

"It's okay," he said, backing them both up. "I'll protect you." Abraham's head was spinning at this darker twist of fate, and his heart pumped like a piston. "You guys, whatever you are, need to leave us alone. We just want Eugene."

"Yes, well, your mistake was finding him." Colt nodded his chin to one side.

His men fanned out in an arc, walling off the escape route behind them. Three of them had lengths of pipe in their hands.

"You should have behaved, Ruger. That would be best for everyone. Get him."

The thugs closed in.

Abraham stepped in front of Mandi, who started texting. He knew how to fight, but he hadn't done much fighting in his own body. Ruger had fought and made mincemeat out of some other people. Now, the time had come for Abraham to see what he could do.

"You better be glad that I don't have a sword," he said.

"It wouldn't make a difference if you did."

Abraham lifted his arms and scanned his opponents. Each and every one was as stout as a telephone pole. *I hope they can't fight as well as they look.*

The black man he'd spoken with at the bathrooms came at him first. He swung hard and heavy punches.

Abraham slipped out of reach.

"Stand still, you big chicken," the burly man said. "Redge is going to bust you up!"

Abraham punched Redge in the throat. Redge floundered backward, clutching at his throat.

The other five men came at Abraham in a rush. He dropped one man with a shot in the ribs, ducked underneath a haymaker, and dislodged the attacker's jaw with an uppercut.

A meaty fist caught him hard in the belly.

Abraham grunted and countered with a leg sweep. Three men were down on the ground. The last two on their feet plowed into him with throaty growls. He tumbled hard onto the street. They wrestled over the pavement, kicking, clawing, and throwing elbows.

He twisted a man's wrist and snapped it. The man let out a painful howl and kicked away.

A rabbit punch to the ribs crumpled another man on the pavement.

"I don't know who you guys are, but you fight like a bunch of daisies."

Abraham tore into them. His big fists broke noses and ribs. Whoever they were, they weren't like Ruger Slade or him. They were cowards trapped in the big bodies, making them ideal bullies. He beat the crap out of them and watched them limp and crawl away. Blood dripped from his swelling knuckles.

"Abraham," Mandi said desperately.

Colt had a long arm around her waist and was pointing a gun to her head.

"Help me."

"Shut up," Colt said. "Listen up. This fun is over. It's time to give yourself up. You don't want this pretty lady to get hurt, do you?"

"No." Abraham lifted his arms.

The back door of one of the cars parked in the alley popped open, and Eugene came out. "I can't believe you missed me. Interesting."

"What is going on here, Eugene? What is this all about? Who are these guys?" he asked.

"Some of my old friends from Titanuus that have proven themselves useful to our cause," Eugene replied. He walked over to Abraham with a very easy stride. "I see you are surprised that I'm not so, well, shabby as I appear. Well, when I came back, I too carried over some of the attributes of Ruger. You see, the experience has done us both very well."

Struggling in Colt's arms, Mandi said, "What kind of snake are you?"

"Why, I'm a snake that can shed his skin and grow it back again. It's something that you wouldn't understand, honey." Eugene looked at Mandi. "I really hate it when innocent people get caught up in our affairs. You made a very big mistake, young lady. You have become collateral damage. And all for what? A truck driver."

"You leave her out of this, Eugene!" he yelled.

"Sorry, but the matter is out of my hands." He looked at Redge as the big man was rubbing his throat. "Get a stun rod and some cuffs. It's high time that we fully restrained this pest."

"If you hurt her, I swear I'll tear all of you apart," he warned.

"Don't make threats that you can't back up, my good man." Eugene took out a handkerchief and blew his nose. "That will prove fatal."

"You won't kill me. I know you need me, don't you?"

"Huh…" Eugene reached over and grabbed the stun rod from Redge. He twirled it in his hand. "Yes, they do need you. Dr. Jack and the others. Yes, they need you. But I don't agree. Tell you what —I'll see to it that Mandi won't be harmed if you behave. Deal?"

"Like I can take your word for it?"

"True, but you don't have a choice," Eugene said.

"I'll be fine," Mandi said. "Don't get yourself hurt."

Redge walked behind Abraham with flexicuffs in his hands.

"What is with you guys and flex cuffs?"

Redge cuffed his wrists and ankles.

"Good." Eugene walked up to Abraham. "Now, say your goodbyes."

"I'm going to get you out of this," he said to Mandi.

Colt scoffed a laugh. "Yeah, right."

"I believe in you," she said back to Abraham.

"Smooch, smooch, smooch—isn't that nice?" Colt said, making kissy lips. "Don't worry. She'll be just fine with me. She'll come around. They always do."

Eugene hit Abraham in the gut with the stun rod.

Fire shot through Abraham's veins, and he dropped to his knees.

"You are still strong. Very strong. Let me try that again, Abraham." Eugene hit him again… and again.

Mandi screamed, "Stop it! You're killing him!"

He fell to the ground with a dark veil falling over his eyes. His heavy lids started to close. All he could see was Mandi kicking and screaming. He read Eugene's lips as well.

"Dispose of her."

Nooooooooooooo!

15

———

TITANUUS

ABRAHAM WOKE WITH A SPLITTING HEADACHE. HIS EYES FELT AS IF
they had sandbags on them. He scratched away the crust and
opened them with his fingers. The bright sun shone into his eyes.
He was lying on a bed of blankets. The sound of a rolling wagon
rattled underneath him. He grabbed a hold of the side and sat up.

"Look who is awake," Vern said. The warrior was riding a horse
behind the wagon. His wavy blond hair bounced on his shoulders
as his puffy lips maintained a permanent sneer.

Bearclaw rode beside Vern. The broad-faced warrior with wild
black hair and a thick beard eyed Abraham like a hawk.

Both men wore their black leather tunics over chain mail.
Their sword belts bounced at their sides.

"Captain! You are awake!" Horace said. The beefy warrior was
driving the wagon.

Sticks rode on the bench beside Horace. Her hair was tied in
twin ponytails. One bandolier of knives was strapped over a
shoulder. Her sword belt was full of more sharp weapons. Wearing
a tight sleeveless leather jerkin over a long-sleeved cotton shirt,

63

the expressionless woman climbed into the wagon with Abraham. "Welcome back," she said. "Did you sleep well?"

"I wouldn't say that." He rubbed his temples with his fingers. "Oh man, Mandi is in trouble. I have to get back home. Where are we? What's going on?"

"We are in Kingsland on the road to the House of Steel," she said as she handed him a water skin. "You've been catatonic for over a week. But the king just summoned us. We didn't know what to do, so we put you in the wagon."

He gulped down the water and wetted his parched lips. His stomach growled like a wolf. "I've been out that long?"

"Yes."

"Has anything else happened?"

"The barn is finished, Captain," Horace said with a look over his shoulder. "The Henchmen and Red Tunics labor in the fields. The weather has been good. The lilies bloom. The songbirds sing. I think it's the calm before the storm."

Staring out at the rolling hills and lush valleys leading toward the city of Burgess, he asked, "Why would you say that?"

"Because we are going to see the king," Horace replied.

Abraham clutched his head. He couldn't stop thinking about Mandi. She was in danger, all because of him. He had to find a way back. Looking at the supplies in the wagon, he told Sticks, "Hand me that shovel."

With a blank look, she reached over, grabbed the shovel, and dragged it scraping over the wagon bed. She put the shovel handle in his hands. "What are you going to do with a shovel?"

He wrapped his hands around the neck of the shovel and looked into the spade as he would a mirror.

Sticks tilted her head to one side and looked at the spot where he was looking.

"I need to go back home," he said. His heart started to race. All he could think about was Mandi being hauled away by Eugene and his goons. He bashed himself in the forehead with the shovel. "I need to go back home!" He did it again, popping himself hard, square in the noggin. "Now!"

Sticks jumped on the shovel and bear-hugged it. "Have you lost your mind? Who hits themselves with a shovel?"

"I do," Horace offered. "Good show, Captain."

"He's insane," Vern said. He'd moved his horse to the left side of the wagon as Bearclaw trotted up to the right. "Possessed. I told you all he's a madman."

"Give me the shovel back!" Abraham said. A trickle of blood ran down his forehead and over the bridge of his nose. "I have to get back home!"

"What is going on back home?" Sticks tried to stop the blood dripping from his forehead with the sleeve of her shirt. "You really made a fine mess of yourself. Horace, did we pack any bandages?"

"Why would we need bandages?" He looked back over his shoulder at Abraham. "Oh, that is bad. Usually Iris brings those. I told you that we should have brought her."

"Yeah, everywhere we go with him, someone ends up bleeding," Vern said. "Or dying."

Sticks glared at Vern. She whisked a dagger out of her bandolier and cut part of the sleeve off her shirt. She put the crude bandage on Abraham's head. She took his hand and slapped it over the bandage. "Keep it there. Now, explain yourself."

"I was back in my old body. Back home. Needless to say, a friend of mine is in big trouble." He studied the concerned faces of the group. "You know the person that used to host this body? Well, the other personality?"

All of them nodded.

"His name is Eugene Drisk. We tracked him down. I tried to get answers, but the weasel flipped on us." He rolled his neck. "Poor Mandi. She's not equipped for this. I have to get there now."

"Perhaps the king will have answers, Captain," Horace said. "Look ahead. The House of Steel awaits."

Abraham climbed out of the wagon bed and into the front of the wagon. He sat on the bench beside Horace, who was driving a team of two horses. Their destination was only a mile away. The House of Steel was a magnificent castle made from alabaster stone. Huge colorful flags made a ring around a humongous sword driven into the earth ages before. Legend said it was the sword of Antonugus, which slew the celestial warrior, Titanuus, the universal being that had formed the world.

"It's a beautiful thing," Horace said as he snapped the reins.

"Yes, it's quite a castle," Abraham replied.

"I'm not talking about the castle. I'm talking about that sword. I marvel."

Abraham checked the blood on his rag. He'd made quite a mess of himself. He sighed. *No more playing around. I have to get back home. And King Hector is going to help.* Another thought crossed his mind. "Ah crap."

"What's the matter, Captain?"

He put the rag back on his head. "Nothing." *Except Queen Clarann is going to be there.*

16

ABRAHAM LEFT HIS ACCOMPANYING HENCHMEN OUTSIDE THE castle's front gate. The King's Guardians, led by their commander, Pratt, escorted Abraham onto the castle grounds.

"What happened to your face?" the horse-necked Pratt asked. He stood half a head taller than Abraham and had shoulders as wide as a deer's rack.

"I hit it with a shovel," Abraham said dryly. He shielded his eyes from the sun, which shone off the shoulder of Pratt's full-plate armor.

"Hmm," Pratt replied. "It looks like you did a fine job if that was your intent. But you shouldn't appear marred up in the king's presence."

"Yes, well, I'll try to be better put together the next time." Abraham wasn't in the mood to chat. He had another mission. He scanned the outlying walls and windows decorating the beautiful castle and saw no sign of the queen. *I hope she isn't there. I don't want to talk about Ruger's illegitimate daughter. Oh man, what if this is what it's all about? King Hector would behead me!*

One of the other two Guardians opened a wrought-iron gate.

The pathway entered a walled channel paved with decorative stones. Stairs led upward toward a terrace. The group was met at the top landing by two more Guardians standing on the other side of another iron gate. They saluted Pratt with hand chops to their temples and opened the gate.

Pratt led the way out onto the king's terrace, overlooking the Bay of Elders. They were alone. "Wait here. I'll announce you." In one stride, he took all three steps leading up onto an elevated patio and entered through the curtains there.

Abraham checked his self-inflicted head wound with his fingertips. Blood had dried on his fingers, but the bleeding was staunched. He gazed down into the bay. Flocks of birds floated in the winds over the choppy waters. He counted dozens of warships docked and out in the sea. He'd never seen so many before.

He rubbed his chin. *Something's brewing. I smell war.*

Abraham leaned his back against the terrace wall and waited for the first person to come through. *Please don't be Clarann.* He wanted to get down to business. No doubt King Hector wanted them to continue their missions, and most likely, this was what it was all about, but he had a mission too: save Mandi and put an end to this mess.

Pratt came through the curtains and pulled them to one side.

Oh Lord, who is behind curtain number one, Monty?

Queen Clarann stepped out onto the patio. Pratt let the curtains go behind her.

Son of a biscuit!

17

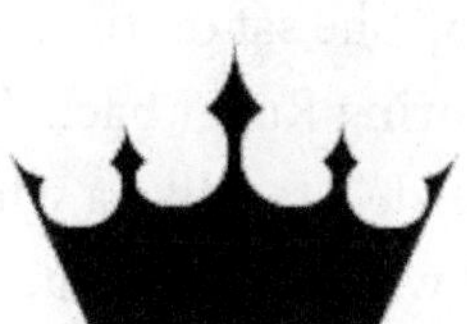

QUEEN CLARANN WAS A FAIR-HAIRED LIONESS WITH ICE-BLUE EYES. She wore a long silk gown that showed off all her natural curves. The beautiful woman dismissed Pratt, who abandoned the terrace.

Abraham took a knee. As his heart thundered in his chest, his palms began to sweat.

She gracefully walked over to him and said, "Please stand, Abraham. It's good to see you."

As lovely as she was, she had a don't-beat-around-the-bush air about her. He rose and faced her.

"By the Elders, what happened to your head? That wound is fresh."

He looked over at the terrace gate where the Guardians were posted and said, "Pratt did it."

"What?" She twisted her head around and glared at Pratt, standing more than an earshot away.

Pratt's eyes grew big, and he stiffened.

"I'm only kidding," he said. He wasn't in a joking mood, but he couldn't help taking a shot at Pratt. "I had a small accident on the way over."

69

"You don't have accidents," she said matter-of-factly.

"I'm not Ruger, remember. Maybe he didn't, but I do." He looked away from her penetrating gaze. "Is the king coming… soon?"

"I've made you uncomfortable, haven't I?" she asked.

He shrugged.

"I have felt horrible for unloading my burden on you. That wasn't right for me to do." She sat on the terrace wall. "I hoped that maybe, well, that might bring Ruger back. I guess I wanted him to know." She shook her head. "I feel like a whore."

"Huh," Abraham said with amazement. "Why would you say that?"

She hugged her arms, looked out over the sea, and said, "Because I am. I'm the cause of all of this. I don't deserve to be a queen, and King Hector is a fool for falling for me."

With a sheepish look, he asked, "Does the king know?"

Her eyes started to water. Teardrops ran down her cheeks.

18

I'm a dead man.

"I'm going to the gallows, aren't I?"

"What? No." She grabbed his hands. "Of course not. Hector doesn't know. I would hate to hurt him like that. He's a true king, and he deserves much better than me. I'm a commoner, not meant for royalty. I should have died."

He patted her back and said, "Don't be so hard on yourself." He wanted to walk away, but being close to her stirred him.

She wore an intoxicating perfume with a lavender scent. Her wine-colored lips looked soft, and her enticing figure, accented in her silky dress, was to die for. The platinum blonde could bring any man to his knees.

"And you don't look like a commoner. You look like a queen."

She choked out a sob and said, "Thank you, even though I know you are feeding me false sympathy."

"No, that's not true, and you know it."

Seabirds landed on the terrace wall. He shooed them away.

"You know, I didn't stick around for the entire story," he said.

"Can you tell me what really happened between you and Ruger? It might help."

Queen Clarann wiped her tears away and said, "It's an awful love story. Ruger and I met through my family's connections with the House of Steel. They are merchants that deal in fine tapestries. That's how I met Ruger, and we fell in love. But the Captain of the King's Guardians is forbidden to marry. His focus must be on the king."

"I thought Pratt was married," he said.

"No, Pratt is a talker who enjoys speaking about his imaginary family." She toyed with the sapphire necklace hanging over her breasts. "He makes it sound real. I overhear them talking some-times. A family serves as a distraction. That's why most of the older knights marry younger women at a much older age."

"It's not such a bad plan," he grinned.

She laughed. "It's not as if they abstain from all relations either. The Guardians are, well, as you know, private. So an unexpected twist of fate occurred when King Hector fell for me. His wife had died, and I managed to catch his eye. Don't mistake me. I love Hector, truly, but the marriage was, well, arranged."

"Let me guess. You and Ruger had an affair?"

"Not at all. Ruger would die first. There was no greater Guardian than him, but before I married Hector, well…" Clarann's chin started to quiver. She took a deep breath through her nose and said, "I seduced him. That wasn't easy either, but my tugging on his heart wore him down. He gave in to me just days before the wedding. I fear I broke him."

"Broke? That's a strange thing to say."

"It wasn't so long after that when all of the crazy things started to happen. Ruger abandoned the Guardians. More possessed people walked the kingdom. The brewing rumors of war grew teeth. I swear I've tainted Kingsland. My wicked heart wanted what it wanted, and now we all suffer for it. Worst of all, Ruger is lost. All I wanted to do was tell him that I was sorry. He needed to know about his daughter too. He never knew."

"You never told him?"

"How could I? It would ruin him."

Abraham scratched his neck and said, "I think he might be glad to know it. It's possible that he might know already."

She looked deep into his eyes and asked, "Is Ruger still in there?"

"No, but he's back home in my world, trying to find a way back here."

"How do you know this?" she said.

"It's a long story, but trust me when I say he's not lost. He's in the wrong body. He's in my old body."

She threw her arms around Abraham and gave him a warm embrace.

Abraham felt himself melt in her arms. The chemistry between them was the kind that should be forbidden.

King Hector's authoritative voice interrupted the moment. "What is the meaning of this?"

Queen Clarann and Abraham separated. She bowed. Abraham took a knee.

"Rise, Abraham!" King Hector said.

He wore the Crown of Stones, which showed the shiny emerald in the front horn. He wore kingly robes, deep red and trimmed with silver fur. Lewis and Leodor walked behind the king, along with another man, who wore juice-purple hooded robes.

The king extended his hand toward Ruger. "A happy queen makes a happy king! I can see the joy on her face. What good news do you bear?" He looked at Abraham's forehead and winced. "What happened to you?"

"I hit myself with a shovel. It's a long story."

"You did a fine job," Lewis said. He was dressed in his cape with new clothing and armor underneath. "I'm certain I could do better."

"Stop it, Lewis, or I'll make a bridle for your tongue," King Hector said. He turned his attention to Clarann. "Well, what are you glowing about?"

"I never gave him a proper thank you, Hector," Clarann said quickly. "He saved our daughter and my life. I finally had a moment to express my sincere gratitude." She dipped her chin. "I'm sorry if I broke the crown's etiquette, but I was suddenly overwhelmed."

"It certainly looks like it," Lewis said.

King Hector ignored his son and said, "Of course you didn't break any formal protocols. You are the queen. You can express your gratitude however you see fit." He put his hand on Abraham's shoulder. "I trust this man. He's more than proven himself."

Abraham nodded. So did the queen. Their eyes met briefly.

Abraham said, "It's an honor, Your Majesty."

"Excellent. Shall we get down to business?" the king said. He turned toward the table on the terrace's upper deck.

The shine of the blue gem on the back horn of the king's crown caught Abraham's eyes. Life sparkled within it. He took a seat at the table with the others. The king sat at the head, the queen to his left, and his son to the right. Abraham sat by the queen with Leodor across from him. The man in purple robes sat beside the viceroy with his face covered by a hood.

"Where is Clarice?" the king asked.

Clarice stepped through the curtains a moment later. The beautiful girl with flowing chestnut hair and gorgeous eyes sat down beside Abraham. "Sorry, Father." She glared at Lewis. "I believe that I was delayed receiving the word."

Lewis smirked. "Of course you were."

King Hector rolled his eyes.

19

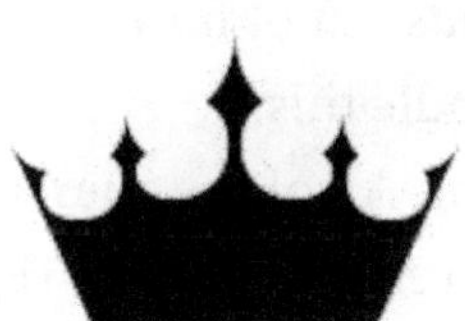

"Abraham"—King Hector opened his hand toward the man seated beside Leodor—"I wanted to introduce you to Melris."

His eyes hidden in his hood, Melris slowly dipped his clean-shaven chin.

"Nice to meet you," Abraham said. He felt Clarice staring at him and gave her a quick look. As her big eyes soaked him in, he looked away. "Let me guess, you're another one of Leodor's cronies from the Sect."

"Hardly," Leodor scoffed. The old mystic's snobbish expression was as froward as ever. He spoke as though he had a bad taste in his mouth. "Melris comes from the outer sect."

"We are the Elders' chosen," Melris said in a soft voice. He had a pleasant yet cryptic manner about him. "We don't pervert the arcane."

"Pah!" Leodor rolled his eyes. "King Hector, I don't understand why you wish to consort with this lunatic. His ilk are an assorted lot of conjurers and enchanters spawned from drunken gypsies. They are tremendous weavers of words, but that is all. Don't let his forked tongue spellbind you."

"I didn't," King Hector said as he drummed his fingers on the table and rested his chin on his palm. "I used the stone of truth on him. Melris answered my questions without fault. He is an Elderling."

"Pfft!" Leodor sank back in his chair and stuffed his hands in his sleeves. "We'll see."

Abraham lifted a finger and asked, "What is an Elderling?"

Leodor flung his hands out of his robes and said, "Oh please, Your Majesty, let me handle this?"

"Be respectful, Leodor. All of my guests in the House of Steel are worthy of the king's respect," Hector replied.

"Certainly, Your Majesty," Leodor droned. "You see, Abraham, Melris claims to be a direct servant of the Elders. Though he cannot speak of them. Or describe them. He has, however, been in direct contact with him. According to the Elderlings, they are born with magic ability and do not require any tutelage or training. They claim that it comes naturally."

Melris held a hand out over the table. His fingernails were perfectly manicured, with a pale mulberry shade. His hands were unblemished and soft. He turned his palm upward, and a beautiful violet flower made of energy appeared.

The women at the table gasped.

"How beautiful," Clarann said with awe.

With a gentle flip of his hand, Melris cast the burning magic flower into the air. It floated higher and higher and then transformed.

"Look, it's a bird," Clarice said.

The bird flapped its wings and streaked into the sky and disappeared.

Hector, Clarann, and Clarice applauded.

"Magnificent," the king said, elated.

Leodor's chinless face tightened. "It's an illusion."

"Illusion or not, I still don't follow what is going on here," Abraham said.

Lewis gave Abraham a haughty look and said, "My father wants Melris to become a Henchman."

"I can't become a Henchman," Melris said as he blew the magic's vapors from his fingers. "I am an Elderling, but they sent me to help."

"And why would they do that?" Lewis asked. "They've never helped before." He shook his head. "There aren't such things as Elders."

"Don't be a fool, son. Of course there are." Hector cleared his throat. "Abraham, Melris is going to assist you on your quest to recover the four remaining stones. He offers knowledge given of the Elders that we can use. His recent arrival couldn't have come at a better time."

"Your Majesty, how can I trust a man that does not wear the King's Brand?" he said.

"Not all in your company wear the brand. They earn it, don't they? Hmm?" Hector replied. "You take Red Tunics and Hirelings, don't you?"

"I suppose that is correct, but we can handle them if they step out of line. I'm not so sure about this guy." He eyed Melris. "No offense."

"None taken," Melris replied.

"As I recall, you didn't handle the assassin Raschel all that well," King Hector replied.

"Yeah, but that's because those two sandbags"—he pointed at Lewis and Leodor—"were behind it all. They hired her. At least they are branded now. But this guy… Well, honestly, King Hector, I have enough personnel to deal with."

"One more won't hurt. Besides, Melris is more than capable of handling himself. He's assured me of that." King Hector stood up and put his index fingers down on the table. A fiery edge built up in his voice. "Melris will accompany you, but Abraham, you are in charge. Melris also has intimate knowledge on the location of the stones. He will guide you on the journey. The two of you can begin sorting out the details on our way out." He adjusted his crown. "Any questions?"

"King Hector, I'm not sure what path we are taking, but we should be going after the horned halfling, Big Apple. That little bald-headed ball of muscle has the answers that we need. That I need." Abraham stood up and planted his knuckles on the table. "Your Majesty, I have problems back home. I need to return as soon as possible."

The friendly demeanor of an Englishman vanished from Hector's face when his eyebrows knitted together and he said, "Sit down!"

Abraham's legs turned to jelly, and he dropped into his chair. *What in Titanuus's Crotch was that all about?*

20

ABRAHAM LEFT THE HOUSE OF STEEL LIKE A DOG WITH ITS TAIL between its legs. King Hector's orders were clear. They were to find the gems to the Crown of Stones at all costs.

"This sucks. This sucks. This sucks," he muttered to himself. He was in his bedroom inside the Stronghold, packing his gear for the long journey.

The triplets, Sophia, Selma, and Bridget, were in the room with him. Each of them was a vixen with piles of dark hair, a rich caramel tan, and seductive *I Dream of Jeannie* eyes. They folded his clothes and helped him pack.

"You seem angry, Master," Selma said. She looked ravishing in her pink tunic dress trimmed in black fox fur. She was sitting on the edge of the bed with her legs crossed and stuffing his clothing into his sack. "Must you go so soon? It's pouring, the rain."

"And it storms," said Sophia, who was dressed in the same outfit but in all black. "You could get hit by lightning."

"Huh huh," he laughed, recalling his battle with Arcayis the Underlord. The powerful mystic had rammed a bolt of blue light-ning into his skull. "Let's hope not." He picked up his son's backpack with the Pirates logo on it. Staring at the logo, he could see his boy's face. The lightning storm had cost him everything. A lightning strike had caused his plane to crash.

Bridget, dressed in white, rubbed his shoulders. "Stay with us, Master. Enjoy yourself by the fire. Let us care for you, for once."

"I've got the king's business to do," he said as he ground his teeth.

King Hector really hacked him off. The man had changed. Abraham couldn't put his finger on it, but adding that blue gemstone to the crown appeared to have enhanced his power and confidence.

"Thanks for the offer."

The upstairs bedroom fireplace crackling nearby set the perfect scene. The triplets converged on him. Their hands and fingers massaged his muscles. They pushed him back into the bed and sat him down.

"Hey, whoa!" he said.

Selma was on her knees, behind his back, rubbing his shoulders. Sophia sat beside him, rubbing his forearms. Bridget was on her knees, rubbing his calves. All three of them smelled great. Their perfume filled his nose with intoxicating effect. His heart started to race.

"Master, it's been so long since you spent time with us. We miss your intimacy. You saved us from treachery," Selma said.

"That wasn't me. That was, well, the other me," he said as he closed his eyes and let Selma rub his temples. "Oh, and by the way, he misses you."

"Really?" Sophia said brightly. All three of them started to glow.

"He's a very bad man, you know. He took my girlfriend back home hostage."

One passion was replaced by another as he thought of Mandi. She was in danger, and he had to get back home. He politely tore his way out of the sensual touches of the three women. He saw Sticks leaning against the door frame.

"Hey… Sticks. We were packing."

"I can see that." Sticks pushed off of the door frame and said, "The Henchmen are gathered downstairs, per your request."

"I'll be right down."

Sticks vanished down the hallway. The triplets giggled as they watched her leave. She wasn't the ravishing beauty that the triplets were, but she wasn't a dog either.

"You guys are harsh," Abraham said and headed downstairs.

Downstairs, all the Henchmen were seated at the great table. The head seat was empty. Sticks sat on the left row beside Prospero, Apollo, Dominga, Tark, and Cudgel. On the right were Horace, Bearclaw, Vern, Iris, and Shades. All of them were in full gear. They were a hard-eyed bunch, to say the least. Last of all was Solomon. His oversized body sat in the chair on the opposite end of Abraham's seat. His matted fur had been combed out. The bigfoot-like troglin had a gentler look about him. He still wore the vest and trousers he'd acquired in Pirate City.

The table was loaded with a feast of roast beast, meats, rolls, and cheese. The two older hirelings, sisters Elga and Eileen, teetered out of the kitchen with bent backs, half hobbling, carrying serving trays. The salty women filled all the goblets with wine and the mugs with hot coffee. They grumbled, hacked, and coughed as they worked.

Abraham sat down and dismissed the hirelings with a wave of his hand and said, "That will be all."

The stringy-haired Elga mumbled in a mocking fashion, "That will be all," and teetered away with her sister.

The galley door to the kitchen slammed behind them.

"Grumpy old women," he said to himself.

He looked down the table. Despite the pouring rain and thunder, the great room had a warm and cozy feel. The huge strong fireplace burned with several roasting logs. Curtains and animal pelts on the walls softened the room's interior. He'd let the triplets handle the decoration. They'd given the Stronghold more of a lodgelike feel.

He lifted his wine goblet. "Let's have a toast."

With befuddled looks, the group lifted their glasses.

"To the Henchmen. Death before failure," he said.

"Hear! Hear!" Horace added.

They drank with unease.

Abraham looked over at Sticks and said, "Let's eat. Pass the potatoes." In a sullen mood, he loaded his plate as they all passed the food around.

Eating utensils scraped against bowls as the food was scooped out in heaps. No one was saying a word. All of them loaded their plates and ate quietly.

Abraham picked away at his food. He sawed up hunks of beef with his knife and fork. He chewed slowly and washed it down with sour purple wine. He couldn't stop thinking about Mandi. He was eating, and back home, she was suffering. He didn't know what to do, and King Hector had sidetracked him.

Vern dropped his utensils on his plate with a clatter and asked, "Captain, what in the Elders is going on? Have you become possessed by someone else again?"

21

"Maintain respect, Vern!" Horace belted out. "You don't question the Captain!"

"Hey, I thought we'd become all chummy now," Vern replied.

"It's not your words—it's your tone," Sticks said.

Everyone at the table broke out in an argument… except for Prospero, who gobbled up his plate of food. Half of the table defended Vern, while the other half attacked him.

Abraham raised his voice. "That's enough!"

The company quieted.

"I'm the same Abraham Jenkins. I have a problem back home. A friend of mine is in danger."

Vern tossed his cloth napkin on his plate and said, "Great. Here we go again, out on another mission while he's worried about another world and not this one."

"Shut up, Vern," Iris said. The mystic, dressed in green robes decked out in subtle arcane symbols, had a frown on her comely pie face. "You took the Brand again, so don't complain about it now."

"Yes, do be quiet. I don't even have a Brand, though I've asked for it." Shades had a mark on one cheek and a scar on the other. He wore no armor underneath his loose-fitting garb. He eyed the fireplace, where the King's Brand was propped up against the mantel. "Now would be a fine time before the mission begins."

"Oh, don't start this again," Iris said.

"Agreed," the attractive black woman, Dominga, added.

"Haven't I proven myself?" Shades said.

Half of the people at the table responded together. "No!"

Shades ran his fingers back through his tawny locks of short hair. "I don't know why you people don't like me."

"It's because of what you did at Baracha, you fool!" Iris said.

Shades rolled his eyes. "You need to let it go. I've saved all of you several times since."

"You imagine things!" Horace fired back.

"Yes, you delusional little creep!" Dominga said.

The bickering resumed.

Abraham opened his mouth to shut them down again.

Then Shades flipped a spoonful of mashed potatoes into Iris's face.

Aghast, she cried out, "You little devil piglet!" She picked up her plate and flung the entire meal at Shades.

Horace jumped out of his seat and said, "Iris! Show some decorum! Shades, I'm going to break you in—ulp!"

A heap of potatoes smote him in the nose. A turkey leg sailed at Shades. He plucked it out of the air and took a bite out of it.

"Thank you, Dominga," he said with a wink.

In the next instant, hands were filled with food. Hunks of meat and bowls of vegetables were being flung from all directions. Rolls and biscuits and bowls of stew went everywhere.

A huge smile broke out on Solomon's face as he filled his hands with hunks of beef and said, "Food fight!"

Abraham sat at the end of the table, watching the meal go to waste.

Sticks crawled underneath the table.

Solomon cowered behind his forearms and hands and moved away from the table, saying, "Don't get food in my fur!"

Hot rolls were chucked like snowballs. The goblets of wine were spilled.

An errant throw sent a bowl of green-pea soup splashing off Abraham's chest.

The Henchmen froze. All of them were covered in farm table grit of one sort or another.

Abraham rubbed his eyes and face. Pea soup dripped into his lap. He clenched his teeth and felt his ears turning red.

All the Henchmen slowly sat back down in their seats.

Solomon took his place at the end of the table. With noodles dangling from his fur, he said, "Sorry, Abraham. I don't know what got into me."

Abraham set the empty bowl of pea soup that had landed on his lap back on the table. "It's all right. Everyone is entitled to a Belushi moment. Now, where was I?"

Sticks crawled back into her seat from underneath the table. "I thought that you were going to tell us about the mission. You hadn't said a word about it since we left the House of Steel. All you said was start packing."

"No, that wasn't it," he said. "Vern questioned me." He gave Vern a hard look. "Just so you know, as well as the rest of you, the real Ruger, it appears, resides in my body back home. I can't explain it. But he lives, somehow. But I don't want to talk about that." He saw Solomon raise an eyebrow. "That's all you need to know."

"In the meantime," Abraham continued, "we are heading north to recover the rest of the stones. And we'll have a new Henchman, so to speak, among us."

The company exchanged confused glances.

Horace said, "What do you mean, Captain? Do you brand another Henchman? Did the king?"

"No. His name is Melris. He should be arriving with those other sandbags, Lewis and Leodor."

"What about Swan and the princess?" Shades asked. He and the Guardian Maiden Swan had connected on their last trip.

Abraham shrugged. "I suppose they'll all be coming along too."

"Captain," Horace said, "the more of us, the harder to navigate in discretion. Are we taking the ship?"

"I don't know."

"It doesn't sound like you are in charge anymore," Vern said in a snide manner.

Bearclaw popped Vern with an elbow.

"The king insists that we let Melris guide us. Not lead." Abraham's jaw muscles clenched. He couldn't stop thinking about Mandi. "Don't have any confusion. I'm in charge."

Iris spoke with the polite airiness of an Englishwoman and said, "What does this Melris do?"

"According to Leodor, he's a mystic from the outer sect. The old chinless wonder doesn't care for him." Abraham smirked. "But apparently, the king summoned him. And Melris calls himself—"

A loud thunderclap filled the room, followed by a quick flash of lightning.

A newcomer spoke a moment later and said in a clear but soft tone, "An Elderling."

Every head at the table twisted toward the front door.

Decked out in the wine-purple garb of a wizard stood Melris. Despite the rain outdoors, his raiment was as dry as a bone.

22

ABRAHAM RESTED HIS ELBOWS ON THE TABLE AND ASKED, "WHERE are the others, Melris?"

"They won't be coming," replied the taller-than-average and slender Melris.

Using a metal rod like a cane, he approached the table. The rod was made out of black iron. It had three feet, like prongs, on the bottom. It didn't clack when it touched the stone floor. Melris's steps didn't make a sound either. "I sensed your distress in working with them. I suggested to the king that they remain behind."

Horace smacked a meaty palm on the table. "I like this Melris."

"I'd like him better if I could see his face," Dominga said as she strained her eyes to look underneath the stranger's hood. "He has skin like a baby."

With his hands, covered in black gloves, Melris lowered his hood. He had short strawberry-blond locks of wavy hair and boyish good looks. Like a rose among thorns, he had not a blemish on him. His lavender eyes had an omniscient spark to them.

"How old are you?" the moony-eyed Iris asked. "You look like a child."

"I'm an Elderling. We don't keep track of our ages, but it would be reasonable to say that I exceed all of the ages of you put together."

Horace pumped his fist in the air. "Hear! Hear! I'm not the oldest one anymore!"

Tark scratched the back of his skull and asked, "Captain, what is an Elderling?"

Abraham was about to speak, but Iris cut him off. "They are supposed to be the direct servants of the Elders. But I've never seen one before, nor any of the other mystics that I've trained with. They are as rare as the Elders. Not that anyone has seen any of them either."

"I believe you are mistaken. You have seen two," Melris said as he made his way around the table. He carefully stepped away from the piles of food. "There is the Fenix, the Elder Spawn. That is an Elder of sorts. Also, you killed the Elder of Slime at Crown Island. The Elders took note of that. That experience will serve you well."

"We've killed Elders?" Bearclaw thumped his chest. "Well, well."

"There are minor Elders and major Elders," Melris replied.

"Which kind were they?" Horace asked.

Melris stood by the fire and picked up the Brand. "It's not my place to say." He studied the crown-like design and set it back down. "Abraham, are you and your Henchmen ready to go now?"

"Er... yes, we are always ready, but it would help if we knew where we were going."

"Yes, it would. We are going to the Wound. Are you familiar with it?"

Abraham teetered on the back two legs of his chair and tried to search Ruger's memory banks. He knew where the Wound was on the map. The canyon could be easily found, located in the northern hemisphere of Eastern Bolg. That was all he recalled. He eyed Horace. "Am I familiar with it?"

"No, Captain. None of us are."

"I see." Melris passed his hand over the log fire, extinguishing the flames. "Shall we go, then?"

Abraham dropped his front chair legs to the floor, got up, and walked to the front door. He felt every eye in the room on his back but Melris's. He opened the door. Sheets of rain were coming down outside. Mud puddles had formed all over the courtyard.

He cupped his hands over his mouth and hollered toward the barn, "Skittles and Zanax!"

A few moments later, two figures crept out of the barn and into the drenching gloom. The Red Tunics Skitts and Zann, brothers, splashed through the mud and made a beeline for Abraham. He called them Skittles and Zanax—one after the candy and the other after the drug Xanax back home—because the names seemed to fit their temperaments. Plus, they were catchy.

The brothers stood before him, soaked to the bone. "Yes, Captain?"

"Get the horses and wagon ready. We are moving out now."

"A nice day to travel," Zann said in a slow and scratchy Southern drawl. "Can't wait to ride in it."

Shielding his eyes from the blowing rain, Skitts asked, "Are we going?"

"You don't think I'm going to pitch my tent, do you?"

"No, sir," Skitts replied. He shoved his brother, and they hustled back to the barn.

Abraham moved back inside, looked at his group, and asked, "What are you waiting for? The sun to start shining? Sunshine or rain, we've got a kingdom to save."

23

THE HENCHMEN HEADED BACK UP THE KINGSLAND COASTLAND toward Titanuus's Crotch. That was still the safest route of travel. Southern Tiotan and Kingsland were in full alert along the border between the two great territories. Not even commerce moved back and forth between the two countries anymore.

Abraham and company had gathered plenty of intelligence while they were waiting on King Hector's direction. They had contacts in the King's Army that kept them informed. There were spies too—spies on both sides. Abraham couldn't help but wonder if Melris might be one of them.

He led the way up the stormy coastline where the Bay of Elders' angry waters crashed. The company moved in the same double-column formation. The Red Tunics towed behind the wagon in the rear. Dominga and Tark scouted ahead. Even the daytime was as dark as night.

Abraham didn't really care. This was the first time since he'd lived in Titanuus that he was mentally detached. He couldn't stop thinking about Mandi and the danger she must have been in. He had no way of protecting her, and his heart ached. She'd been good to him without him giving her any sort of reason.

Solomon caught up to Abraham with his long-drenched arms swinging. He was traveling on foot but had little trouble keeping up with the horse, with his giant stride. "A word?"

"Of course." Abraham peeled his horse away from Sticks and Horace, who were always fixtures in front of him. He led his horse toward the sandy beaches and the crashing waves. "What's on your mind?"

"We haven't spoken since your last episode. At the dinner table, you mentioned an encounter with the real Ruger Slade. That threw me." Solomon slung the water from his hands. "Stinking fur. It adds another hundred pounds when it's wet. You know, I think we could make a killing selling umbrellas."

Abraham's horse nickered and shook its neck.

"A great idea. A fortune for the taking," Abraham said glumly.

"You're all eaten up. More so than before. We all sense it. So fill me in."

"It's a long story."

"We have a long journey."

Abraham told Solomon everything that had happened when he was back home. If he left out any detail, it wasn't intentional.

Toying with the wet hair underneath his chin as though it were a goatee, Solomon said, "Interesting. I sympathize with your distress, but at least you are back on board with getting out of this place. I was beginning to feel like a lone wolf."

"Yeah, well, the both of us might be a pair of lone wolves. I don't feel like the king still has my back either. He's more interested in the gems." He shifted in his saddle. "And Mandi is all alone."

"It sounded to me like she has Ruger to help her. Maybe it won't be that bad. It's best to assume that she's safe."

Abraham frowned and cast a look behind, to where Melris rode on the wagon Iris was driving. "What's your take on that guy?"

Solomon wiggled his protruding eyebrows and said, "Weird but smooth. I can't really make much of a judgment on him."

"Yeah, me either. I haven't even bothered to talk to him."

"Compared to Leodor and Lewis, he's a breath of fresh air."

"Agreed. But at least I knew what to expect from them."

"You can't have it all," Solomon replied. "So, what is the plan?"

"Junction City is on the way up to the Wound. I'm hoping to stop there and pick up the trail of Big Apple."

Solomon nodded. "Yeah, if that guy thinks we are a threat, he's going to keep tabs on us." He cast a glance back at Melris. "Tell you what. How about I try to feel the strange fellow out? You seem too tense right now. I'll take a crack at it."

"Go ahead. I don't feel like talking—not much, anyway."

Solomon drifted back into the ranks, and Abraham took his spot in the front.

"Trouble, Captain?" Horace asked.

"No, we otherworlders were only touching base," he told both of them. "Keep your lips sealed, but we'll go to Junction City and see if we can sniff out the horned halfling there. Just don't let the newbie in on it."

"Aye, Captain."

Sticks nodded at him and said, "My lips are sealed."

24

THE HENCHMEN WERE RIDING ALONG THE BOTTOMS OF THE EASTERN hills of the Spine, a few days from their destination in Junction City. Abraham, as well as the others, would scan the stark mountain range as strange sounds and calls would echo down from its jagged ravines and valleys. Abraham had no desire to navigate the treacherous mountain terrain again. The mere thought of such a trek in the odd, barren, and humid climate gave him the willies. The company traveled at a brisk pace through the grassy plains.

Domingo, who had been scouting from the front with Tark, galloped back to the main party. A worried look crossed her pretty teardrop-shaped face.

Halting his horse and the rest of the company, Abraham asked, "What is it?"

"I can't say," she said with a quick look over her shoulder. She pointed behind herself. "That stretch of wheat grass that we are about to cross through has a stink about it."

"A stink?" Horace sat with a mirthful look. "Perhaps that's Tark?"

Dominga made a gentle eyeroll and said, "No, it's not an odor so much as a feeling. There is a silence. The grasses do not even rustle."

"The wind is not blowing," Sticks said.

"Come on, I'll show you what I'm talking about." Dominga led them another half mile through the fields.

They found Tark standing behind a long rise. His horse grazed a few yards behind him.

She followed the path of pressed-down grass right toward him. "Did you see anything?"

Tark kept his smoky eyes on the expansive field of tall brown and fertile green grasses. "Nothing. It's alive but stagnant. But these goose bumps on my arms haven't departed either."

Abraham rode up on top of the rise. The fields were like a desert that went on endlessly in all directions. It would be a perfect place for hunting varmints and deer.

"I don't *feel* anything." Ruger's body had a strong sense when it came to danger. "Not that I think you are mistaken."

"I've been at this a long time," Tark said, rubbing his forearm. "When my hairs stand on end, I'm usually right."

"True," Dominga agreed.

"We can go around the field, but that might take an extra day," he said. "I hate to do that when we can make a straight path for those mountains. We'll be home free then. Besides, we can't risk the open roads and crossing Hanchan soldiers. It wouldn't surprise me a bit if Commander Cutter and his men were keeping an eye out for us. That guy's a bad penny. He'll show up again, I figure."

"It's your call as always, Captain," Tark said.

Abraham eyed the horizon. Leagues away was a bordering set of mountains, much smaller than the Spine. Those ranges made up the borders that separated Hancha from Eastern Bolg. The goal was to cross the open range, navigate the mountains, and make their way to Junction City. With the sun setting behind them, the Spine cast a shadow over the range. A pit started to form in his stomach. He eyed Sticks. She had the assault rifle slung over her shoulder.

"Ready that weapon," he said. "Horace, tell the troops to have the crossbows ready. I'll lead."

Horace turned his big horse around and hefted his spear. He circled the spear tip and thrust it in the air.

Immediately, Bearclaw and Vern loaded their crossbows. Behind them, Apollo and Prospero did the same, and so on with all the well-equipped Henchmen.

Abraham gave Tark and Dominga a nod. With crossbows in hand and resting on their laps, they resumed their scouting position at the forefront. Flanked by Sticks and Horace, he followed their lead. The entire company ventured two hundred yards deep in the eerie silence. The sound of his heart pumped in his ears.

"Why are we moving so slow?" Vern asked. "It's just a bloody field. At this rate, we'll never make it to the mountains until tomorrow morning. Let's ride."

"If you want to ride out ahead, feel free," Abraham said. "As a matter of fact, maybe it would be best to put you on permanent scout duty."

Vern replied, "Look, I'm just saying we could move quicker. It's not like we are going to get attacked by a bunch of varmints."

"Tark warned us," Sticks said.

Vern rested his crossbow against a shoulder and said, "He gets spooked all of the time."

"Did you see that?" Sticks asked. She pointed the barrel of her assault rifle toward a small rise in the grasses to her left. "I saw the grasses move."

"So did I, Captain," Horace said.

Up ahead about thirty yards, Tark and Dominga came to a stop. They pointed their crossbows at the grasses.

A chill raced up and down Abraham's spine. The tall grasses rose up in a circle that surrounded them. Aboriginal men stood up in the field, wearing the grasses like hats. They were lean, tall, and muscular. Their brown bodies were painted with white patterns, with swirls, streaks, and dots on their bare faces and chests. Some of them had long throwing spears hoisted up on their shoulders. Others had primitive bows and arrows.

Horace spat black juice onto the ground. "Pitters."

The name didn't ring a bell. "We've fought them before?" Abraham asked.

"Aye, years ago," Horace replied. "They live in the low ridges of the Spine and hunt in the fields. We waltzed into one of their hunting grounds once before. They didn't like it."

"What happened?"

Horace lowered his spear. "Three of us died that day."

25

ABRAHAM COUNTED AT LEAST FIFTY PITTERS WHOM HE COULD SEE. Hundreds more could have been hiding in the tall grasses.

"Will they negotiate?" he asked Horace.

"No. We tried that last time where we encountered them on the other side of the Spine. They don't speak."

"We can run for it or circle the wagon. They aren't faster than horses, are they?"

"They are fast," Horace replied. "We'll have to bust through their front ranks, but Captain, they won't stop until they catch us."

"Maybe, but we can at least fight with the mountains at our back. With our weapons and armor, we can whittle down their wooden weapons."

"Agreed, we can kill them," Horace replied.

Abraham lifted his hand. "Everybody, get ready to run to the hills. Run for your lives," he quipped. He dropped his hand and kicked his horse in the ribs. "Eee-yah!"

The Henchmen's horses, led by Tark and Dominga, bolted into a full gallop. The wagon, drawn by a team of two beasts, rattled to life. Iris drove the wagon, with Melris clinging to his seat. As one, the company thundered through the grasses.

The Pitters called out in a cacophony of wild hooting. They snaked through the grasses, keeping pace with the horses. As their bowstrings were plucked, a barrage of arrows whistled through the air. Smooth as silk, they drew arrows from their animal-skin quivers and fired again.

An arrow pierced Sticks in her thigh, and she let out a sharp gasp. A Pitter closed in on her from a forward angle with his spear held high. She shot the wild man in the face with the rifle, and blood sprayed out of the dying man's back. He stumbled and vanished into the tall grasses.

The Pitters chasing them started to fade behind. The ones ahead came at them at an angle. With hollering hoots, they closed in on the fleeing gang of hardened fighters. One lanky Pitter crashed spear first into Horace's beast. The spear snapped on impact. Horace rode the beast over the man and gored another charging Pitter with his spear.

Bearclaw and Vern fired into the frenzied throng. They slowed and lined up their horses beside the racing wagon then threw their crossbows into the back. Bearclaw waved his arm at Skitts and Zann, and the Red Tunic brothers sped up to the wagon.

"Get into the wagon, load those crossbows, and keep firing." Bearclaw readied his twin-bladed Viking-style battle-ax and peeled away. The Henchmen formed a battle ring around the wagon and horses.

Vern whisked out his sword and followed Bearclaw back to the front of the wagon. They swung the King's Steel into their rushing enemies. Steel and bone clashed. Hot blood sprayed the fields. The Pitters fell but kept coming in gnashing swarms.

Solomon snatched up one Pitter and threw him into two other pursuers.

Skitts and Zann jumped from their horses into the wagon.

Zann loaded the crossbows, and Skitts aimed and fired. They worked in perfect tandem. Pitter after Pitter fell, gurgling in their own blood.

Abraham pulled Black Bane free of its sheath. The darkened steel of the broad blade shone with its own inner light. He leaned over his saddle and swung at an attacker. The savage's head leapt from his shoulders.

"Eat dung, Pitter!"

The horse-riding Henchmen stormed ahead at full speed toward the mountains. Spears and arrows whistled by. An arrow skipped off Horace's armor. Their armor saved most of them. The fine metal, crafted from the King's Steel, offered the ultimate protection. No finer metal existed in all the land.

Black Bane sank into the neck and clavicle of another Pitter. The savage dropped like a stone.

Two Pitters zeroed in on Sticks and her horse. One of the wild men grabbed onto the horse's reins and tugged while the other latched onto the back of her saddle. Sticks slung her weapon over her shoulder and pulled free a long dagger. She cut one Pitter across the forearm, but he hung on, with his feet dragging across the ground.

"Give off my horse!" she yelled.

Abraham dug his heels into his horse and chased after Sticks. "I'm coming!"

Sticks gave him a quick look and rolled her eyes. She leaned backward and lunged at the savage clinging to her saddle. She stabbed the wild man in the neck, and he fell away. She pulled herself forward and flicked the same dagger into the second Pitter's chest. The man held on. She whisked out her short sword and chopped his arm off at the forearm.

The Pitter let out a wild cry and slipped into the grass. Sticks's horse trampled over him.

Abraham gave her a thumbs-up. She shook her head with a disappointed look.

He caught up to her and spoke over the wind and the pounding hooves of the horses. "Forgive me! I need to remind myself that you can handle yourself! You are a fine marksman with those daggers."

"I could have shot them, but you said to save the bullets. But I needed the practice," she said, with her twin ponytails bouncing on top of her head.

"You're a natural! You don't need practice. You have a gift. In my world, you are what we'd call a crack shot!"

"Crack shot?" Sticks gave him a funny look.

The Henchmen pulled away from the front waves of the Pitters. The savages in grass hats fell behind them but didn't slow their chase. Nothing lay between the company and the mountains. They had broken free.

Abraham twisted his head around and made a head count. Solomon, Cudgel, Apollo, and Prospero were bringing up the rear. Bearclaw and Apollo were riding on either side of the wagon. Skitts and Zann were in the wagon, loading crossbows. Iris was driving the wagon, and Melris was sitting beside her. Sticks and Horace were riding beside Abraham, and Tark and Dominga were keeping the lead out front.

"It looks like we are in the clear," Abraham said.

"Aye, Captain!" Horace bellowed. "But we could kill them!"

Abraham made a light-hearted chuckle. He caught Dominga looking back at him. She smiled and waved.

A huge pantherlike creature as big as a horse launched itself out of a concealed spot in the grasses. It took Dominga and her horse down.

Tark screamed, "Nooo!"

26

A SECOND PANTHER BEAST POUNCED ONTO TARK AND HIS HORSE. HE
tumbled from his saddle into the tall grasses.

"Yah! Yah!" Abraham yelled.

He and Horace raced neck and neck to the aid of Dominga and
Tark. They arrived a few seconds later.

"What are those things?" Abraham asked.

"Wild panthers!" Horace said.

Each giant cat had the light coat of a lion and a tuft of thick
brown fur on top of its neck.

Horace lowered his spear and charged the panther that had
sunk its sharp fangs into Tark's horse's neck. "I'll kill them!" He
bore down on the panther before it sprang away at the last second.
"Missed!"

"Horace, watch out!" A third panther sprang out of the grasses
and knocked Horace from his saddle. More huge cats appeared
and converged on the Henchmen. They attacked the horses and
brought them down by biting their legs. Abraham pulled back on
his reins and wheeled his horse around. The Pitters and their
panthers encircled the stalled company. "Bloody meat pies!"

"What do we do?' Sticks said.

"Circle the wagon!" He waved his hand around in the air. "Henchmen, circle the wagon! Let loose the horses! These cats will eat them alive!" He jumped off his horse and swatted its rear flank with his sword. "Yah!"

The horse bolted.

"Aaayeeee!" Dominga screamed.

Abraham's head snapped around. The silky black woman was riding on the back of a panther. Her fingers were lodged in its thick patch of neck hair. It twisted around, bucked, and bit and clawed at her. With a kick of its hips, the panther bucked her into the air.

Dominga flipped into the air and landed on her feet. She pulled short swords free from her scabbards and got into a fighting stance.

The wild panther charged her. She split its nose and went down in a flurry of slashing claws.

Abraham sprinted toward the panther. He caught up just as it bowled Dominga over. He swung Black Bane hard into the beast's hips. The blade cut clean through the skin, taking bone and sinew with it.

The panther kicked with its back claws, knocking Abraham off his feet. It turned around, saliva dripping from its slavering jaws. Its piercing green eyes lapped him up with hungry intent. It pounced.

Abraham lifted his sword and held it fast.

The panther impaled itself on the blade. Its claws tore at Abraham in wild death throes. Warm blood oozed from its wound over Abraham's hands. It died and sank down on top of the man.

With a grunt, Abraham pushed himself out from underneath the massive beast. Dominga grabbed his arm and tugged. Her upper arm had huge gashes in it. The wounds were nasty.

"I hope you aren't allergic," he said.

Grimacing, Dominga asked, "What's that mean?"

"I'll explain later."

The Henchmen were embroiled in a heated battle around the pair of horses and wagon.

Solomon had a wild panther by the neck and was punching it in the face.

Dominga fired mystic hornets of energy from her fingertips. The humming swarm bore into the Pitters. The savages hopped and jumped and slapped at the glowing insects.

Iris's attacks served the Henchmen well. Cudgel pummeled the ill-equipped savages with bone-jarring swings of his spiked mace. Teeth clacked together and shattered. Skulls were crushed.

Apollo and Prospero swung their long swords with devastating effect. Apollo disemboweled two charging Pitters at the same time. Prospero hacked the arm off of one and sliced out the knee of another.

Horace lumbered out of the grasses, holding his gory spear. Blood was on his face and beard. The wild hooting increased all around them. "We can kill them, Captain!"

Abraham joined his men. "Death before failure!" He turned Black Bane loose on the enemy.

Slice! Chop!

Hack! Glitch!

The dead fell in heaps. The army of Pitters didn't dwindle. More came at them from all directions.

"How many of them are there?" Sticks said.

"Who cares! More food for the Elders!" Bearclaw said.

"None can withstand the might of the King's Steel!" Vern shouted as he ran his blade through a Pitter's skull. "We are invincible!"

A stone tomahawk tumbled through the air and clocked Vern in the skull. He collapsed like a tent.

"Vern!" Dominga cried. She ran to the man and stood over his body with her swords in hand.

Solomon moved alongside her at the back corner of the wagon.

Skitts and Zann kept firing the crossbows into the horde.

Abraham swung Black Bane through a savage's chest as a wild panther charged him. "Oh no, another bad ol' puddy tat." He split its nose in twain before Horace gored it with his spear. "Thanks."

Horace charged back into the fray.

There was no end to the sea of Pitters. They continued to crop up by the dozens.

"Black Bane, if you are listening, we could use a hand," he said.

The only things keeping the Henchmen in one piece were their superior skills, weaponry, and armor, but that wouldn't hold forever. The Henchmen, after all, were only human. He banged the tip of his sword on the wagon's wheel. "Black Bane, wake up!"

The sword quavered. The runes in the blade glowed like embers and went dim. Abraham cut down another attacker and shook his head. Perhaps his predecessor, Eugene Drisk, had it right.

"Dirty donuts! I should've brought more Henchmen."

27

THE BATTLE RAGED. THE SECONDS FELT LIKE A MINUTE. THE Henchmen were pressed, their backs to the wagon, fighting for their lives.

Vern was down.

Tark was nowhere to be seen.

Solomon's fur looked like a pincushion of arrows.

Sitting in the wagon seat, Melris yawned. The Elderling stood up and spread his arms wide. His wine-colored robes hung from his arms like a sheet, and his long fingertips needled the air.

While fighting, Abraham watched the young mystic out of the corner of his eyes. Arrows shot by the enemy veered away from the strange man. Melris's robes rustled with a life of their own. *What is he doing?*

Melris pushed back his billowy sleeves. He flipped up his hands.

Dozens of Pitters in close-quarters battle near the wagon were lifted from their feet, along with their big cats. The savage horde levitated in the air, higher and higher. The confused throng of sweaty painted bodies swam and twisted in the air. They hooted and panted with wide-eyed astonishment.

The clamor of battle fell silent.

The rest of the Pitters looked up in the air with the whites of their eyes locked on their clan. They watched as the cluster of suspended men and wild animals were gathered together in the air.

With Sticks and Horace at his side, Abraham and the other Henchmen watched the marvel take place in the sky above. The knot of hooting Pitters and their wild panthers were bunched together. The distraught cats let out angry growls and lashed out at their masters.

"You don't see that every day," Solomon said.

The Pitters stranded on the ground gathered underneath their brethren with their necks bent toward the sky.

Abraham glanced at Melris. Facing away from the living tangle in the sky, the Elderling turned up the corner of his mouth. He dropped his hands. From over a hundred feet above, the Pitters and wild panthers went into a hooting and mewing freefall.

The Pitters on the ground let out a feverish gasp. Many scattered. The rest were crushed underneath their brethren. It became a pile of dead men, their limbs broken and twisted. The living survivors writhed underneath the pile as they tried to claw their way free.

A ball of purple flame started in the palm of Melris's hand. The size of a tomato, the ball grew to the size of a pumpkin. With a swipe of his hand, he lobbed it toward the pile of Pitters and big cats. It sailed through the sky and landed square in the middle of them. The flames exploded. They consumed every man, living and dead. Their flesh turned to ash. The pile became a bonfire of burning bones and awful stink.

The dozens of surviving Pitters fled.

Horace wiped his bloody spear tip in the grass and said, "I don't think Leodor could have done that."

Iris covered her nose and said, "I agree."

28

TITANUUS

Back at the House of Steel, Lewis and Leodor were sitting in a small living room, drinking wine. A board game with chess-like pieces sat on a small round table between them. Leodor's wizened face and knitted eyebrows were focused on the board.

Lewis stared into the fire nearby, flipping a dagger up and down in one hand and drinking from the other. "Come on, Leodor, make a move."

"I will when I'm ready," Leodor replied in his snobbish manner. He started to move one of the game pieces but moved it back. "When I'm ready."

"You act like the very heavens will fall if you make the wrong move," Lewis said.

"One never knows for certain the weight of their decisions. So the Elders say."

Lewis rolled his eyes. He stood up, walked over to the fire, set down his wine, and sheathed his dagger. He spread his fingers in front of the flame. "Don't try to segue into another speech about your precious Elders. I'll believe them when I see them."

"You've seen one."

"That *thing* on Crown Island? It was merely a monster, worshipped, well fed by foolish men. What sort of person feeds a monster? That is stupid."

"It's still an Elder." Leodor placed his piece on another position of the checkered board. "Gratius Victorious."

Lewis stiffened. He picked up his wine goblet and swallowed the remains. He walked over to the gameboard and looked down. "Hmm… It seems that you have erred, my friend." He moved one of his white ivory pieces, shaped like a knight in armor. He smirked. "Gratius Victorious."

Leodor stiffened in his chair. His fingertips clawed at the thinning hair on his head. "How do you do that? I don't understand it."

"I'm brilliant." Lewis refilled his goblet. "And I play better when I'm tipsy." He bumped into the table and knocked several game pieces over.

"More like drunk." Leodor started resetting the board. "Play again?"

Lewis yawned. "I don't know. Believe it or not, I'm getting tired of beating you. I'm getting tired of everything."

"Is that so?" Leodor said with an arched eyebrow. "And could it be that you miss adventuring with the Henchmen?"

"Pfft. Hardly. Perhaps I miss leading the King's Guardians, but the Henchmen, no. I'm glad Father saved us from another doomed mission. Aren't you?"

Leodor shrugged.

Surprised, Lewis plopped down in his seat across from the older man and said, "Really? This is a startling admission coming from you. What is going on in that age-spotted forehead of yours?"

"I can't say. But my chest nags me."

"Well, my horrid brand itches too. Maybe it's because they all died."

"They are the kingdom's hope. Your father places his faith in them." Leodor finished setting up the board. He moved a piece. "Your move."

Lewis frowned. "I don't want to play again. I want to drink. A night on the town wouldn't be so bad."

"But we are restricted. Besides, I can't leave. The Sect would find me and peel the skin off of my back. No thank you. I'm safest here or among the Henchmen."

Lewis moved a piece. "It's ludicrous that you think that way. Ah, I know what it is. It's that Elderling, Melris, isn't it?"

Leodor shrugged in his robes. "No. I could care less about that imposter." He moved a piece.

"Do I sense a note of jealousy rolling off of your slithering tongue?"

"Don't be silly. I care nothing about some enchanter off of the streets."

"An enchanter that conveniently appeared in the king's chambers undetected. That is no easy feat, my friend."

"Why are you calling me 'friend' all of a sudden?"

He paused in thought and said, "I have no idea. Perhaps it's because, at the moment, I don't have any." He moved a piece on the board. "Pathetic. I prefer your company compared to drinking alone."

"Even worse, I prefer your company without drinking at all. Oh well, I suppose we should consider our confinement a blessing from the Elders." Leodor moved an onyx game piece.

"Don't start with the Elder talk. Save your breath for some other fool that is dumb enough to worship the very dung-covered ground they walk on." He slid a piece diagonally from one checkered square to another. "Gratius Victorious."

The tired-eyed Leodor made a sound as though he were choking. "Three moves. You bested me in three moves!" He backhanded all the pieces off the table, sank back in his chair, and stuffed his hands in his robes.

"I told you I get better when I'm drinking." He sloshed his wine in his goblet. "It's a gift."

"A shame that you can't use it toward something more beneficial."

"I can. I'm a genius in military organization. For five years, I kept the Guardians organized and crushed any uprisings. I'm quite suited for the field, if I don't mind saying so myself. My gift is anticipation followed by focused action."

"Well, you are the king's son. And he's no fool."

"If it's any concession, I've never beaten my father."

Leodor straightened up in his chair. "Interesting."

Lewis guzzled down more wine. "How's that?"

"Because I have beat him several times."

"Hmm, I can see your frustration. Perhaps you are getting too old."

"With age comes wisdom."

"More importantly, power. You know, we were so close to having the kingdom to ourselves." Leodor rubbed his chest. "Do you really think that we will die if we work against the Brand?"

"Something terrible will happen. I'm certain of that. The Blue Demon will come, they say."

"Another myth, I say."

"Are you willing to risk it? To be honest, I find it refreshing knowing where I must stand. I am tired of all the scheming."

Lewis set down his goblet. "My, you are getting old."

As the door to the living room burst open, Princess Clarice entered. "There you are. I've searched all over for you."

"Why is that?"

"You know why. We can't just sit here. It's time to escape."

29

Lewis moved to a plush sofa near the fireplace, stretched out, and sank into the cushions. "This castle isn't big enough, apparently. Over five hundred rooms, and she still found us." He stuffed a pillow over his face and in a muffled voice said, "Go away."

Clarice shut herself inside the room, took a seat on Lewis's sofa, tugged on his trouser leg, and said, "Hear me out."

With the pillow still over his face, he replied, "I'll do no such thing. Talk to Leodor. He might take you up on it, but not I."

"Listen to me!" she urged. "We are Henchmen. Part of a group. It's not natural for us to be so far apart. I can feel it. I sleep with demons in my dreams."

"Does your brand itch and burn?" Leodor asked.

"It nags me like buzzing flies that won't go away," she replied earnestly.

Lewis lifted the pillow off his face. "Speaking of buzzing flies that won't go away…" He threw the pillow at his half sister. She slapped it aside.

"I know you feel it too, Lewis. We aren't supposed to be here. We are supposed to be out there. It's driving me crazy."

"Not me—I'm fine. If it bothers you so much, then have a drink. Either that or find a suitor. You're about at childbearing age. Go make some babies. You'll soon forget about all of this."

She punched him in the leg.

"Ow! Do that again, and I'll toss you into that fire." He sat up and rubbed his eyes. "So, where is that hound of yours, Swan? Let me guess, she's snapping chicken necks."

"She'll snap your neck," she replied. "I gave her the slip. Seriously, Lewis, Father is wrong to keep us here. We don't belong at the castle. We are Henchmen."

"He's only saving face. The real reason we are here is because of you. You are the one being protected. He couldn't have cared less about us." Lewis got up and prepared another goblet of wine. "If you want to run away again, I won't stop you. It will be our little secret."

"The king will only send us after her again," Leodor replied.

"I assure you that won't be happening," a woman said. She stood in the doorway.

"Leah," Lewis said with delight. "What a pleasure it is to see you."

Leah was the head of the Guardian Maidens. She was a striking beauty, all warrior, all woman, wearing a bronze cuirass that matched her coppery locks. He strolled across the room and kissed her hand. "I've missed you."

"Yes, so much that you ran into the arms of an assassin, I heard," Leah said. Her big beautiful eyes probed his.

"I was seduced. Bewitched. But as I recall, you rejected my advances, time and again."

She wiggled his prominent chin with her fingertips and said, "That's because your reputation precedes you, Lewis the Lewd."

Clarice and Leodor let out a giggle.

With his hand still clasping Leah's, he said, "You cut to the heart."

Leah gave him a rueful smile and said, "That's why I'm the captain of the Guardian Maidens." She slipped from his fingers and ventured deeper into the room. She stared down at Clarice. "Planning a little excursion?"

"No, I was only visiting with my brother," Clarice replied nonchalantly.

"Half brother," Lewis fired back.

"Please, Clarice. You've been trying to duck the Maidens ever since the Henchmen left. But I promise you this—you'll never slip me. Not like you did the others that failed me recently. Hazel is dead, thanks to your foolishness." Leah sat down on the sofa beside Clarice. "You'd do well to forget about it."

Clarice huffed, folded her arms across her chest, and said, "You don't understand. You aren't a Henchman."

"No, I'm a Guardian Maiden. We are bonded and have a special brand of our own."

"I'd like to see that brand," Lewis said with a dashing smile. He moved to the wine hutch and pulled out a new bottle. "How about I pour you a glass? It's from the Old Kingdom. Centuries old. The best."

"You know that the Guardians don't drink on duty, and I don't drink off duty either." She gave him a friendly nod. "But I appreciate your offer."

Lewis sat down between the women and said, "I'm with you one hundred percent, Leah. I've been telling the little princess that her efforts are nothing but foolishness. It might be best to lock her up in the dungeons."

"If only I could," Leah said.

"Hey, no one is locking me up anywhere." Clarice jumped out of her seat and pointed at the other three persons in the room one at a time. "You're a coward! You're a coward! And you're a coward!"

"You dare!" Lewis said. He jumped up to his feet and pulled his sword. "You might call me many things but never a coward!"

Leah rose from the sofa and said, "Agreed."

"I don't mind it so much. Cowards are survivors," Leodor added.

"You sit here on your arses, hiding behind the castle walls, while the kingdom is in flux!" Clarice pulled her rapier. "Our brothers and sisters, Henchmen, need us! I challenge you"—she pointed the tip of her blade at Lewis—"and you"—she did the same to Leah—"to a duel of swords. I win, then you have to follow me after the Henchmen. I lose, I'll leave you alone."

"You are a delusional little gal," Lewis said with incredulity. "First, you can't defeat either one of us. Second, we would make it a hundred yards from the castle. The King's Guardians, not to mention scores of other soldiers, would see us."

Clarice smacked his blade with her blade. "Coward!"

Lewis's high-boned cheeks reddened. "I'm losing patience." His grip tightened on his hilt.

"There is no point in this foolishness," Leah said. "Lewis is right. There is no way out."

"Leodor can get us free of the castle's walls and far from the soldiers' sight," Clarice said.

Leodor picked up the game pieces he'd knocked from the table. He placed them in the appropriate positions back on the board. "It's true. I can."

"Leodor!" Lewis whined. He'd been a part of Leodor's portal incantations before. "Why would you say that? She's only guessing."

"It's true. I can. But just because I can doesn't mean that I will."

"So, if I outduel Lewis and Leah, then you will teleport us out of here?" Clarice said.

Leodor shrugged. "I don't see why not."

Lewis and Leah gave Leodor incredulous looks.

Lewis shook his head and said, "No matter. It wouldn't go that far." He pointed his sword at Leah. "We'll finish this in the proving grounds."

30

Iris stitched up a nasty gash in Horace's forearm where a wild panther's claw had torn it open. "You should be more careful," she said. "Get a suit of the king's chain mail that will cover all of your arms."

"My forearms are too beefy," Horace said. He was chewing a wad of tobacco in his jaw and spat.

Iris glared at him. "I told you I don't like that stuff."

"I know, but it takes my mind off the pain. I'll spit it out later." He winced. "Ow, woman. Are you stitching from the inside out or outside in?"

"Spit it out," Iris said.

"Ah…" Horace took the wad of tobacco out of his mouth and tossed it into the campfire. "There. Happy?"

Abraham managed a smile. He sat near the campfire, warming his hands over it. The company had made camp at the base of the mountains. The stark jagged hills were a natural border between Hancha and Eastern Bolg.

Sticks, Solomon, and Tark helped Iris bandage the wounded.

Not one Henchman had escaped without new scars. The battle with the Pitters had been nasty.

Dominga and Cudgel were cooking over another campfire.

The Red Tunics, Skitts and Zann, pitched Abraham's tent.

Abraham stood up and made his rounds, making sure that no one was going to die.

"How are you guys doing?" he asked Vern and Bearclaw.

Vern was holding a bandage on his head that Iris had made for him. That stone tomahawk had clocked him good. "My head pounds like a drum, and my ears are ringing. Sadly, I still breathe."

"I know the feeling. You?" he asked Bearclaw.

Bearclaw was scraping a stone over the blades of his axe. "I sewed up my thigh. But my wounds were minor. The king's armor kept my bowels intact."

"Good. Get something to eat. Sticks is making Pitter panther stew," he said. "Good stuff. Can't you smell it?"

"Aye," Bearclaw replied.

"Yeah, we could eat for months after slaying all of those Pitter panthers." He scanned the camp.

Melris stood on the edge of the camp in the shadows, staring at the mountains. The gentle winds stirred his robes. Abraham hadn't said a word to him after the battle, for too many had wounds to attend to.

Abraham walked to the Elderling. "I think it's time that we had a chat."

"Certainly." Melris kept his eyes fixed on the rocks. His hood still covered his head. "What do you wish to talk about?"

"First, take that hood down. I feel like I'm talking to a ghost."

Melris complied. He wasn't nearly as haunting with the hood down. He had a boyish quality in his face that made him more approachable. Like Sticks, he wasn't one for showing expression. "Is this suitable?"

"I like to see your eyes when I'm talking." He locked eyes with the man. Melris's eyes had a twinkle like purple stars. "Uh, I suppose I should thank you for that trick you pulled out in the fields."

"Trick?"

"You know, levitating the enemy and doing a watermelon drop with them. That was amazing, but the timing could have been better."

"That wasn't a trick. I learned it from Trinos," Melris replied. "So, should I have executed it sooner or later?"

Incredulous, Abraham said, "Sooner. And who is Trinos? Never mind."

"I merely sped up the process of elimination. Your company would have prevailed with minimal losses by my estimation."

Abraham's voice became harsh. "Listen, Commander Data, it's not my company, it's *our* company. You are a part of it. We fight— you fight. You don't sit in the wagon and watch the birds fly by."

"I see," Melris said. "Is there anything else?"

"Look"—he thumbed back toward the camp—"I know these people. They are Henchmen. But I don't know you. You aren't a Henchman. You are an Elderling, whatever that is."

"We are direct servants of the Elders, born with the land's magic coursing in our veins." He leaned to one side, past Abraham. "And you are mistaken. Shades, Skitts, and Zann are not Henchmen. They don't have the Brand, but you trust them."

"They earned it. They proved themselves."

"I took the lives of sixty-eight enemies singlehandedly. Have I not *proven* myself?"

Abraham nodded. He had to admit Melris had the right answers. He pushed his fingers through his hair and said, "Let's run through a few things. I need to know that we are on the same page. First, who is in charge?"

"You are in charge. I am merely a guide. I hope that you don't feel threatened by me."

"No." Abraham absentmindedly put his hand on Black Bane's handle. "It's good we are clear about that. As for the Henchmen, we all perform like a military unit. I know what to expect from them, but I don't know what to expect from you." He glanced down at the iron rod Melris carried. "What does that do?"

Melris flipped the rod around like a sword. "This is a rod of devastation. That should speak for itself."

"I see," he said, taking his eyes off the thing. "Listen, Melris, if we fight, you fight. We fight for the king. We fight for one another. 'Death before failure' is our credo."

"I admire your spirit." Melris turned his back and faced the mountain. "I shall do my best to fit in. In the meantime, I am solely focused on recovering the stones from the Wound. If you'll pardon me, I must meditate."

Abraham shook his head. His thoughts wandered back home. He was worried about Mandi. "I don't need this." He started to walk away. "I need to get back home."

Melris turned. "You desire to find a portal?"

Abraham stopped in his tracks. "Yes."

"I know something about that."

31

"SPEAK TO ME." ABRAHAM DRAPED HIS HAND OVER THE MAGE'S shoulder. "Let's talk by the campfire. I'm getting hungry. Let me ask, do you eat?"

"Some," Melris said with an uncomfortable look.

Abraham locked his strong fingers on the Elderling's shoulders. Melris was a slender six-footer. The man's velvety robes felt thicker than him. Abraham wasn't about to let him go now. He wanted information.

He led the man to Horace's campfire. "Sit. Speak."

Melris quietly sat down in front of the flames.

Abraham waved at Sticks and Solomon. "Bring some food. You'll want to hear this. At least, Solomon will."

Solomon lumbered over and squatted down beside Melris. "Fellowship by the fireside?"

"More than that," Abraham stated. "Ol' Melris is going to shed some light on the portals."

Solomon's brows rose.

Sticks brought over two bowls of Pitter panther stew. She handed one bowl to Abraham. "Hopefully, this will be better than the story you told about that man running from the giant rock and losing the golden idol."

Nodding his head, Horace said, "Yes, that was a bad one. Why would the treasure hunter throw a hireling the prize? That was a foolish thing to do. I'd die before imparting my treasure to a hireling."

Abraham spread his hands out and said, "The hireling died."

"Yes, but you said that he never got the idol back either," Sticks said as she dug her spoon into her bowl. "The treasure hunter lost the small idol and the golden coffin."

"That was the Ark of the Covenant. Not a coffin. It's the place where Moses kept the Ten Commandments," Abraham said. "I don't want to explain this again. It's not about the treasure."

"It's always about the treasure," Horace said as Iris walked over with a bowl of stew and handed it to him. "That's what treasure hunters do."

"Never mind."

Abraham started eating. As much as he wanted to hear about the portals, he had to eat or pass out. He considered passing out, as that might get him back to Mandi, but Ruger's body wouldn't allow it. The salty broth with chewy panther meat hit the spot.

"All right, Melris," he said. "What do you know about the portals?"

"King Hector is on the right path. His cause is just even though not all Elders agree. The portals are created by another world, a world of invaders." He refused a bowl of stew that Iris tried to hand him. "I assume that would be your world, Abraham Jenkins."

"Mine too," Solomon said. "But we didn't have anything to do with it."

"No, of course not. You are only fish that were caught in the net," Melris said.

Shades slipped into view and leaned against the wagon. Using a knife, he cleaned his nails.

Melris continued, "The king was wise to eliminate the other-worlders such as you. But the numbers have grown to many."

"You are saying we should be killed?" Abraham said.

"At first, that was the best course of action, but the Elders reconsidered since you wield Black Bane," Melris replied.

"What does that have to do with it?"

"The sword was crafted by the Elders. It can't be wielded by just anyone. It is bestowed on the one that can protect Titanuus."

Abraham rubbed a palm on the blade's handle. "Huh. I didn't know that."

"I can't explain all of it entirely, but the sword possesses special qualities," Melris added.

"You can say that again," Abraham said.

"The metal is from the blade of Titanuus. The sword shattered in his battle with Antonugus ages ago. Black Bane is but a sliver. The rest lies in the ocean deep." Melris held his gloved hands over the flames. His hands began to glow, and he flicked his fingertips.

The embers of the fire drifted into the air above them and formed tiny bright-orange stars above the group's heads.

Melris massaged the air. Flames snaked out of the fire and formed the outline of two flaming sword-wielding warriors. They were covered in full-plate armor and battle helms made of brilliant lights. They battled among the stars.

"Titanuus and Antonugus battled in the heavens for centuries. Finally, Titanuus fell."

One warrior gutted the chest of the other.

"Titanuus suffered a mortal wound and fell from the heavens and into the waters of an empty world."

The orange embers cooled and disappeared.

"Titanuus was formed. His blood gave us birth. But now, the very life of Titanuus is under a darker threat, an invasion from another world." Melris sighed. "This is a bigger threat than Antonugus."

Abraham rubbed his head. Another headache was coming on. "So what are we supposed to do? And how many people like me are out there?"

"It is hard to say. Even the Elders don't know, but anyone could be an otherworlder like you."

The Henchmen grouped at the fire exchanged glances.

"The Elders call it soul swapping. Their essence is moving out of one body and into another. Through the portals. How it happens we can't explain. But I am here to investigate," Melris said. "The portal has been opened in another world by means we don't understand. Only the Crown of Stones, we hope, can counter it."

"Can't it be closed from the other side?" Abraham said.

"Possibly. But sometimes, when a gate is opened, it is impossible to close. But the Crown of Stones, we hope, will suffice."

"This is crazy." Abraham set down his bowl. "The only thing that makes sense is that I'm crazy and none of this is real. If we close the gate, everyone will be stranded here, like me and Solomon."

"That, I can't say for sure," Melris said. "Even the Elders don't know. But the Crown of Stones should be able to control both opening and closing. But the other world is opening them on their own."

"Well, isn't that just great." Abraham kicked at the dirt with a heel. He suspected the Big Apple would have more answers. He had to find him again and figure out what his motivation was. He pinched the bridge of his nose. "I've heard enough. I'm going to sleep."

"Captain!" Horace said.

Two winged shadows appeared in the sky. They dropped down on Shades, hooked their talons into his arms, and flew him away. They were gone by the time Abraham pulled his sword free.

All he could hear was Shades yelling, "They found me! They found me! Help meeeee!"

32

Lewis, Leodor, Leah, and Clarice gathered in a small training ground inside the House of Steel designed for the Guardians. The proving ground was located in the sublevels of the castle, having the appearance of a modified dungeon. Cells were there with no bars. The limestone walls were slick with moisture in some places. Racks of weapons and armor filled the stony cavities.

Clarice stood on a square platform of risen stone, fifteen by fifteen feet wide. She buckled on a suit of padded armor. She tied her flowing brown hair back in a ponytail.

Leah warmed up her bare arms with two wooden practice swords. She spun them in her grip with fluid expertise.

"Seriously," Lewis quipped. He carried a jug of wine in his hand. He took a long sip. "You are challenging me with children's toys? I thought this was going to be a real fight." He set the jug down, walked over to a weapons rack, and snatched up a wooden sword, which was little more than a polished stick knotted up with a leather binding around it to make a handle. "How dangerous."

Leodor took a seat on the edge of the platform and yawned. "Can we get this over with? I'm ready to retire for the evening. I had to be up when the roosters crow. I'm not myself without proper sleep."

"Says the man that always looked tired." Lewis propped a foot up on the steps of a small set of bleachers facing the arena. He set his jug down to stretch. "Don't fret. This won't last long."

"No, it won't," Clarice said. She spun two swords in her hands. "Who goes first?"

Lewis gestured toward Leah and said, "Ladies first. And do me a favor. Teach her a lesson so I don't have to."

"You'll have to do your own dirty work." Leah hopped up onto the platform and squared off on Clarice. "Are we using two swords or one?"

Clarice said with a shrug, "Since I made the challenge, I'll let you choose."

"We can keep it interesting." Leah flipped her swords with her wrists. "Two swords it is."

Lewis rolled his eyes. "Is this going to be a fight or a show? Two swords. Pah."

"Just keep score." Leah eyed Clarice. "How many strikes to the victor?"

"Best of five," the princess replied.

"Five? You seek to delay the inevitable." Lewis crossed his arms while still holding his sword in hand. "Take your mark."

The women faced off. They each held two wooden swords and took a battle stance. Their eyes locked.

"The rules. The rules." Leodor sauntered over to the bleachers and sat down. "Be clear about them."

"Yes, yes. We'll adhere to the standard. No strikes above the neck or below the knee. A point, if earned, will be deducted. Agreed?"

Both women nodded. Clarice's forehead started to bead with sweat.

"Someone is nervous. Let the battle begin." Lewis pulled his shoulders back and smirked. Leah was taller and longer, giving her a key advantage in reach. "Engage!"

Leah lunged forward, stabbing at Clarice's chest.

Clarice parried the attack by batting the swords to either side. She countered with a twin downward thrust and struck both of Leah's shoulders.

"Hit!" Lewis said. He gave Leah an incredulous look and said, "I hope you are awake now."

Leah's nostrils flared. She rolled her neck from side to side and fixed her stare on Clarice.

Clarice had a stone-cold look in her eyes.

"One strike, Clarice. Take your positions," Lewis said firmly.

The women resumed their battle stances.

"Engage!"

Clarice thrust. Leah parried. The wooden swords clacked off one another like the sound of popping wood. Violent thrusts and parries were exchanged. Leah pressed the attack. *Thrust. Thrust. Chop. Thrust. Thrust. Chop.*

With astonishing agility, Clarice glided away from the attacks. She twisted her swords between Leah's attacks and smote her hard in the belly.

"Hit!" Lewis shouted. "Two strikes, Clarice. No strikes," he said with disappointment, "Leah. Try hitting her back this time. You are captain of the Guardian Maidens, aren't you?"

Sweat glistened on the skin above Leah's breasts, which heaved underneath her figure-enhancing bronze cuirass. A snarl formed on her face. "At least I'm still a captain." She resumed her battle stance and faced off with Clarice. "You've been practicing."

Clarice stared Leah down like a panther hunting its prey. "I'm a Henchman. Fighting for your life is practicing," she replied coldly. "Death before failure."

Lewis chuckled. "She's a volatile little chipmunk, isn't she. Engage!"

The two women fought. Swords impacted one another with wooden fury.

Leah pressed the attack. Her thrusts were parried, spun away from, or countered.

Clarice snaked her body away from the flurry of skilled attacks. She shuffled away, ducked, and countered. The women battled back and forth, using every square inch of the arena platform.

The sword-on-sword strikes echoed hollowly in the proving chamber.

Leodor sat on the edge of his seat, tired eyes wide, fists clenching.

Lewis yawned. He followed the yawn with a belch.

Leah overextended herself on a thrust.

Clarice whacked her opponent in the ribs.

"Hit!" Lewis shouted. The women disengaged and faced one another in the middle of the platform. "Three strikes, Clarice. The victor," he said with noticeable disbelief.

"Good fight," Leah said to Clarice. "You've grown much, and I underestimated you. I let you get in my head. It won't happen again." Panting for breath, she gave Clarice a hug. "I'm proud of you."

"Thanks," Clarice said. She broke off the hug and faced her brother. With a confident smile, she said, "You're next."

33

"WHAT JUST HAPPENED? WHAT WERE THOSE THINGS?" ABRAHAM shouted.

Shades had vanished into the midnight sky. Strange hulking winged creatures had swooped down and snatched the rogue away in a blink of an eye.

"I've never seen the likes of them before," Horace said as he poked his spear toward the sky. "He's gone now. Could be anywhere."

Abraham spun around on his heel. "Does anyone know what in the hell those things were?"

All the Henchmen were on their feet with weapons ready. All eyes were searching the sky and the surrounding scenery. Prospero and Apollo shrugged, sheathed their swords, sat down, and resumed eating.

"He's gone now," Iris said. The rose-colored fire in her hands went out. "I don't suppose there is much we can do about it."

Sticks slipped her daggers back into her bandolier and said, "'They found me.' You heard him say that, didn't you?"

"Yes." Abraham gave her a probing look. "What did he mean? Who found him?"

"I know Shades as well as any," she said, "and he's been edgy. I got the feeling that he was worried about someone coming after him. I even caught him checking the skies from time to time. I found it weird."

"I noticed that too," he said, still searching the skylines. "He seemed very desperate to get the Brand. Do you think that might have something to do with it?"

Horace stuck his spear into the ground. "No telling now. He's gone. Better get some rest, Captain."

"What? We just lost a man. I'm not going to sleep on that. We have to get him back."

"If you say so, Captain," Horace replied. "But he's not a Henchman, so I wouldn't fret."

"Skittles and Zanax aren't either, but I'm not going to abandon them either."

He scanned the faces of his hardened crew. They all clearly held a grudge against Shades. Despite the rogue's loyal efforts, he still hadn't won them over.

A pit grew in Abraham's stomach. He hadn't put his faith in Shades either. He'd refused to brand him. He clasped his hands behind his head and surveyed the stars. "Blue blazes."

"Your friend bears the mark of the Targon," offered Melris, who hadn't budged from his spot in front of the fire.

Abraham dropped his hands and gave Sticks a curious glance. She shrugged. So did Horace. The word *Targon* didn't jostle anything in Ruger's memory banks either. He stood over Melris and asked, "What is a Targon?"

With his eyes fixed on the fire, Melris said, "The Targon are slavers from the Old Kingdom. They serve the High King of the Mountains. They prepare the finest specimens for the king's service."

"By specimens, you mean people, right?" Abraham asked.

"I'm sure they mark beasts for service as well. The slaves to the Targon are like cattle. Hence the mark. Like the King's Brand."

"Well, aren't you a fountain of information? Why didn't you try to stop them, Melris?"

"I was as surprised as you," the Elderling replied.

Abraham paced around the campfire. The Old Kingdom was in the northeast territory, days away. He didn't owe Shades anything, but the rogue was part of his team. Abraham couldn't abandon him.

"Do you have any idea what will happen to him?" he asked.

"I cannot say. Perhaps he will be made an example of. I'd assume the worst. The Targon are ruthless people." Melris stood up and faced Abraham. "Sorry."

"What are we going to do?" Sticks asked. "Even with horses, we can't track something that is flying."

"I'm tired of my crew getting snatched away." Abraham clenched his jaws.

Sticks was right. They had no way to catch the Targon and no way to tell if Shades would still be alive either. He watched the clouds passing in the sky. He had a mission to complete. He needed to get back to Mandi. *Lord, what am I going to do? I need some help on this one.*

"Clearly, Shades has a past that pre-existed his time with the Henchmen. It's no surprise for such a sneaky fella," Iris said as she began gathering the empty bowls of stew. "I don't think it was meant to be. They don't call him Shades for nothing. It's probably not his real name."

"Since I've been here, Shades has done no wrong."

"You weren't in the prison," Iris said.

"Love"—Horace put his hand on Iris's shoulder—"careful how you speak to the Captain."

Iris moved out from underneath Horace's meaty hand and said,

"I follow, but that doesn't always mean that I have to agree." She hustled away.

Melris tilted his head toward the sky. The bottom end of his rod started to glow a faint purple.

Abraham's neck hairs stood on end. High above, something circled in the air. He gripped the handle of Black Bane. "Is that them? Are they coming back?"

"No," Melris said in his soft voice. "That is something far more dangerous."

The great creature in the sky dove toward the camp.

"The sky lives," Horace said.

Abraham pulled his sword and said, "Henchmen, to the ready!"

34

Lewis stepped up onto the training platform with the wooden sword resting on his shoulder. He hiccupped. "A shame to let all of that good wine go to waste on this meaningless exercise."

"It's far from meaningless," Clarice said. "If I win, we are all leaving."

"Don't count on it," Lewis said.

"You gave your word!" she fired back.

"I'm talking about you winning. It's not going to happen."

Leah dabbed her sweaty face with a towel and asked, "What will it be? One sword or two?"

"As you can see, I only brought one, but I'm perfectly fine letting this little rodent fight with two," he said, a noticeable slur in his words.

With an incredulous expression, Leah asked, "Are you certain? She's as quick as a cat."

"Yes, I saw the little kitten whip you like an old dog." He leaned into Leah's pretty face. "I think you and I should spend time together. I could teach you my excellent swordplay."

Leah patted his cheek and said, "Let's see how you do against your little sister first."

"Half sister."

"Prince," Leodor said, "your timing is going to be way off, on account of your inebriation. I'm employing the Rictarn Tactic. It should spare you from immediate humiliation."

"Are you instructing me on the usages of steel? Or wood, rather. A mystic. Now I've heard it all."

"I spent some time in the army when I was younger. All servants of the crown required training back then."

With a side look, Lewis replied, "Obviously, you were horrible at it."

Leodor lifted his scrawny shoulders. "True. My body aches just thinking about it."

Leah stepped off the platform and said, "Shall we get on with it?"

Lewis and Clarice faced off in their battle stances. He kept his sword on his shoulder. She had both blades out in front of her.

"I'm going to enjoy throttling you," Clarice said.

"The first competitor to score three hits wins," Leah reminded them. "Engage!"

With the quickness of a springing cat, Clarice stabbed at Lewis with both blades.

Lewis brought his sword down like a flicker of a snake's tongue. *Whack.* He hit Clarice hard on the top of her skull.

Clarice jumped back, grimacing. "What in Titanuus was that?"

"It would have been your funeral if this sword were real," Lewis quipped.

Tossing her towel over her shoulder, Leah said, "That's a point for Clarice."

"I thought I lost a point," Lewis said, "and I don't have any to lose."

"No, these are Gin-gin rules," Leah said. "If you don't have a point to give, your opponent gets your point." She smirked at him.

"So be it," he said.

Clarice rubbed her head on her forearm. Her eyes were watering.

"Did you feel that through your pelt, little badger?"

"I'm going to pelt you," Clarice replied.

"Resume your places," Leah said.

The fighters stood a few paces apart, Lewis towering over his sister like a cat over a mouse.

"Engage!"

Clarice parried Lewis's downward strike with both of her swords. *Clack!*

Lewis chopped harder into her swords. The strength of his long sword arm knocked her parries aside. Stretching and striking, he swatted her behind.

Clarice let out a yelp and skipped away.

"Hit!" Leah said. "One strike, Clarice. One strike, Lewis. We are tied."

"Bravo," Leodor said from his seat.

"Take your positions."

Clarice's nostrils flared. Her eyes narrowed with growing hatred.

Lewis turned up the corner of his mouth.

"Engage!"

Clarice's swords struck out in a blinding whirlwind of fury. *Clack. Clok. Clack. Clack. Clok.*

Lewis caught every blow on the length of his sword. With one hand behind his back, he danced backward around the ring, blocking every strike she made. "You are fast. Your skill is average." He ducked one sword strike and sidestepped another. "Your footwork could use much work as well," he added as he glided around the ring.

Clarice broke off her assault. Panting, she backed away and lowered her swords.

"Are you quitting?" Lewis asked.

"I want to see you fight and not dance."

"Oh, if that is your wish, let me grant it." He gripped the sword with both hands and charged.

Clarice's eyes grew. She parried the fierce blows that Lewis rained down on her with wroth force. He knocked her swords down. She brought them up again and absorbed more punishment. She backed toward the rim of the stage, cornered, and one foot slipped off.

"Hit!"

"What?" Clarice exclaimed.

"You came off of the platform. That's a hit," Leah explained. She gave Lewis an approving look. "One strike, Clarice. Two strikes, Lewis. Take your positions."

Clarice moved to her spot with her shoulders hanging. Eyebrows knitted together, she shook her head and resumed her battle stance.

Lewis moved into his spot and said, "One more strike, and I can go to bed. I know what you are thinking, ratling. You seek to dupe me and catch me off guard. But I can see the fire burning in your eyes. I won't be fooled." He moved into his stance and put both hands on his sword. "But you can try me."

"Engage!"

Clarice came at him.

Lewis knocked both swords out of her hands with one mighty swing. He put the sword on her neck.

"Hit!" Leah said.

Leodor clapped. "Bravo. Bravo. I'm not a fan of you, Lewis, but that swordplay was exquisite." He smoothed his thinning hair back. "And I really didn't feel like casting a dimension spell. They are very dangerous."

Clarice kicked both swords off the stage and stormed out of the room.

Lewis dropped his sword on the deck. He stepped off the platform, put his arm around Leah, and reeled her in. "Well played, my dear."

"Indeed," she replied.

As Leodor's tired eyes awakened, Lewis kissed her full on the lips.

35

A WINGED BEHEMOTH NESTLED IN THE MOUNTAIN'S ROCKY LEDGES. It sat perched over a hundred yards high on the hill. Its beastly shape contoured with the hill.

Sword in hand, Abraham moved toward the base of the mountain with his eyes glued on the creature. Sticks and Horace flanked him.

"It's a big thing, whatever it is," Sticks said.

"We can kill it," Horace added.

Abraham's arm hairs stood on end. His earlobes burned. Fear didn't course through Ruger's veins. Excitement did. The thought of battle aroused him. He tried to quell Ruger's natural enthusiasm. "That thing is bigger than an elephant. And it flies as well."

"What's an elephant?" Sticks asked.

"Melris, you seem to have some inner knowledge. Can you tell us what that thing is? Is it another one of those Targons?"

"No, I sense the beast is of a different complexity. I will shed more light on it." He shot a pale purple beam of light—like a flashlight—out of his hand.

Iris gasped.

"The Fenix," Abraham said as he stared in horror at the hideous beast.

The ugly creature had eight eyes, four on each side of the head. The eyes burned with citrine fire. A long, broad snout was that of a hammer-headed bat. Its fur was ruddy and brown. Saliva dripped from the fangs protruding underneath its thin black lips like a bulldog's. Great black wings were folded behind its back.

The Henchmen loaded crossbows.

"Take aim, Henchmen," Horace said.

Fingers started to squeeze the triggers.

"No, wait," Abraham said. "I think that is Simon."

"How can you be sure?" Solomon asked from his position behind the wagon.

"Because we killed all of the others," he replied.

"No doubt, this creature, if it is the same, it comes to kill us," Solomon added. He stretched his long arm out and pushed forward Skitts and Zann, who sat in the wagon with crossbows ready. "Go ahead. Shoot that thing."

"No, don't shoot it. Everyone, stay calm." Abraham motioned downward with a hand.

"Abraham, that thing is ten times bigger than the last. It couldn't be the same one. Even if it was, you killed its father or mother or whatever," Solomon added.

Speaking in a slow Southern-like drawl, Zann said, "Well, I'm not taking any chances." He squeezed the trigger.

Clatch-zip!

The bolt sailed true and struck the Fenix in the nose. It let out a moan like a wounded lion. Fog spilled from its great mouth. The inky white mist spilled down the mountainside like an avalanche of snow.

"You idiot!" Abraham said. "Everyone back away. Everyone back away!"

The Fenix launched itself into the sky.

Zann stood up in the wagon and shouted, "Woohoo! See, I scared it away."

Backing away, Melris kept his light on the creature and followed it through the sky. "The breath of the Elder Spawn is subtle." The light from his hand went out.

Abraham lost sight of the Elder Spawn. "Everyone, get out of here before that breath freezes your limbs."

"And the Fenix makes a snack out of us." Solomon bolted toward the fields.

The Henchmen hurried after the troglin. With a screech, the Fenix dove down from the sky. Swooping over the camp, it unleashed its vaporous breath. Its vapors splashed out like falling rain. A sticky substance coated the fleeing Henchmen and their camp.

Horace fell first, and his big belly squashed the campfire.

Iris fell next, followed by Sticks, Vern, and Bearclaw.

Abraham's limbs moved like molasses. He watched more Henchmen fall one by one. His lids grew heavy, and his flight came to a stop. He fell to his knees with his sword locked in his grip. Melris moved in front of him. Bolts of fire flew skyward from his fingertips. The Fenix dropped out of the sky and landed on the Elderling.

Abraham screamed, "Nooo!"

Shards of pain sliced through his head. He fell on his back. The Fenix loomed over him. Hot saliva dripped from the monster's mouth and onto his armor. Its rancid breath could have woken the dead.

"Man, you really need a Tic-Tac," he said.

Abraham's new world went black.

36

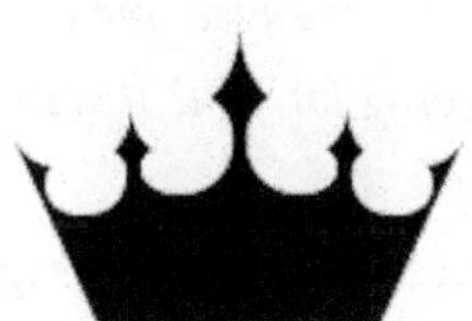

ABRAHAM WOKE TO THE SOUND OF THE WIND RIPPING THROUGH HIS hair. Giant talons were latched around his body. The world waited to greet him hundreds of feet below.

He squirmed inside the viselike grip. "No. Nooo!"

In the fleeting moment when he'd blacked out, he hoped he would return to Mandi's side. Instead, he flew through the sky like a rodent being taken to a hawk's nest. He pulled his arms up. Somehow, impossibly, Black Bane remained in his grip.

The Fenix had a furry coat over its belly. Its legs dangled low, making it too far for Abraham to take a stab at it.

He decided to take another stab at it, a different kind of stab. "Simon! Simon Fenix! I know it's you! Take me down!"

He'd named the elder spawn after the movie character Simon Phoenix, from the movie *Demolition Man*. Before the great dragon-bat thing departed, he'd called it that at least one hundred times when they bonded.

"Simon! It's me. Abraham. Take me down!"

"What is all of the shouting about?"

Black Bane, the sword, was speaking in Abraham's mind.

"Well, look who decided to join us," Abraham said with his mouth to the wind. "I can only imagine that you have nothing to offer."

"I wouldn't say that. I always have something to offer. Mostly advice... about women. Er... what is your name again?"

"Abraham Jenkins." He looked down at the treetops they were flying over. "I don't guess that you ever remembered yours?"

"I can't say I do. Perhaps it changed one too many times. So tell me, Abraham, how are things going for you? It sounds quiet. No banging around. That's a good thing."

"Not really. I'm captured by a giant dragonlike creature. I think it's taking me back to its nest. The funny thing is you helped me kill its mother before. Now, I think it's about to kill me."

"Hmm... it sounds dangerous. Can't you hit it?"

"Sure, but I might fall a thousand feet."

"In my past, there was a dragon, with shining black scales the size of small shields. It had a great belly, for a dragon, that dragged over the grasses. I used to run. It would fetch me but never kill me."

Straining his neck as he searched for some possible way to escape, he asked, "So what happened to it?"

"I believe it married a druid. A fetching woman, not a sample I prefer, but very ghostly and exotic. Rose-petal lips. Skin as soft as—"

"Not helping!" Abraham squirmed in the Fenix's clutches. "Listen, Black Bane, I need to get down on the ground before this thing takes me back to its nest. Or wherever. Can you help?"

"Did you call me Black Bane?"

"Yes!"

"Interesting. I have the worst trouble with names, though I do recall being referred to as that before. You see, the other personalities would call me that from time to time. But I keep forgetting. Thanks for reminding me. Now, where were we?"

"I need to get out of this creature's grip and back onto the ground."

"And you said that it is a dragon?"

"Yes!"

A jolt of energy coursed through the sword and into Abraham's body.

"Gah!"

The Fenix's claws opened wide.

Abraham plummeted toward the earth. "Black Bane! This isn't what I had in mind. I'm falling!"

"You are free of the beast, aren't you?"

"I'm going to die any second now!" Holding the sword in two hands, he screamed at it. "Help me!"

"I thought that I did. Let me see what I can do. The magic resources in this world are tricky. If I only had my spell book... Yes, I recall having a spell book."

Abraham twisted his head around just in time to see the green treetops rushing to greet him. All he could think to do was scream, "Nooo!"

The Fenix swooped underneath him, and he grabbed onto a handful of fur. Hanging on for dear life, he pulled himself up into a sitting position.

"Simon! It's you, isn't it!"

Over the sound of the wind, he heard a rattle of acknowledgment coming from the Fenix's throat. A catlike purr rumbled beneath him. The ugly beast craned its neck and locked four eyes on Abraham's own.

"It is you!"

He started floating upward. His fingers grasped the thick patch of fur on Simon's back while his feet started to rise into the air. An unseen force was pulling him upward.

"Hey, what is going on?"

"Is my spell working, er, what was your name again?"

"Ruger! I mean Abraham! Your spell is a little late. I'd be looking like roadkill only seconds ago. Turn it off!"

"Turn it off? That is an odd phrase. So, your present condition is safe?"

Abraham kept trying to pull his body down, but it kept floating up. "I'm riding on the back of the dragon. I think I'm safe. It would be better if I could get him to land."

"I see. Hold on, Ruger."

"The thought had occurred to me," he replied as he recalled a line from an old spy movie. His body suddenly dropped onto the creature's back. He found himself sailing through the starlit skies. With the wind kissing his face he said, "James Bond, eat your heart out."

As he sailed the skies on the back of the great living beast, a feeling of exhilaration swept through Abraham. He'd flown planes and felt the special freedom that it gave, but that was nothing like riding on the back of the Fenix. Its body churned with warm life. Its outstretched wings beat the winds with power. Abraham let out a triumphant cry at the top of his lungs.

"Interesting."

"Huh." Abraham came to his senses. "What's that, Black Bane?"

"I can hear the thoughts of the Fenix. It is talking, but it's more of a childlike gibberish."

Abraham stroked the pelt on the Fenix's back. "That makes sense. It's only a few months old."

"Maybe so, but it's a strong-willed thing with a deep intelligence of its own. So, you want him to land?"

"Tell him to take me back to the camp. No, wait. Tell him to follow after the Targons."

"Targons?"

"They snatched away one of my Henchmen. Shades. Only a few minutes before Simon appeared. If he can find the scent, maybe he can catch them. They would have been heading toward the old kingdom."

"I'll ask."

For a moment, all of Abraham's concerns faded away. He felt no guilt. No pain. No crosses to bear. Now, only he and the open sky remained.

Simon the Fenix veered away from his eastward path and turned north.

"Whoa," Abraham said. Black Bane's grip was warm in his hand. The runes in the blade had a soft glow. "What's going on?"

"I communicated your desires to the beast. I believe he understands. Apparently, he has a nose like a dwarven setter."

"What is a dwarven setter?"

"Funny that you should ask. A big dog, I think. It's fascinating that I can recall the breed but little to nothing else. But I can still picture many comely women clearly in my mind. How are the women in this world? Are they fetching?"

"Some of them are as fine as wine and sweet as honey."

"It sounds like a fine place to be. What I wouldn't do to sample some cuisine. I don't hunger, but I admit, this metal coffin leaves me quite bored."

"Perhaps when I find a way back to my world, it will send you back to your world too."

"Eh... I'd rather be here. Where I come from is a hellish place—hot, dry, and overrun by evil."

"What about the women?"

"I'll take my chances elsewhere."

Simon's wings beat faster, and they gained speed.

The wind tore through Abraham's hair. "Man, he's moving. He must have picked up on something." With the warm winds caressing his face, he felt like a kid on a roller coaster.

Black Bane didn't reply.

Simon let out a rumble in his throat and dived. His wings stretched to their limits, over thirty feet wide. In a spiral, he glided downward.

Abraham felt the warm handle of the sword grow cold. The fiery glow in the sword's blade went cold.

"Black Bane?"

No response came.

"Asleep again. Well, thanks."

In the fields below, a train of people was moving at a brisk pace. A caged wagon pulled by a horse was among them. Abraham squinted. A man huddled in the cage, but in the night, at that great distance, he was hard to see.

He patted Simon's neck. "Take me closer."

The great batlike dragon swooped lower. He flattened out one hundred feet above the party, like a silent shadow sailing over their ranks.

Abraham caught a better look at that rolling cage. Shades was on his knees with his fingers locked around the bars, looking up at him. The rogue was being led by large men in heavy cloaks with bulges in their backs. He waved at Shades.

Shades made a subtle wave back.

There was no sign of the tigerish creatures that had snatched up Shades earlier, which Abraham had figured to be some sort of wraith or demon. Only the big people in hooded robes were there, moving at a brisk pace. At least twenty of them were there.

Simon circled around.

"Let's make another pass," Abraham said into one of the Fenix's earholes. He had no idea whether the Elder Spawn understood him or not, but he seemed to feel a connection. "A little closer this time."

Simon dipped closer to the ground. The Fenix practically skimmed the ground at fifty feet in height.

The slavers, or whatever they were, didn't tilt a head.

Shades waved his arms wildly.

Abraham tilted his head toward the man and said, "What?"

Shades pointed into the air.

Abraham whipped his head around. A tiger-faced man with the wings of a bird, holding a spear, flew right at him. Abraham knocked the spear aside. The big-bodied attacker's momentum knocked him off Simon's back. Abraham tumbled toward the ground.

37

ABRAHAM LANDED FLAT ON HIS BACK, AND THE FALL AUDIBLY knocked the wind out of him. Fighting for his breath, he rolled over onto his side, sucking for air. He fought his way to his hands and knees, still gripping Black Bane in his hand.

The Targon formed a ring around him. They had the faces of great cats and bodies like Olympian wrestlers. Muscles bulged underneath their robes. They lowered their spears at Abraham. Their hands had fur on them. The fingers' nails were sharp and black.

Abraham sucked for air and finally managed to say, "Hello, kitty."

A Targon with a face like a leopard's rushed over and kicked him in the ribs with the toe of his boot. It sprang away with its green eyes narrowed and whiskers twitching.

"That's the King's Armor I wear. It takes a licking but keeps on ticking." Abraham rose to his feet. He counted eight of the Targon.

A loud screech erupted in the skies above them. Simon the Fenix was locked in battle with four flying Targon. The winged lionlike men cut through the air with the agility of small birds. One jabbed its spear into Simon's hide.

Simon's tail snapped through the air. The barbs growing on the end of his tail struck a Targon in the chest. *Thump!* Blood sprayed from the wound.

The Targon died in midair. His wings collapsed, and he plummeted from the sky.

The battle above was enough to catch the Targons' attention, allowing Abraham to catch his breath. He couldn't be sure, but some of the Targon appeared to have wings, while the others didn't. He brandished his sword with a few twists in the air and said, "Listen up, Thundercats. We can do this the easy way or the hard way. And to be clear, the hard way will be fatal."

Two Targon charged him with spears lowered.

Abraham chopped the tip off one spear and sidestepped the other. One Targon impaled the other on the end of his spear.

The battle above kept raging.

Abraham fought for his life below. With roars like lions', the cat-men charged. He split a panther-face's skull. The other five attackers wrestled him to the ground. Teeth bit into Abraham's thigh. A clawed hand slashed his face. He fought through the wild sounds of angry mewing.

He punched.

Kicked.

He slid a dagger out of his belt and stabbed an exposed belly.

The Targon were fierce fighters, cat-quick and nasty. They were light on their feet, perhaps too light…

Abraham rolled on top of a Targon and thrust his weight down. Ribs cracked underneath his power. The cat-man hissed. A claw swiped his face. Abraham gored its chest with the dagger.

"Bad kitty."

Ruger's endless endurance and superior strength slowly overtook the litter. The Targon were big but not strong. Unlike men, they weren't heavy boned either. They were light on their feet. Perhaps that was why they were able to fly.

A Targon sprang onto Abraham from high above. He stepped underneath it and cut clear through its abdomen.

A spear whistled through the air. Abraham slipped his neck aside, though he hadn't seen it coming. Ruger must have had something like a sixth sense. The Targon regrouped. Five of them were left. They jumped Abraham like a bag of kitty litter. Two came at him, spears lowered. Two more flanked to one side and hurled their spears at him.

Abraham jumped forward, avoiding the hurled spears. With sword in one hand and dagger in the other, he hacked down the two charging felines.

Wet blood dripped from his blades. He took the fight to the other attackers. Cloth, fur, and flesh ran red. Black Bane slaughtered. The Targon died with their bright cat eyes fixed on the sky.

Abraham stood in the blood-slicked grasses, searching for more enemies. None came.

He lifted his sword in both hands over his head and said, "Thunder! Thunder! Thundercats! Hoooo—oof!"

A flying Targon flew into his backside, and they tumbled over the grasses. Abraham's grip failed him. He was in a fight for his life against a Targon that was bigger, stronger, and faster than the others.

Abraham punched its face.

The Targon locked its fingers around Abraham's neck and squeezed. The black nails bit into skin.

Abraham latched his fingers around the Targon's neck and squeezed with all his might.

Holy sheetrock, this thing is strong!

The flying Targon had the face of a leopard and carried a superior air about it. It showed no fear in its eyes—only victory. With raw strength, more like an animal's than a man's, it growled in its throat and squeezed hard. The Targon's nails dug into Abraham's thick neck muscles, which did not give.

Abraham wedged his fingers into the thick muscles of the Targon's neck. The cat-man glared into his eyes, its face turning red and purple like Abraham's. His facial fur didn't stand on end. Victory lurked in its eyes, fueled by vengeance.

With a grunt, Abraham squeezed with all his might. "Urk!" The veins in his forearms sprouted like worms. Ruger's engine turned on. Losing air, his engine started to fade. The cat-man's raw power was suffocating him.

What is this thing made of?

The steel-strong limbs in Ruger's body started to give way. Triumph showed in the cat-man's eyes. It had Abraham. He could do nothing.

Farewell, Titanuus.

38

The Targon's eyes widened. It let out a ragged mew and slumped over to one side of Abraham's body.

Gasping, Abraham kicked away from his dead attacker. Shades held Abraham's dagger in his hand. The tip dripped blood.

Rubbing his throat, Abraham said, "Good timing. How'd you get out of that cage?"

"No cage can hold me," Shades said. The light-in-stature man extended a hand. "And it is I that should be thanking you, Captain." He flipped the dagger and offered it pommel first to Abraham. "The Targon would have made an example out of me."

Abraham wiped his blade in the grass and sheathed it. All the Targon were dead. The ones that had flown in the sky lay dead on the ground.

Abraham saw no sign of Simon. "Where did the Fenix go?"

"To dinner. He had a Targon in his talons and flew that way." Shades pointed toward the Spine. He made a gritty look. "Your head looks like it's been ripped off and stuck back on again."

"Yeah, well, it feels like it too." He spotted his sword lying in the grass and picked it up. "Man, I thought I was a goner. Those Targon weren't so bad, but the winged ones are tougher than nails."

"The Targon possess natural skill that they rely on more than routine training. Their weakness is their refusal to wear armor." Shades patted down the robes of a dead cat-man. "Like the great cats of the wild, they have incredible instincts, making them excellent trackers. The winged ones are felines supreme, the strongest of the lot. They lead the hunts. If it weren't for that bat thing, I fear you would not have made it. Or would have been enslaved the same as me." He winked at Abraham. "You have interesting friends. But this brood is a bunch of slavers." He moved to another body, rummaged the robes, and fished out a small leather purse. "And slavers have money."

"What is your tie to them?"

Shades shrugged and said, "Well, the Targon seek talent to serve the King of the Mountains."

"In the Old Kingdom."

Shades arched a brow and said, "Yes. You know that."

"Melris had knowledge of the Targons' history."

"I see. Well, the Targon are a very secluded race, as is the King of the Mountain. They have a strange relationship, eons old."

Abraham studied the dead. "These Targon are striking. They don't come across as something that is wicked."

"If you think these men catch your eye, you should see the women. But they aren't any different than the rest of the races. There is good and evil in all of them. This group survived on money." He spilled out the contents of a purse into his hand. Silver shards shaped like guitar picks gleamed dully in his palm. "A decent score."

"So, how did you wind up at the King of the Mountain?"

"Easy. My parents sold me straight out of my homeland in Hancha. That's right. My own flesh and blood sold me for a few rotten songs." He started juggling four shards then added the fifth, sixth, and seventh. "I made money on the streets as an entertainer of sorts." His hands and fingers moved in a blur. "I was good at it. Actually, the thieves' guilds had their eye on me at first, but the Targon came and snatched me away.

"For the king, I worked as a jester and sleight-of-hand magician. I can perform acrobatics, act, and be an expert marksman. In truth, it hadn't been a very bad life. If you took care of the king, he took care of you. At least, so long as your skills remained worthy. He had an assortment of great talent, but the older ones, when they lost a step, would disappear."

"So you escaped?"

Shades touched the star tattoo underneath his right eye. "Escape is not so easy. Like the King's Brand, the Targon slavers have a brand of their own. It allows them to track you no matter where you go." He caught all seven coins in the palm of his hand and lifted a finger. "It's magic, but I learned its secret when I worked as a scribe for one of the king's sages. That's when I learned that another mystic brand can cover the slave brand's detection. I planned my escape and sought to become one of the king's legendary Henchmen." He ran a finger down the scar under his left eye. "That's when I acquired this."

"So that's why you want the brand?" Abraham sheathed his sword. "It figures." He started limping away.

Shades hustled over to him. "I earned the Brand. The same as the rest. I delight in the company of the Henchmen. I'm a faithful follower. And need I remind you, I just saved your life and risked my own." He moved in front of Abraham. "Captain. I need this. The Targon will be back. They'll publicly flay the skin from my bones. I'm not one to beg, but please."

Abraham moved past him. "I'll think about it."

39

Two mornings later, the Henchmen reunited at the base of the mountains on the side of the Eastern Bolg territories. Abraham and Shades were waiting on them at the bottom of a key mountain pass. Tark and Dominga were the first to track them down.

All the Henchmen had survived the encounter with Simon the Fenix, as his paralyzing breath wore off.

The Henchmen gave Shades a half-hearted welcome back.

Abraham got slaps on the back and hearty handshakes. He brought them all up to speed.

Iris rode in the back of the wagon, tending to Melris. The Elderling had been crushed underneath Simon the Fenix, which was bigger than two elephants. He lay in the wagon, underneath a blanket, with his eyes closed and breathing gently.

"How is he doing?" Abraham asked. He was back on his horse, riding by the wagon.

Sticks was doubled up behind him. They had lost many horses battling the Pitters and the wild panthers.

Iris was stirring ointment in a small bowl with a mixing spoon. She applied the bluish salve to Melris's lips. "He's not dead, and so far as I can tell, he's fully alive. When that beast landed on him, he was crushed into a dip in the ground. His ribs are bruised, but nothing else appears to be broken. Methinks his bones might be soft, like a baby's. Perhaps the Elder of Fortune is his mentor."

"You can't wake him up?" he said.

"I've tried using strong-smelling scents. Nothing stirs the man's sense. I do the best I can to keep water in him." Iris stroked Melris's face. "He's pretty for a young man. I've never felt skin so soft." She tugged on his cheek. "Yet firm as leather."

Abraham nodded. "Let me know when he wakes."

"I will."

They were only two days' ride from Junction City. Abraham's wheels were turning. With Melris down, he could start his hunt for Big Apple. The Elderling had been very persistent about moving straight to the Wound, but his present condition presented the perfect opportunity for Abraham.

"What are you waiting for?" Sticks asked. She gave him a little squeeze from behind.

"What do you mean?"

"I know you're heading straight to Junction City. Now's the perfect time. I'm ready. Let's do it."

Abraham glanced over his shoulder. Vern and Bearclaw were walking alongside Solomon. He waved at the troglin.

Solomon lengthened his stride and caught up with Abraham and Sticks in no time. "Any revelations?"

"No. I wanted to let you know that we are going to ride ahead to Junction City. We want to keep a low profile," he said.

Solomon wiggled his eyebrows and said, "I see. Because I'm giant and hairy, you don't want me around. Ha. I'll get over it. So, you are going after Big Apple, huh?"

"I've got to take a crack at it. That little dingleberry threw us completely off track. He knows more than he lets on. I'm certain the rest of the Sect knows more too." He twisted his head around and looked at the wagon. "And Melris, he's not sharing his entire story either, I'm sure."

"I'll keep an eye on things." Solomon covered more than half of Sticks's back with his paw of a giant hand. "I assume you are taking this butterfly with you, but who else?"

"Shades will come."

"Are you certain?" Sticks said. "He brings danger."

"We had a long talk the past two days. I'm certain."

"Are you going to make him a Henchman?" she asked.

"I'm thinking about it."

"If you want my opinion, I like Shades," Solomon said. "He brings some flavor to an otherwise drab party."

Abraham nodded.

"What does *drab* mean?" Sticks asked.

"Dreary," Solomon replied.

"I'm not drab," she said.

"No, you aren't drab… or happy or sad or angry. I don't know what you are." Solomon chuckled. "It's sexy, and it's not." He eyed Abraham and discreetly asked, "Does she show any kind of emotion? You know…"

Abraham managed a smile and said, "A gentleman never tells."

"You can if you want," Sticks said.

"Oooh, spicy. Now, I like that." Solomon grinned widely. "And she didn't even bat an eye. I like the mystery that comes with this woman." He punched Abraham in the arm, which jostled Abraham in the saddle. "You lucky dog."

"You could have stayed back with the triplets, you know," Abraham said.

"And miss out on all of the fun of being a Henchman?" Solomon tossed his head back. "Ha! I'm seeing this through. Unlike you, I want to get back home."

Abraham instantly thought of Mandi. "Yeah, me too." He felt Sticks's grip tighten around his waist. He'd become a man torn between two worlds and desirable women aplenty. The question was which world was more important—back home or Titanuus. Telling the difference between the two had become impossible. *The only thing I can do is move forward and hope I do right.*

Abraham turned his horse around and brought it to a stop. The Henchmen gathered in front of him.

"Red Tunics, start a fire," he said as he dismounted. He found Shades quietly standing among the group, his hands clasped as he rolled his thumbs over one another. "Horace, fetch the King's Brand."

Several of the Henchmen rolled their eyes, and others sighed.

"Shades, come forward."

40

"HOW ARE YOU FEELING?" ABRAHAM SAID TO SHADES.

Shades was slumped over in his saddle, clutching his chest. "I don't recall the last brand hurting so much. I feel like my chest is on fire."

"Consider it payback for what you did to us in Baracha," Sticks said. "If it were up to me, I'd have stuck the hot iron all over you." She was still doubled up in the saddle with Abraham. Only the three of them were traveling.

"I bet you didn't crack when it burned you either," Shades said.

"Never."

The trio was on a roadway leading to Junction City. They rode through light rain along a muddy road with deep wagon-wheel ruts. Their wet cloaks did little to keep their clothing from becoming damp.

Abraham had left Horace in charge of the Henchmen—as long as Melris remained asleep. They were to wait three days on the north side of Junction City for Abraham to return. If they didn't return, Horace could come after them. Shades had been to a tavern called the Broken Wing. Their hunt for Big Apple would start there.

Sticks sniffed the air. "What is that burning smell?"

"We are downwind of Junction City. Those are the smokestacks you smell," Shades said. He pointed ahead. "Once we clear that next rise in the plains, we'll be able to see the city."

Abraham kicked his horse into a trot. Even though he had a mission to complete, he wouldn't mind a hot meal and soft bed. Having Sticks riding behind him got his juices flowing too. She leaned on him from time to time, pressing her breasts into his back.

I'm a dog. Sticks in one world and Mandi in the other. Cheesy time-traveler romances, here I come.

Over the rise, he got his first glimpse of Junction City. "Whoa."

The horse came to a stop, though that wasn't his intent.

Junction City resembled Burgess in layout: stone buildings and stone-paved streets. Huge smokestacks made of cut rock were spread throughout the city, towering over everything else. They were at least one hundred feet high and half as wide as they were tall. Giant plumes of smoke billowed out of the tops of the stacks. The smoke colors varied among a putrid yellow, filmy moss, and dingy white.

A river ran behind the city and snaked through the valley.

Travelers entered and exited the city from all directions, on a variety of roads. The town bustled with activity on all corners.

"A thriving place, eh?" Shades said.

Abraham crinkled his nose and asked, "What are they burning?"

"Refuse. Wood. Coal. People." Shades bobbed his hand. "It keeps the people warm at night."

"Coal? That's interesting. Do the stacks always burn?"

"I haven't spent much time here, but I'd suppose so. Maybe not. I traveled here when I was a boy. Made another pass after I escaped. With hundreds of thousands of people, it's a good place to get lost in." Shades leaned over his saddle horn. "And it appears to be growing."

"Do they have an army? Does the King of Eastern Bolg live in there? I don't see a castle."

"The king lives on the other side of the Little Vein River. Junction City has its own garrison though it's a trading city, open to all territories. Aside from Kingsland, of course. You won't see any blue banners with lion's heads and white wings here. I'm certain of that. Shall I lead?"

"Take us to the Broken Wing. I don't want to waste any time."

"Aye, aye, Captain." Shades gave his horse a kick and led them toward the city.

One hundred yards out, a group of four riders wearing leather armor dyed gray and skull-cap helmets rode right toward them.

"Who are they?" Abraham asked.

"Representatives of Junction City's garrison. They are called the Gray Guard. They aren't the friendliest bunch either." Shades lined his horse between Abraham and the oncoming men. "It's best that you let me do the talking."

Abraham recalled Shades's work on the *Sea Talon* when they'd been boarded by the trio of brothers called Captain Alphonso. They were from Tiotan, and Shades had bribed them.

He gave the rogue a nod and said, "Go for it."

The soldiers closed in at a full gallop.

"They aren't slowing," Sticks said. "Shouldn't they be slowing?"

"I would think so." Shades stopped his horse.

Abraham did the same. He dropped his hand to his sword. "I don't think that's a welcome wagon. They look like they want to kill somebody."

His heartbeat pumped in his ears. Something was up. Big Apple must have known they were coming.

Sticks's hands slid away from his body as she pulled his dagger from his belt. "I need to borrow this."

41

THE GRAY GUARD THUNDERED PAST THE VISITING TRIO AT FULL
speed. They didn't even give the small company a glance. They
rode fast and hard and disappeared over the rise.

"See? I told you that I would handle it," Shades said. "Did you
even notice that they didn't have weapons drawn?"

"Weapons that we could see," Abraham said. "I wonder where
they are going? There isn't much of anything between us and the
others."

"There isn't much traffic coming from the south either," Sticks
added. "But the Henchmen can handle themselves."

Abraham flipped out a hand. "Lead the way."

Their horses' hooves hit the cobblestone streets several
minutes later. Junction City was a nice city, by medieval standards.
The people were just in an array of robes and fine linens.
Merchant carts and merchant wagons rattled over the streets.

Abraham's forehead started to bead. He watched a wagon full
of coal roll by. The churning fires in the smokestacks created an
extra layer of warmth in the city. They created a stuffiness too. A

mild odor lingered in the street. The wind shifted direction, bringing forth the smell of burning wood.

They stabled the horses and walked the streets. Men and women shouted back and forth from their windows. Children raced through the streets, pushing a metal ring with a stick.

A group of gawkers gathered around a salesman who stood on a small platform and had a curtain stage behind him. His thumbs were in his suspenders. He had a tall hat and handlebar moustache. Behind him was a contraption that looked very much like a bicycle.

"Oh no," Abraham muttered as an icy shiver raced down his spine. He saw men and women pulling carts like rickshaws.

Women shielded themselves from the sun with medieval umbrellas.

A lanky fellow with hair down to his waist carried a wooden sign that said Showgirls. He twisted it around his body in a showy fashion.

People from all walks of life were strolling through Junction City as well: scale-covered Myrmidons, bruising barbarians, pale-faced zillons and troglins appearing here and there, cat-faced Targon gliding through the crowds.

He gave Shades a worried look.

"Let's hope they aren't slavers," Shades said coolly.

Sticks nudged Abraham's ribs with an elbow. She pointed her eyes toward the top of a smokestack. A dragon like the ones the zillons flew basked in the warmth of the stack's smoke.

"It seems they take all kinds in this town. Shades, how many taverns do you think this city holds?"

"Dozens. Is that where you want to start looking?"

They walked by a haunting garden protected by a wrought-iron gate. A Sect temple loomed in the background.

"We could always start there. They know where the trouble is," Sticks said. "They'll be distracted since we killed Arcayis."

"True, but someone must have stepped up. No doubt they will have named a new Underlord," Shades added.

"Yeah, I think the Big Apple would have answers to that too. That mission had his stink all over it," he said.

A trio of jugglers waltzed by, tossing fruit and knives between their hands.

Shades walked right between the juggling act, plucked two knives out of the volley, and tossed them each into separate fruits. The move left the jugglers gaping.

"We are keeping a low profile," Abraham warned.

"Sorry, I couldn't help myself," Shades quipped. "Ah, here it is." He moved toward a tavern painted a dull red.

A heavy-set woman sat in an Adirondack-style chair, fanning herself. Beside her was a pretty young woman in skimpy clothing with the dark eyes and straight hair of an Asian. She stood behind a booth, selling wooden tokens.

"You, sir. Big strong man. For only five silver shards, you can drink all you want from our chain of taverns." The young woman slipped from behind the stand, grabbed his hand, and rubbed her nubile body against him. "Your choice of ale, grog, and fruity mixers." She glanced at Sticks. "We have many prettier girls too."

Abraham tried to pull his hand away, but the little woman wouldn't let go.

Sticks belted her in the stomach.

"Hey! Don't you hit my ladies!" The big woman sitting in the chair started to rise. Her face was turning as pink as her robes. She had a scratchy, husky voice. "I'll have the bruisers skin you alive!"

Shades slipped some silver shards into the fat of the woman's palm. "We'll take three tokens. And there is a little something extra for you. You'll have to forgive my little brother. He doesn't get out much."

"She's a he?" the fat woman asked.

"In most territories." Shades gave Sticks an ornery look while the woman counted the coins in her hand.

She bit down on one shard with her bad teeth and nodded her saggy chin. "That's good coin. Targon. I'll take it." She kicked the young girl in the ribs. "Will you get moving and give these fine customers their tokens?"

The girl fished the coins out of a box in her booth and gave them to the older woman. She bowed and moved away.

The big woman in the chair stuffed the tokens into Shades's hand. "Have yourself a good time, you handsome little fella. The Broken Wing welcomes you! Ha ha!" She swatted Shades on the behind as he entered. She did the same to Abraham and Sticks. "You two fellas have a good time as well."

The Broken Wing was another decrepit tavern filled with broken tables and chairs that had been mended back together time and time again. Oily-skinned men and women drank, ate, smoked, and cursed at the tables. The bar on one side of the tavern and the granite-block fireplace on the other side of the bar were the main fixtures.

The food smelled fried and greasy. The smell of baked hot rolls tickled Abraham's nose. A scent of spiced pumpkin lingered in the sweltering air.

That was the first thing Abraham noticed. The second was the strands of eye-popping bikinilike clothing worn by the fetching women. They walked the floors with hips swaying and eyelashes batting. Trays of drinks were balanced delicately in their hands. The strumpets were a mixed lot of women, Myrmidons, zillons, and cat-faced feline women who had to have been Targon.

Abraham swallowed the lump in his throat.

A woman slipped behind him and purred in his ear. She had white fur with tiger stripes, pink eyes of a rose, a wisp of black clothing, and a human body to die for. "Hello, handsome," she said. "Let me find you a seat. I'm Lila."

"It's no surprise that you picked a dwelling full of trollops," Sticks said to Shades.

"And it's no surprise that others easily mistake you for a man." Sticks punched the man in his arm.

Mesmerized, Abraham let the gorgeous tigerish woman seat him at the table. He wet his lips and said, "Thank you."

The Targon waitress caressed his face, gently scratching it with her clawed fingertips. With a sexy purr in her voice, she said, "Just whistle if you need me." She strolled away.

That was when Abraham noticed the third pertinent thing. He turned to scan his surroundings with a smile all over his face. As he swiveled around in his chair, he found himself looking at the broad side of a huge man's back.

Their elbows bumped.

The man turned.

It was Commander Cutter from Hancha.

42

ABRAHAM WAS A SECOND FROM RAMMING HIS ELBOW INTO Commander Cutter's broad face when Sticks jumped into Abraham's lap and kissed him.

Commander Cutter shoved his elbow into Abraham's shoulder. The blow knocked him and Sticks onto the floor.

"Watch what you're doing, whore," Cutter said in a grizzly voice. Without even looking at them, he picked up his pint of ale and guzzled it. He wiped his forearm across the white scar on his chin. The man was a mass of muscle, with a short haircut and strong angular features. He wore a black cloak and grabbed his bastard sword, propped up against the wall. "Let's go, Black Squadron. This whore hole is getting too crowded for a big fella like me."

Abraham and Sticks continued to kiss. She started to get into it, and his heart raced—not because of her but more because of the presence of the Black Squadron. They were a company of Hancha's elite soldiers. They wore burgundy tunics with upside-down black ankhs over suits of chain mail. The Henchmen had encountered them before in a small town in Hancha. Commander

Cutter had hunted them from Pirate's Harbor. Shades had burned that tavern down as a distraction. They crossed them again after their victory in Cauldron City. Commander Cutter challenged Ruger Slade, but Slade the Blade had refused.

Commander Cutter and his small company of four departed the Broken Wing to the disappointed flattering and musings of the serving girls.

Abraham sat up. Sticks broke off her kiss but still straddled him. He scanned the room. No more members of the Black Squadron remained to be seen.

Shades stepped into view and offered his hand. "I see our mighty friend is back."

Abraham took Shades's hand and stood up with Sticks's legs still locked around his waist. He gave her the big eye and asked, "What's gotten into you?"

"Perhaps it's the competition. I saw that hungry look that you gave the Targon."

"My my, Sticks has a jealous bone. I never thought I'd see the day," Shades said cheerfully. "She's human after all."

"We have bigger things to worry about." He set down Sticks even though he was so riled up that he didn't want to. "Shades, get us a room with a view of the street. A balcony would be great." He cast his glance all over the bar. "I've got a feeling that if Cutter is here, so is Big Apple. It's no coincidence. Keep an eye out for Lord Hawk too. Probably a bunch of members of the Shell about. We better lie low."

Shades scored a room on the second level of the tavern. Using a key, he let them inside. "It's all yours. I'll send up some food."

"Where are you staying?" Abraham asked.

Shades winked at him and said, "With all of these ladies strolling about, I won't need a room. They'll offer me one of theirs." He closed the door.

The room was large, with a queen-size bed covered in a purple quilt and pillows. Two storage chests sat along the wall, along with a desk and mirror and a table for two by the window. A single door opened to the outside balcony.

Abraham opened the door and said, "I bet I could be rich if I invented the sliding door for this country."

Sticks sat down on the edge of the bed and started taking her cloak off.

"Uh, what are you doing?"

She took the long braids out of her hair and combed them out with her fingers. She flipped her head down and tousled her hair and flipped it back. Her dark-auburn locks hung on her shoulders. Her tomboyish good looks started to stand out. She removed her bandolier and unbuckled her tunic.

Abraham swallowed. "Uh, Sticks, Shades will be back with food at any moment."

She raised a brow, made a quirky smile, and said, "No, he won't."

"We need to find the Big Apple and see what Cutter is up to. I know they are here. We have a mission."

Sticks pulled off her trousers. All she wore was a cotton shirt that hung down past her waist. She walked over to him, took him by the hand, and led him to the bed. She pushed him down onto the bed, tugged his trousers off, and straddled him. "I have a mission too. I want you, and I want you now."

43

ABRAHAM AND STICKS HIT THE FESTIVE STREETS OF JUNCTION CITY. Some sort of celebration was going on. People marched over the paved roadways, playing instruments, wearing costumes, and carrying a variety of flags and banners. He got a vibe like what he'd gotten before when he visited Mardi Gras on Bourbon Street in New Orleans.

Sticks clasped Abraham's hand and he walked with her arms swinging.

What is going on with her?

The expressionless woman showed little emotion in her face or otherwise. But when she wanted something, she didn't hesitate to take it. She might not say much, but she carried a passionate intensity in her eyes. Those eyes said it all, and she had taken Abraham.

Still, the hand holding and arm swinging seemed awkward. She led the way.

"Come over here," she said in a chipper tone.

Along the streets were small booths where women painted the faces of men and women celebrating in the parade. He overheard people talking about a contest of costumes going on. The more he looked about, the more odd characters he saw. People were dressed like dragons, birds, rodents, cats, and even clowns of a sort. Some disheveled drunken men even mimicked the Gray Guard soldiers while they sang at the top of their lungs, swinging arm in arm.

The array of custom clothing was bright and colorful in some cases, dreary and dark in others. The women strutted about shamelessly in tight silken bodysuits that left very little to the imagination. They rubbed up against Abraham when they walked by with smiles and flirtatious giggles.

What is this, Comic-Con?

"Come on, Abraham, sit down," Sticks said. She patted a stool.

"What are we doing?" he asked as he pulled his head away from a cute teenage girl with roses in her hair, who tried to apply makeup to him. "Hey, I'm not into that!"

"Shush, we can't look like ourselves and risk being seen." She planted her rear end on a stool beside him. "Now, what sort of creature would you like to look like?"

"I don't know. Back home, we had a holiday called Halloween. We'd dress up in something scary. I liked doing scary." He saw some men strolling by with ugly masks on. "Can't I do that?"

"No." She sat with her back straight and her cheeks sucked in as the girl attending her put on a base layer of makeup. "A mask will distort your senses."

"What are you going to be?"

"A cat," she said.

"Really, a cat? That's not very original."

She eyeballed him and replied, "Back in the Broken Wing, you seemed to like them."

He'd seen more women dressed up as cats at Halloween parties than anything else he could recall. In some cases, it might have been sexy, but it wasn't very original.

"It's fine," he said.

Sticks frowned. "Fine? Is there something else that you'd rather I be?"

"No, I'm good with the whiskers. Go for it." He looked at the girl powdering him up. "Give me a white face with two blazing silver stars over my eyes."

The girl shrugged and quickly got to work. A few minutes later, the makeup job was over.

"How do I look?" Sticks asked.

She had her face painted white and was given black whiskers and a red button nose. The makeup artist accented her eyes with black and gold, giving her a very desirable feline look.

"Pretty hot. I take back what I said about the cat thing."

"What are you supposed to be? I don't recognize that image. Is it something from your world?"

"Yeah, I'm Ace Frehley. Do you like it?"

She lifted her shoulders as she paid the young woman. "I think a cat would have been better."

"Nah, Space Ace is the way to go." He played the air guitar. "Lead the way, cat lady."

Sticks led them through the raucous crowd. Bars and taverns ran from one end of the road to the other. The bars associated with the Broken Wing each had a blue front door.

They crossed the street, and as they did so, Abraham caught four dudes in Kiss makeup marching by. They flashed him the Kiss sign. He gingerly flashed them back.

Oh man, this isn't good. This is crazy. I'm crazy.

They spent the next few hours moving from bar to bar, trying to locate Commander Cutter and his men. The tavern floors were sticky. The sweaty people coming in and out started to smell. Smoke in the barrooms became a thick fog.

Abraham sipped on his beer. His eyes burned. Sticks would sit hip to hip beside him. He felt lost, but in a good way. People would look right through him. He bobbed his head to the thumping beat of the music. *I could get used to this.*

They made it through four bars and spent a little time in each before moving on to the next.

Commander Cutter was nowhere to be found. They hit three more blue-door taverns. Sticks made her rounds and asked a few questions. Abraham sat quietly and observed. The townsfolk of Junction City lined up shots of liquor and played drinking games. Hearty men bounced shards into glass tumblers and drank.

The party atmosphere was like ones he'd seen at college. It reminded him of his time with the team after baseball games. It was close to home—too close. A headache started to build between his eyes. He set down his beer and wetted his lips. He needed water.

Sticks came back and joined him at the table. "Are you well?"

"I don't know."

A woman in a long red coat with a matching wide-brimmed hat came in. Men with leather boots, moustaches, and cowboy vests strolled in after her.

"Did you find out anything?" He gripped the table with the end of his fingers. "Big Apple is here. I know it." His chair started to turn underneath him. "Sticks, is the room moving?"

"No," she said.

She sounded as though she were on the other side of the bar. "I need to get out of here. I need fresh air." He stood on wobbly knees.

A man shoved him down into his chair and said, "You aren't going anywhere."

44

ABRAHAM GRABBED THE MAN BY THE CHEST AND REELED HIM IN. THE man wore a mask with the face of a chimpanzee. A hooded cloak covered his head and shoulders.

"Who are you?" Abraham asked.

"Easy, easy," the man behind the monkey mask said. He lifted the mask.

"Shades." Abraham shoved the man back. His own head started to spin a little.

Sticks tucked away her daggers. "What are you doing, fool?"

Shades made a meow sound and said, "I like the makeup, kitten. Quite the improvement. Is there any chance that it's permanent?"

"Shut up," she replied.

Abraham shook the fog from his head and asked, "Where have you been?" He looked the man up and down. "And why are you taller?"

Shades plopped down in a chair, bent over, and lifted his cloak. One-foot-high wooden stilts were fastened to his boots. "It's all part of my disguise, Captain." He stared hard into Abraham's face. "No fancy makeup required. Uh, what are you supposed to be?"

"Ace Frehley. A famous bard back home."

"Ah, I see. It's quite fetching." Shades rolled his eyes. "So, have you had any luck tracking down Commander Cutter?"

"No." Abraham fanned himself. "I need some water. What about you?"

"As a matter of fact, I came from his very spot."

Abraham sat up.

Sticks leaned forward. "Well?"

"Two blocks over is a tavern called the Showboat. There are many pretty dancing girls." He shrugged his pale eyebrows. "They have Commander Cutter and his brood captivated. Shall we press on?"

Abraham rose to his feet and headed to the door. He stumbled out into the street and gulped for fresh air.

Shades and Sticks followed behind, with Shades asking, "What's wrong with him? Did the Captain have one too many?"

Sticks hooked a hand around Abraham's waist and said, "No, I don't think so. What's wrong, Abraham? You aren't going to black out, are you?"

He took a deep, long breath through his nostrils, and his head started to clear. He straightened back up. "No, I'll be fine. Whew, I don't know what came over me." He wiped the cold sweat from his brow on a sleeve. "The bar was suffocating. I don't know what it was."

"I'll lead the way," Shades said with an uneasy glance. He pulled his monkey mask down. With his stilts on, he stood only a few inches shorter than Ruger. "I like being taller. I can get a better view of people, and it's not as smelly. Trust me when I say there is nothing worse than standing underneath a dirty man's armpit."

The word Showboat was painted on a wooden sign hanging over the tavern's blue door. A burly bouncer type in common garb stood outside the door, with arms crossed and a wary look in his eyes. The bruiser had a mohawk and goatee. The bouncer grabbed Shades by the collar and said, "You again? I don't like you."

Shades flashed the token. "I have this."

"I don't care. I don't like your face!" The bouncer spat as he talked.

"It's only a mask," Shades said as he wiped the spit from his mask. "I can take it off."

"No." The bouncer shoved him away. "Get out of here before I break your legs."

Abraham and Sticks were the next in line.

The bouncer eyed them both, took a long, hard look at Abraham and said, "You're a big one. Bigger than me." He nodded and eyeballed Sticks. "Lucky for you, I like cats. I have a couple myself in my flat. Lilly and Tiger." He stepped aside. "Enjoy, but don't make trouble, or I'll bust you up."

Abraham nodded, took a deep breath, and shuffled inside.

Incense burned in the tavern like a bad perfume. The bar sweltered. Big bodies were crammed behind small tables. The tavern dwellers faced a stage full of dancing girls on the opposite end.

Sticks zeroed in on two stools open behind the bar. She dropped on one before another man and woman could take them. She hitched her thumb and said, "Find another spot."

The man started to say something back to Sticks but had second thoughts when he looked up at Ruger. The couple left.

Abraham took a seat. "Man, these places smell."

The bartender was an Asian-looking woman who wore a white shirt underneath a black vest. She set down a pair of steaming towels on a plate before them.

He and Sticks exchanged a glance.

"It's for your sweat!" the bartender said in a smart-alecky Chinese-like accent.

"We have makeup on," Sticks fired back.

"So!" The bartender gave them both a disappointed look. "You got coin or just hogging stools?"

Abraham and Sticks flashed their tokens.

The bartender filled two shot glasses with a wine-red liquid. "Cherry brandy. Drink up. It's good for the sweats. Go ahead, drink it."

Abraham didn't want to drink, but he tapped his glass against Sticks's and said, "Bottoms up." After they both drank, his face soured. "Ugh, that tastes like cough syrup."

"No syrup. Cherry brandy. Do you want ale? Devil's fire? A prairie fire. I'm busy. Tell me what you want," the bartender said.

Sticks lifted two fingers and said, "Ale." She turned her back to the bar and faced the stage. "Looks like Shades was right. There's Cutter."

Cutter sat behind a small table, like a man among boys, hunched over. His bastard sword was propped up against the wall nearby. A group of his Black Squadron were with him. They were all armed, but judging by the women on their laps, they were having a good time—except Cutter. No woman accompanied him. His eyes were on the stage.

The exotic dancers moved their nubile bodies to the thumping beat of bongos, chimes, and the sound of a flute. They were short ladies, representing many of the races, and they would weave their way through the crowd in an enticing manner.

Cutter shrugged off their advances. He'd look them up and down and push them aside.

"It looks like he's a picky one," Sticks said.

"He's probably waiting on someone and doesn't want to be distracted," he said.

"I bet I can distract him," Sticks said.

"What do you mean?"

She departed for the stage, saying, "Watch and see."

45

Sticks vanished into the crowd, leaving Abraham scratching his head. He turned his attention back to Cutter's table. Cutter's men pawed the women and pulled them into their laps. Some of the dancers squirmed away, and others didn't.

Cutter slugged down his ale and scratched his ear. The man had a high-and-tight military cut and was built and looked like a bulldog.

Abraham eyed the man's bastard sword. *I wonder how good he really is.*

Ruger Slade was rumored to be the best swordsman in the world. The competitive spirit of Abraham embraced that, and he had a feeling that the body of Ruger did too. The raucous atmosphere stirred something inside him. He touched the pommel of his sword, wanting to test his mettle.

The thumping beat of the music shifted to a sultry melody. The rowdy men in the room fell silent for a moment. They craned their necks as the light on the stage dimmed.

A woman appeared on the stage who stood out among the

other dancers. Her hands carried flames. She swayed to the beat and moved the flames from one hand to another.

Abraham narrowed his eyes. The woman's face was painted like a cat. A skimpy two-piece outfit hugged her sensual curves. It was Sticks.

With a body that was the envy of all the other dancers, Sticks made her way off stage and into the crowd. She moved with the sexy prowess of a feline. Sweat glistened on her flat belly. Her hips swayed with every step, leaving men's tongues hanging out of their mouths.

Sticks's captivating movements had his heart beating in his throat.

"I really like this cat version of her better," Shades said in his smooth Australian-style accent. "She's a real dog otherwise."

Abraham twisted his head around and said, "I didn't think you were allowed in here."

"Pfft, do you think that sack of meat could keep me from slipping into a tavern?" Shades took off his mask. "They have a back door, you know. The cook let me in. She was a cutie."

The bartender set down a steaming cloth, a mug of ale, and a shot of cherry brandy in front of Shades. "You need anything else?"

"How about some mix?" Shades said.

Abraham turned his attention back to Sticks. She was making her way through the crowd and moving the flames from hand to hand. She would blow out the candles on the tables in an enticing fashion and light them again with her own flame.

Shades nudged Abraham. "Have some mix? It's good stuff."

Abraham found himself looking at a bowl of peanuts. His jaw hung.

Shades cracked open a shell, ate the nut, and tossed the shell on the floor. "Have you had some? I bet they don't have a treat like this in your world."

As alarming as the sight of peanuts was, it didn't hold a candle to the performance Sticks was giving on the floor. Lust filled the eyes of men. They hooted and hollered for more.

Shades crunched down on his bowl of mix and said, "She has a fine rear end, doesn't she? It's her best asset, if you ask me."

"What is she doing?"

"She's working on the big fella, Cutter. You know, she's going to seduce him." Shades grinned. "You know, squeeze him for information."

Abraham didn't hide his shock.

"Don't worry, I'm sure she'll hate every bit of being with a large fella like that," Shades added. "But a Henchman has to do what a Henchman has to do."

"She's going to sleep with him?"

"We are spies. We do what we do."

"Great," Abraham said with a disappointing shake of his head. "I'm dating Jane Bond."

"Don't worry, there are more Sticks in the sea."

"Don't you mean *fish*?" Abraham asked.

"Sure. You do remember that Sticks and I had a thing for a good while," Shades added. He tossed more shells on the floor. "It's best not to get so attached. But we are a tight group. Hard to avoid those love triangles that surface."

Abraham swatted the bowl of peanuts out of Shades's hands. The mix scattered, and the bowl shattered.

"You pay for that!" the bartender said. "That was my number-one bowl. It will cost you extra."

Abraham turned his back on the bartender with his nostrils flaring. He focused on Sticks. He'd just slept with her, and now she was seducing a room full of men. It shouldn't have bothered him, but it did.

"Don't let your skull boil," Shades said as he slipped the bartender some shards. "It's the king's business. Make the most of it." He handed Abraham a mug of ale. "Have a drink. You're too rigid to blend in."

"Ooh, I see the problem. Big man with star face has a slutty woman," the bartender said. "I would like to hire her." She started wiggling her shoulders. "She make my customers very happy."

Abraham took a deep breath. *Don't let it eat you up. None of this might be real anyway.*

Sticks made her way toward Cutter. The warrior's gaze swallowed her body as he rubbed his chin. The expressionless woman went right at him. Her eyes locked with his and burned with sultry intensity. She held her hands in front of Cutter's face, flames dancing in her palms. Cutter blew them out and grinned. She hopped into his lap. He picked her up with a smile on his face and walked by Abraham and straight out of the bar.

46

"WHAT WAS THAT ALL ABOUT? I THOUGHT HE WAS WAITING ON somebody," Abraham mused.

"He was," Shades replied. "Her."

The four remaining soldiers of the Black Squadron started to depart. The hard-eyed soldiers, who had a Henchmen-type quality, escorted dancers out of the bar.

The soldiers walked by with drunken grins on their faces.

Shades tripped the one third from the back. The man tumbled into the backside of the man in front of him. The first soldier went down as well.

"Say! I saw you do that!" the soldier in the back said.

"I did too," said one of the pretty dancers. She pointed at Shades. "It was this little weasel."

"I reckon this little hound needs to be taught a lesson," said the soldier in the back.

Abraham punched the talking man in the face. The man fell like a stone.

Shades kicked the soldier he'd tripped in the side of the face.

He said to Abraham, "Take care of this mess. I'll catch up with you." He bolted for the front door.

"Wait!" Abraham said. He started after Shades. One of the soldiers on the floor tackled his legs and drove him back into the bar. He punched the man in the ribs. The soldier was well padded up with a tunic over chain mail.

He hit the man harder.

The man let out a groan.

"Stop fighting! Stop fighting!" the bartender said. She cracked Abraham over the head with a ceramic jug, and ale spilled all over him.

The dancing girls screamed and scattered.

The soldiers in front came to their feet and rushed Abraham.

Abraham wrestled against two men. They whaled on one another.

"You want a fight? We'll fight! No one attacks the Black Squadron and lives!" the first soldier said.

A burly patron smashed a chair over the talking soldier's back.

Abraham twisted away from the man he'd been punching and shoved the man into the crowd.

A bar brawl broke out.

The bartender jumped up on the bar and screamed, "See what you did?" She thrust a finger at Abraham. "You are paying for this!"

Abraham dropped some silver shards on the table and bolted out of the front door.

The wee hours of the night had come, but the streets were still bustling with celebration. He saw no sign of Shades or Sticks.

"Great!" Abraham rushed through the streets, trying to find his friends.

A parade of costumed people marched by, blowing horns and tossing confetti.

All four Black Squadron members spilled out of the Showboat. They spotted Abraham from across the street. One of them pointed at Abraham and shouted, "There!" They pulled their swords and ran after him.

Abraham jumped in with the parade.

The Black Squadron, drunk or not, weren't fooled. They plowed into the paraders and shoved them aside. They hacked at Abraham with their swords.

A sword tip came within a whisker of Abraham's nose. *That was too close.* He bolted away from his pursuers and ducked into a dead-end alley. With his back to the wall, he pulled his sword just as the Black Squadron closed him in.

"You're dead now, painted fool," said the tallest man in the front. "No one crosses the Black Squadron and lives."

"Wouldn't the Gray Guard take issue with you killing one of their citizens?" Abraham fired back. "Murder is a crime."

"Not when it's self-defense, plus"—he glanced at his men—"I have three witnesses, and you have none." He advanced with his sword ready to parry.

Two street urchins bolted out of the alley. Three cats bounded after them.

"I'm really good with this sword," Abraham warned. "You might want to reconsider and walk away."

"Just because you're big doesn't mean you're good with a blade. I've cut down much bigger, you painted-face oaf." The soldier waded in and lunged. It was a good jab from the ox guard position.

Abraham slid to the side, swung, and cut the man's head clean off.

The dead soldier fell to the ground with blood spurting from his neck.

The remaining three soldiers gaped. Their astonished eyes were blinking.

Abraham twisted his blade in the air and said, "A lucky stroke. Who is next?"

Two Black Squadron soldiers crept in as one. With their eyes narrowed, they came in at high guard position.

They were skilled and seasoned soldiers. Abraham could tell even though their drunkenness made their movements sloppy. On a sober night, they might have proven a better fight.

As one, the soldiers advanced and thrust downward.

Abraham blocked both swords. He shoved them backward, turned his hip, and slashed Black Bane through their guts.

The disemboweled men dropped to their knees.

"That was fast," the last soldier said. His sword hand trembled. "Who are you? You're as good as Cutter."

"I'm Ace Frehley. Rock star." Abraham held Black Bane like a guitar and started to air jam. "Black Squadron, I hear you calling. What's it going to be? I tell you what. I'll even close my eyes."

With a sneer, the soldier gripped his sword with two hands, tilted his head, narrowed his eyes, and said, "Say, I recognize you. We tracked you in Hancha. You're Ruger Slade."

The sweat and spilt ale must have washed away part of Abraham's makeup. "No, I'm Space Ace."

The soldier tipped his chin. "Sure. If you say so." He took a step closer. "Go ahead. Close those eyes, Ace."

Abraham shut his eyelids. The sound of running boot steps caught his ears. The heavy steps weren't closing in. They were going away.

The Black Squadron soldier was running away like the six-fingered man in *The Princess Bride*. He raced toward the end of the alley.

"Crap!" Abraham sprinted after the man. The last thing he wanted was for the soldier to warn Cutter. "Coward! A member of the Black Squadron shouldn't run."

The soldier disappeared around the corner at the end of the alley.

Abraham barreled into the street and headed in the direction where the man had run away.

The soldier was gone.

Abraham wiped his sword off on his cloak and sheathed it. "What a cluster."

47

ABRAHAM JOGGED THE STREETS AND SIDEWALKS, DUCKING INTO alley after alley but finding no sign of the soldier, Shades, or Sticks. His search went on for minutes as he drifted anxiously through the city. Standing inside an alley, he kicked a crate.

"Bloody meatballs!"

He didn't have any doubt that the soldier had run off to warn Cutter. He could only hope that Sticks wouldn't blow her own cover. Cutter had gotten a good look at her before.

Abraham turned over a barrel and sat down in the shadows of the alley. He watched the thinning parade of people strolling by. He took a deep breath, leaned his head against the wall, and closed his eyes. Another headache was coming on. He thought about Sticks. Mandi. The thought of both women being in danger tore his heart in two.

He beat his head against the wall.

"What are you doing?"

Abraham's eyes snapped open to see Shades in front of him with his monkey mask on. "I could ask you the same."

"I'm not kissing stone with the back of my head. What's the problem?"

"One of the Black Squadron recognized me. I killed the others, but he ran. I lost him." He sighed. "I'm certain that he'll tell Cutter that we are here. Sticks could be in more danger."

Shades looked out on the street and back at him. "I found the dwelling where Cutter is. I managed to catch up with him. Would you like to see it?"

Abraham jumped up. "Why didn't you mention that in the first place?"

"I didn't want to interrupt your sulking. Besides, she can take care of—"

Abraham shoved him out of the alley. "Lead the way."

Shades picked up the pace and led him to a ratty tavern on the river side of the city. It had a double-door front entrance with one door closed. Two drunken women staggered outside. A stairwell leading to the top room's balcony started at the bottom of the tavern's alley. He pointed at the balcony, which wrapped around the rickety tavern. "They went up there. Headed to the back."

Just inside the alley at the bottom of the stairs, a Black Squadron soldier was leaning against the wall.

"I think he's good." Shades waltzed right at the man.

Abraham tried to hook the rogue's arm, but he slipped out of reach.

The man didn't move when Shades approached.

Creeping forward, Abraham said, "Is he sleeping?"

"You could say that." Shades tapped the man on the chest. "Are you asleep?"

"What are you doing?"

Shades lifted the man's head back, showing his cut throat. "I caught up with the rat at the bottom of the stairs. He didn't see me coming. They never do."

Abraham recognized the soldier that had fled in the alley. "I guess my secret is safe with him."

Some familiar gusty laughter could be heard from inside the rundown tavern. Abraham put his ear to the wall. More hearty laughter belted out again on the other side.

"That's him."

"Him?" Shades asked.

Abraham pulled the mask off Shades's face. He put it on and said, "Watch my back."

He staggered into the tavern doorway and leaned heavily on the door frame. The eyelets in the monkey mask were small, but the visibility was decent. Hunched over, he teetered in the bar area. The tables were half full of dwellers in sordid clothing, with bloodshot eyes. The smoke was as thick as pea soup.

In the back of the bar, by a cold fireplace, Big Apple sat on a barstool. A woman's muddy blouse was stretched between the stubby horns on his head. He puffed on a thick cigar. The bare-chested, musclebound halfling tossed his head back, chortling. Women were wrestling in a mud pit. His eyes were lit like fire.

"I'll be," Abraham muttered. He pushed some talents onto the bar and sank into a stool.

Big Apple was surrounded by a bunch of goons who looked like executioners from a medieval dungeon. They wore black hoods, and chains crossed over their backs. Each of them carried a mace.

The bartender, an ugly guy with a pitted face, slid a tankard of beer his way. He looked just like Sam from Pirate Harbor and gave Abraham a wary eye.

Abraham managed a loud belch underneath his mask.

The bartender moved away.

He moved down to the end of the bar, where he could get a better eye at the festivities. Three women were in the ring of mud, slugging it out with a fat man in white. *It can't be.*

A man walked behind Abraham and rubbed shoulders against

his. He and his escort took a seat near Big Apple. Abraham immediately recognized Lord Hawk. The leader of the Shell wore his
signature black vest over a maroon shirt. The gorgeous Myrmidon
woman, Kawnee, escorted Lord Hawk. They glanced at Ruger, but
he looked away from both of them, focusing on the action in the
ring.

It looks like the gang is all here. His fingertips tingled. *Now what?*

Big Apple clucked away as though he'd never laughed before.
The obnoxious horned halfling shouted over every blurry-eyed
patron in the room. "Fight, fat man! Fight!"

Abraham dared a glance at Big Apple's table.

Lord Hawk was whispering in Big Apple's ear. He subtly
pointed at Abraham.

Oh no, they recognized me. He scooted away from the scene from
one stool to another.

Big Apple huffed smoke out of his nose, pointed his stubby
cigar hand at Abraham, and said, "I want you! Don't move a
muscle."

48

ABRAHAM POINTED AT HIS OWN CHEST IN A "WHO, ME?" GESTURE.

"Yes, you, monkey face!" Big Apple said boldly. "I want you to get in the mud ring with my girls. I've never seen them wrestle a monkey before." He stiffly clapped his hands. "Get in there."

Abraham shook his head.

Big Apple tilted his head to the side and asked, "Are you telling me no?" He looked at Lord Hawk. "Is he telling me no?"

Lord Hawk leaned back in his chair, hooked his arm over the back of his chair, and said, "I believe that he is. He's a large man too. Like one of those mountain gorillas. You know, I bet he thinks he can handle the likes of me and you."

Big Apple grabbed a mug of ale from his table and slung it into the fireplace. He jumped up and stood on top of his stool. "Me! You think that you can handle me 'cause I'm little?" He flexed his arms and chest. The horned halfling's muscles bulged like a little Hercules. "Come and see if you can take me."

Abraham waved his hands in front of him. He noticed Lord Hawk toying with the handle of the revolver on his hip. Kawnee sat beside him with a playful smile on her fish face. He slid off his stool and backed away. His body, on the other hand, had other ideas. Ruger's body wanted to fight. He wanted to fight all of them —kill them all. They reeked of evil.

I'd probably be better off if I killed them. But I need answers.

"Hey, monkey face," Big Apple said. "Why don't you take that mask off?" He looked him up and down. "And stand up straight. I want a better look at you. You can't fool me by hunching over."

This is going bad.

He backed toward the door. The air surrounding him turned ice cold. He twisted his head over his shoulder and looked up.

In black robes, the towering wraith, Fleece, stood behind Abraham. No face could be seen inside the hood, only pitch-black darkness. The tatters of Fleece's robes moved with a ghostly life of their own.

Frost came out with Abraham's breath. His skin crawled. Arcane power emanated from the wraith. It had power, true power. Abraham started backing the other way. His hand found the pommel of his sword as he moved out of the radius of cold.

"What is the matter, monkey man?" Big Apple asked. "Don't you want to dance with my servant, Fleece?"

Abraham glanced back at Big Apple.

The horned halfling tugged at the jewel-studded collar on his neck. His eyes narrowed on Abraham. "Are you going to get in the ring now, or are you going to wind up like one of them?" He pointed into a corner.

Two men were leaning in a corner, shriveled to husks. Their eyes and mouths were wide open, as if gasping in torment and horror.

He swallowed. *They know it's me.*

Fleece drifted toward him. The cold air came back. Chills ran down Abraham's spine.

He cleared his throat and, through the muffled mask, said, "If you insist, I'll wrestle."

Big Apple's eyes brightened. He clapped his hands together with a loud smack. "That's the spirit!" He made an impish laugh. "Huh-huh-huh-huh-huh. You made the right decision, monkey man. Now, go show those girls what you can do."

Lord Hawk put a boot to Abraham's rump and shoved him forward.

He feigned tripping on his robes and sprawled out on the ground, hitting it with a loud thump. His sword belt clattered against the floor.

"Whoa!" Lord Hawk came to his feet. "This fellow is loaded down like a soldier."

From his hands and knees, Abraham said, "I'm a Gray Guard. Out having a good time. I don't want to get reported to my commander. They frown on this sort of behavior. I hope you understand."

"Gray Guard?" Big Apple asked. "Did you say Gray Guard?"

Without looking back, Abraham said, "Yes." *Oh man, this is going to be bad. I should have said anything else. Mercenary. Black Squadron.* He started crawling toward the mud pit. "Does that matter?"

"We aren't very fond of the Gray Guard. Look where you are, man," Lord Hawk said. "This is a hive for criminals. The Gray Guard likes to keep an eye on guys like us. You know what, Big Apple, it's all coming together."

"What is that?" Big Apple said.

"This man is a spy."

You got it half right. He kept moving toward the mud pit. "I'm not a spy. I only want to have a good time. I swear I won't say anything."

Two of Big Apple's goons blocked Abraham's path. One of them stepped on his fingers. He let out an exaggerated scream. "Gah! Please don't hurt me! I said I would wrestle."

"He doesn't sound very brave for a Gray Guard. The Gray

Guards I know would die before they humiliated themselves," Lord Hawk said.

"We'll take him on anyway!" one of the sultry women in the mud ring said. Mud dripped over her voluptuous body. She slung her hair back, revealing a few missing teeth. "We aren't particular." She slapped the belly of the fat man, who was tied up by the arms of the other two women. "Just look at this ox!"

"Shaddup, you stupid wench," Big Apple said. "I see what you are saying, Hawk. This fella is very… wimpy."

"Cowardly," Kawnee added. "I don't even think he is worthy of the mud ring."

Something stirred inside Abraham's gut. It was Ruger. No one was going to call him a coward and get away with it. The acting job was over. *Enough is enough. Screw it!* He grabbed one of the goons by the ankle and jerked the man to the floor.

49

BEFORE THE SECOND GOON TOWERING OVER HIM COULD ACT, Abraham reached up and punched the man in the crotch.

The goon doubled over with a loud "Oof!"

Abraham socked the man in the jaw, stood up, and with his chest heaving, said, "Nobody calls the monkey man a coward!"

Lord Hawk pointed his revolver right at his chest and said, "Don't do anything stupid."

Abraham played dumb. "What does that do?"

"It blows your head open like a rotting melon."

Big Apple chuckled. "I like the monkey man. Let's see him wrestle."

Abraham had a plan. Covered in mud, his face wouldn't be seen. He took off his cloak and wrapped his sword belt in it. After setting that aside, he stood in front of them, wearing breastplate and trousers. He couldn't let them see his brand. "I'm ready."

Big Apple, Lord Hawk, and Kawnee lifted their eyebrows.

One of the women in the ring said, "Ooh yeah, bring him on in. I want the monkey man."

"I saw him first," said another one of the muddy ladies.

Suddenly, Big Apple's goons on the floor tacked Abraham. One of them grabbed his hair and pulled. The other one hit him in the gut.

The three men wrestled over the floor in a knot of angry flying limbs.

Abraham bent one goon's wrist backward and snapped it.

The man let out a howl of pain.

He cracked the last goon in the jaw. The blow knocked the man out cold.

"Fighting dirty, huh?" he said. "I can take it."

He looked at Big Apple and Lord Hawk. Their eyes were bigger than saucers.

"What?" he asked.

Something wasn't right. He glanced down. The monkey mask lay at his feet.

He looked back at them and smiled. "Did you miss me?"

"Ruger Slade!" Lord Hawk pointed the gun at him and squeezed the trigger.

Abraham jumped high.

The bullet blasted out of the barrel and ricocheted off Abraham's breastplate. He landed on Lord Hawk and drove the man to the ground. He punched Lord Hawk in the throat and wrenched the gun from his hand. He jumped up and turned the gun on Big Apple. He thumbed the gun hammer back. "Don't move!"

Big Apple lifted his hands and said, "Don't shoot!" As his remaining goons started to flank Abraham, he said, "Back off! I don't want him shooting me on account of you idiots. You got me, so what do you want?"

"Answers. Sit down."

Big Apple plopped down on his stool and puffed on his cigar. "I might not have the answers that you want."

"You have them. I know you have them. You wouldn't have sent us on a wild-goose chase to Cauldron City if you didn't."

Big Apple chuckled. "I was hoping that you would have been killed. It seemed unlikely that even you and your Henchmen would be about to kill Arcayis. That was impressive."

Lord Hawk got up, rubbing his jaw. "It would have been more if the Black Squadron would have had the stones to finish you off. That's why I sent them. You scared the crap out of them. That's for certain. Kill Arcayis. Didn't see that coming." He shot a look at Big Apple. "I thought he was strong."

"Maybe he would have been stronger if he was the Underlord," Abraham suggested.

Big Apple's eyes lit up. "You don't think Arcayis is the Underlord? That's an interesting theory. Why is that?"

"Leodor didn't buy into it. That's good enough for me. The Underlord is still out there, alive and well." He eyed Big Apple. "Perhaps it's you."

"I assure you that I am not the Underlord." Big Apple blew a smoke ring. "I'm not your enemy. I just don't want to go home. I don't want to be Edgar the invalid again. That's why I don't want you finding the king's stones." He spread his arms out. "Be content with who you are. You are Ruger Slade, the best swordsman in the world. Enjoy it. Join me."

"He can't join. He's branded," Lord Hawk said in a condescending way. "He must follow the king's orders. That's how I understand it. This man has no choice but to bring us down. After all, we are the king's enemies."

"Kingsland is dying. Eventually, it will fall," Big Apple said. "A new world is coming to take over. You can do what you want with us, but you can't stop it."

"Tell me who is behind it. It's the Underlord, isn't it?" Abraham looked between both men. "Or is it someone from *back home*?"

"Perhaps they are one and the same," Big Apple said. "You might as well put the gun down. You aren't the sort of man to shoot me in cold blood. You're just another pawn like me, trying to find his place in this world. Well, your place is with a dying king-dom. My place is with a rising one."

Abraham knew that both men had more information than they'd ever let on. He'd have to torture them to get it out of them. That wasn't his style, but the Henchmen weren't above it. He studied Big Apple's impish face. He was cocky but careless.

"Humor me," Abraham said. "Is there a portal? You know, a permanent one." He wiggled the gun. "This didn't magically appear, did it?"

"I don't know." Big Apple stared at the gun. "But I do know there are more of those out there. Do you really think King Hector stands a chance against that? Swarming men loaded with modern-day artillery? The time will come. It will be a slaughter."

"You know, *Edgar*." He watched Big Apple's eyes narrow—now was the time to get all the information he could out of them. He might not get another chance. "You are wearing on my patience." He lowered the gun barrel and shot the stool between Big Apple's legs.

Big Apple jumped over to the fireplace hearth. "Hey! Hey! Hey! What are you doing?"

"Stand still!" Abraham fired again. The bullets blasted away chips of the fireplace's heart. "Where's the portal?" he yelled. "Who's the Underlord?"

The women in the mud pit stuck their fingers in their ears and raced out of the bar, screaming.

"Quit wasting my bullets!" Lord Hawk said.

Big Apple cowered inside the fireplace. "I don't know!"

Abraham fired into the fireplace again.

Blam!

"Tell me what I want to know!" Abraham's frustration boiled over. "Tell me now!"

Blam!

Big Apple yelled at him. "Nooo!"

Abraham pointed the gun at Big Apple's leg. "Now I'm going to hurt you!" He squeezed the trigger.

Click.

"You're empty, fool!" Lord Hawk said.

Big Apple grinned and touched the gemstones on his collar. "Fleece, get him!"

Abraham threw the gun at Big Apple's head. The weapon bounced off the man's hard head and horns. He dove toward his cloak and sword.

Fleece swooped in above him. His shifting mass of swirling robes enveloped Abraham's body.

He crawled on, fighting the icy numbness and pain coursing through his extremities. The wraith was draining the life out of him. He clawed his way toward Black Bane. He could see the pommel sticking out from underneath his cloak. He groaned and cried out as the might in his arms was sapped away.

Abraham flattened on the floor. He rolled over on his back. His fingers clutched in the air as he writhed.

The wraith loomed over him, a huge, haunting apparition. In the darkness beneath its hood, two eyes like bright stars appeared.

Abraham's blood froze. He couldn't move.

Big Apple and Lord Hawk looked down on him. The horned halfling was smoking and grinning. Lord Hawk kicked Abraham in the ribs.

"You wanted to know who the Underlord is," Big Apple said. "Like I said, it wasn't me." He pointed his cigar at the wraith. "It's him." He ran his stubby finger over the collar on his neck. "And you'll never guess who controls him. Me. Ha ha ha. Now I have you, Abraham. Don't I? Don't we all?" He waved his meaty palm. "Bye bye, Abraham Jenkins. Bye bye, Ruger Slade."

Screaming at the building intense pain, Abraham lost his sight and descended into darkness.

50

———

BACK HOME

Darkness. Pain. Abraham could hear himself breathing. Slow. Easy. Quiet. He didn't open his eyes. He was seated. Soft-rock radio was playing. The familiar sound of rolling down a highway caught his ears.

I'm in a car!

He kept his eyes closed. Something was restraining him. It must have been a seat belt. He wiggled his fingers. His wrists were bound in front of him.

Blazing saddles! More flex cuffs!

He didn't move. The last thing he wanted to do was alert his captors to his condition. He'd need to take them by surprise. He needed to listen and learn about Mandi. His nostrils flared. The faint smell of sweet perfume, good stuff, lingered in the air. It didn't smell like something Eugene Drisk would wear—or his goons, like Colt.

Mandi?

Abraham couldn't be certain. Mandi always smelled good. All he could do was hope this was her.

The car he rode in accelerated and pushed him back in its seat. The car had a throaty roar in the engine.

"That's it. Open it up, babe," a man said in a casual and quiet manner. "It's a long drive. Might as well have some fun."

Someone was tapping on the steering wheel to the rhythm of the song's beat. She was humming the words of a Rupert Holmes song. "Shh," she said. "I'm listening."

The woman who spoke clearly wasn't Mandi. She had a firm voice and carried authority. Abraham didn't recall having seen any women in Eugene's group either.

Who are these guys? What have they done with Mandi?

"I don't know about this yacht-rock radio. It's not a good fit for the Hellcat," the man quipped.

"Of course it is. It's the perfect cruiser," the woman said quietly.

"If you say so," the man replied. "You're always right."

Sounds like I've been abducted by a pair of newlyweds. Oh man, how much time has passed? I've been days in Titanuus.

Abraham took a peek. Moonlight shone through the car's glass. Through his narrow eyelids, he could see a nice-looking brunette with medium-length hair driving the car. Both her hands were on the wheel, fingers tapping. He slid his eyes over to the passenger side. The man in the seat sat with his head higher than the head-rest. His shoulders were almost too wide for the racing seat.

Another big goon. I can handle him. I think.

He closed his eyes.

He'd have to wait it out and see where they took him. In the meantime, he'd listen. He would make a move the first chance he had. The only problem was the flex cuffs. His ankles were free, and he could still run. Even with his hands bound, he could fight if he had to.

I'll play possum. Knock them out and steal the car.

The car motored down the road mile after mile.

As glad as Abraham wanted to be, he wasn't. He was back

home, but at what cost? Ruger Slade's body was back in Titanuus. Big Apple had him. And the Underlord had been revealed. Sticks, Shades, and all the Henchmen would be in danger now. Plus, his enemies would have Black Bane. Everything was a mess.

What am I doing?

Perhaps he was better off back home than in Titanuus. Or was it vice versa? He had a hard time telling.

One step at a time. Keep it simple. Find Mandi. Save Mandi.

Another song started playing on the radio.

"Ah, I love this song," the man said. "It's good but twisted by today's standards. There's an interesting bit on Wiki about it."

"I didn't think you liked yacht rock," she said playfully.

"Not me. The car."

"Ah, I always take pleasure learning new things about you. Benny Mardones. 'Into the Night.' Check," she replied.

Benny Mardones? Seriously?

Abraham dared another peek. The woman driving was staring dead at him in her rearview mirror. He snapped his eyes shut. *Devil's donuts! I know she saw me. Just act like you're still asleep.* He shifted in a slumbering fashion and rolled his head over to one side. *Please buy it.*

The voice of Benny Mardones died.

"What did you do that for?" the man on the passenger side asked.

"Because Sleeping Beauty has awakened."

51

The car seat's leather groaned as the man twisted around in his seat.

"No. Hey, Mandi," the woman said. "Wake up."

Someone stirred beside Abraham.

"What is it?" Mandi asked.

"Your boyfriend's awake, but he's playing possum," the woman driving said.

Mandi unclicked her seat belt and scooted toward Abraham.

"I've got your back," the man said. "Any sudden moves, and I'll zap him."

Abraham kept his eyes closed. He felt Mandi's warm hands on his face.

"Ruger. Ruger." She gently slapped his cheeks. "Are you back?"

He opened his eyes. "I'm not Ruger. I'm Abraham."

Mandi threw her arms around him and hugged him tightly. "I'm so glad you are back! I didn't think I'd see you again."

"I didn't think I'd see you either. I was worried." He got a good look at her face when she pulled back and saw her cheeks were bruised and swollen. "What happened?" He kicked the man's seat in front of him. "Did they do this?"

"Heavens, no. That's my cousin, Sid, and her husband, John. Remember I told you about them," Mandi said.

"Hi," Sid said.

John turned farther in his seat and extended his hand, which was as big as Abraham's. He was a nice-looking guy, clean shaven with angular features and wearing dark sunglasses. "Call me Smoke."

Abraham took the man's strong grip and asked, "Got a knife, Smoke?"

"Sorry about that," Mandi said as she whisked a knife out of her boot. She cut off the flex cuffs. "You twitch a lot. And when you wake up as Ruger, you're very intense. You still aren't used to this place."

Abraham rubbed his wrists, looked at Mandi, and said, "Thanks, warrior princess. Care to catch me up to speed? What happened to Eugene and those goons?"

"Man, this is eerie," Smoke said. He looked dead into Abraham's eyes. "You are completely a different person. I can see it and hear it. Him and Ruger aren't the same. Maybe it's strong hypnosis."

"Or he's a shifter," Sid chimed in.

"No, he's in the same body." Smoke's nostrils flared. "He doesn't reek of evil either. But those other dudes did."

Abraham looked at Mandi and said, "So, your cousin's husband can smell evil? How convenient."

"It's not so much a smell as it is a feeling," Smoke replied coolly. "It comes on primarily when dealing with the supernatural elements. I want to hear more about this fantasy world. Titanuus?"

"John, don't push it," Sid warned.

"Come on, hon, if there is a portal to a fantasy world, then we have to go," Smoke said. "It can be a second honeymoon."

"What about the kids?" Sid said. "Can they go on the honeymoon too?"

"No, that would be a vacation. But I don't see why not. I'm sure Keith and Sally could use the break," Smoke replied.

"We aren't going to another fantasy world," Sid replied. "We don't even know if this one is real."

"Are you talking about my fantasy world or this world?" Abraham asked.

"Take your pick," Sid said dryly.

"Titanuus is real," Abraham stated.

Smoke tapped Abraham's knee with the back of his hand. "I believe you, dude. We'll find that yellow brick road and take you back there."

"I don't want to go back. I mean, I do, but I don't. Mandi, what is going on? Bring me up to speed."

Mandi held his hand and said, "It's a bit of a story, and I'm not the best at it, but I'll try." She glanced up. "Let's see. We were in the alley in Pittsburgh. Eugene and his otherworlder goons got the drop on us. They had a gun to my head. Eugene gut-punched you with a stun rod."

"Yeah, that's the last thing I remember."

"You went down, and I was scared. Colt and those guys, they were possessed with a strange darkness in their eyes." She shivered. "I tried to fight them off, but I'm not that strong. The only thing I did was send Sid a text before all of that happened. I jammed my phone in my pocket." She swallowed. Her voice trembled. "I wanted them to at least find my body if they killed me."

He squeezed her hand. "I'm so sorry, Mandi. This is all my fault." He touched her bruised cheek. "You need to stay out of this."

"She won't be able to stay out of this until it's over," Smoke added.

Sid elbowed him.

Smoke shrugged. "Sorry, but it's true. It's like Rocky said: 'It ain't over till it's over.'"

"I agree. I'm in this to the end," Mandi said. Her beautiful eyes were intense. "Don't try to talk me out of it. Besides, when you went down, Ruger came back."

"He did?" Abraham asked.

"Yeah," Mandi said. "Eugene's goons were carting us both to the cars that pulled into the alley. More men in black SUVs came."

"I hate black SUVs," Sid said.

Mandi continued, "Just as they were about to load you into the car, you came to life like a wild tiger. I'm not sure how you got out of the flex cuffs, but you did."

Smoke interrupted. "I can show you."

"Mandi, ignore him," Sid said.

Mandi cleared her throat. "Man, could you move. I mean, you could move before, but when Ruger takes over, it's different. He's merciless."

"You can't treat evil any other way," Smoke said. "You have to bash their face in with a shovel. Strike first. Strike hard. No mercy."

"Take it easy, Karate Kid," Sid replied with a chuckle.

Smoke shook his head. "No, that's Cobra Kai I'm quoting."

"Weren't they the bad guys?" Abraham asked.

Smoke twisted around in his seat again and said, "Now there is a new series on YouTube that spins the story around from Johnny Lawrence's side of things."

Sid punched Smoke in the leg again. "Let her finish the story, please." She looked in the rearview mirror at Abraham. "Sorry, but my husband hasn't gotten a lot of guy time lately, since the kids are still little."

"It's okay," Abraham said. He wet his lips. "But you'd get plenty of that in Titanuus with the Henchmen."

The leather groaned in Smoke's seat when he started to turn.

"No," Sid warned.

Smoke looked mysterious but had some playfulness about him. The more he talked, the more Abraham liked him.

Abraham took a water bottle that Mandi offered him and twisted the cap off and drank. "Ah, that's better. You were saying?"

52

MANDI'S FACE LIT UP AS SHE TOLD THE STORY. "YOU TURNED THOSE thugs into broken pottery. I've never seen a big man like you move so fast."

Smoke cleared his throat.

"Every punch you threw broke something," she said with excitement rising in her voice. "I heard ribs snap. A man's jaw broke. Three men were knocked out cold with one blow. I didn't see all of it, but those dudes were going down like the Hindenburg. Colt had a gun on me and told you to back off. I don't know what overcame me. I guess I got Ruger syndrome, because I drove my elbow in his belly.

"That's when you, or Ruger, pounced. A gunshot went off, but you had him on the ground and were beating the hell out of him." Mandi took back the bottle and drank. "Whew, Sid, turn the air conditioner up. Anyway, Eugene was screaming at his men. That's when you locked eyes on Eugene." She tensed. "There was murder in your eyes. Not like when you fought those men—that was focused. Intent. But once you looked at Eugene, it was nothing but deep hatred. My toes tingled. Eugene shrank under your gaze, dove into the car, and locked it. You punched out the windshield."

"Cobra Kai," Smoke said subtly.

Sid shook her head.

"Anyway," Mandi continued, "Eugene stomped on the gas and peeled out of the alley. We grabbed another car and chased him through the city. That was my first car chase, but I think I did pretty good. Then you grabbed the wheel and almost turned the car over. I swatted you back and said, 'Let the woman do the driving.' You actually listened, but your arms were bleeding all over the car. You started to bandage it."

Abraham checked his forearm and saw some scarring, but the wounds were mended.

"We took care of that," Sid said. "It's a special healing foam that we use. It's more effective than stitches."

Abraham lifted a brow and said, "I see. So, what happened in the chase?"

"I caught Eugene's bumper on a corner. He rolled over, and we rolled over in the middle of the street." Mandi rubbed her cheek. "That's how I got this bruise. We squeezed out of the SUV, and you rounded up Eugene. He was squirming his way out of the car's window. You knocked him out cold. I don't think you meant to.

"By this time, the cops were coming. I told you that we needed to run. You tossed Eugene over your shoulder and started running. I'm pretty sure that you didn't know where you were going, but you ran like a deer and almost lost me more than once. Somehow, we beat the cops and ducked into a parking garage and hid. You laid Eugene down in the stairwell. Your eyes could have bored holes through him. Ruger hates that guy."

Abraham could understand why. Eugene had used Ruger's body for his own selfish and immoral purposes. Somehow, Ruger had a sense of what was going on with a body he hosted or through the eyes and actions of another. They were all connected.

"As we huddled in the stairwell, things went south. You blacked out again," Mandi said. "Stone-cold comatose."

"What have I been doing all of this time? Sleeping?"

Mandi shrugged. "Lucky for me, I had texted Sid, and they picked us up a few hours later. We've been on the run ever since."

"Super Uber," Smoke muttered.

Sid drove the car off the highway while Abraham sorted out his thoughts. They pulled into a shopping plaza. A Pizza Hut and a Baskin Robbins were there. Smoke got out of the car and hustled inside.

"We're stopping for pizza?" Abraham asked Sid. His belly growled.

Sid turned in her seat. She was fetching, like Mandi, but taller and more athletic. She carried a dangerous air about her, and a gun was holstered on her hip. "Smoke has a very strict dietary regimen that he must adhere to."

Abraham watched Smoke walk out of the Pizza Hut with four pizza boxes. He moved into the Baskin Robbins. "Pizza and ice cream?"

"Milkshakes," Sid said.

"Huh." Abraham peered through the window. "Where are we?"

"Morgantown, West Virginia," Mandi said.

"What are we doing here?" he asked.

"Smoke wanted to catch a Mountaineer basketball game. We are hiding out too, lying low until the channel's clear," Sid said. "Our people will let us know when we can move. In the meantime, we'll keep trying to fish more info out of Drisk."

"You sound like someone with a law-enforcement background, but Mandi said you were bounty hunters?"

"I used to be FBI. Circumstances changed the day I met him." Sid pointed her gaze toward the window.

Smoke was coming back. He had four pizza boxes and four milkshakes in one arm. He opened the car and slid in like a big cat.

"Did you get milkshakes for the rest of us?" Sid asked him.

"No. I got you guys a pizza. Pepperoni," Smoke said as he filled all the available cupholders with the milkshakes. He handed one pizza back to Mandi and eyed her and Abraham. "Do you want a milkshake? I'll go back."

"I'm fine," Mandi said.

Abraham almost answered the question then instantly asked, "Where in Titanuus's Crotch is Eugene Drisk? You didn't leave him alone, did you?"

53

SID DROVE THEM DOWN A LONG STRETCH OF COUNTRY ROAD. THEY stopped at an old white two-story farmhouse with a wraparound porch. The house was pitch black inside. The large gravel driveway had a few abandoned vehicles. A red storage barn stood nearby, and one of the doors was open. A red Massey Fergusson tractor was stowed inside.

Everyone got out of the car. The winter air was cool, crisp, and breezy. Snowflakes lingered in the air.

Abraham's legs were cramping. The back seat of the Dodge Hellcat hadn't been made for a big man like him. He felt as though he'd run a marathon, and his body ached all over. Ruger had pushed him to the limits again.

He closed the door to the phantom-black Hellcat and said, "Nice car."

"Thanks," Sid said.

He eyed the porch. The farmhouse looked abandoned. He expected to see someone on the porch, but nobody was there. "You didn't leave Drisk alone, did you? There's a guard here, right?"

"No, no guards," Smoke said. He tossed the pizza boxes in a

small dumpster then moved to the trunk. "Mr. Drisk isn't going anywhere."

"You can't trust that guy. He's like me. He'll squirm out of wherever you put him!"

"No, he won't." Smoke studied Abraham's eyes. "Are you taller than me?"

Smoke stood a half inch taller if Abraham had to guess. He was about six-foot five himself.

"No."

"Good," Smoke replied. He eyed Sid.

The trunk popped open.

Eugene Drisk lay inside the trunk. His eyes were closed. His mouth, wrists, and ankles were bound with flex cuffs.

Smoke lifted the man out of the trunk as if he were stuffed with feathers. He dropped Eugene on the ground.

Abraham took a long look inside the trunk, seeing a few shotguns, assault rifles, and metal briefcases—an arsenal. "Are you sure you're just bounty hunters? That's some serious artillery."

"The Challengers have great trunk space, don't they?" Smoke closed the lid. "The things we hunt, let's just say, are full of surprises." Smoke picked up Eugene by the back of the pants like a piece of luggage. "Let's go inside and start a fire."

Abraham headed toward the house.

Smoke pushed him toward the barn. "That way."

The inside of the barn was in good shape. No straw or livestock was there. The floors were solid planks of wood. Some of the stalls had been converted into camping rooms. A kitchenette and a coal-burning stove were there.

Mandi closed the barn door.

"I'll start the fire," Sid said as she walked by Abraham. She was only a few inches shorter than he. She briskly made her way to the Buck stove sitting in a corner of the barn. Some blankets and mattresses lay on the ground. It made for a livable indoor camping environment.

"You guys have been staying here?" he asked.

"The last few days," Mandi said.

"I've been out that long? Geez. The time is a mess. An hour in one world might be a day in the other." He scratched his face. "I guess we need to make the most of it."

Smoke propped Eugene up in a chair and tied him up to a support beam. He lightly smacked the man's face. He pushed open his eyelid. "He's still out."

"I told you that serum was too strong for an old man," Sid said with a shiver. When they got a fire going in the stove, she rubbed her hands in front of it. "Get warm, you guys. We'll probably be here a while. Smoke overdosed him again."

"Better safe than sorry," Smoke said. He walked over to Sid and gave her a kiss. "I'll let you give him the shot next time."

Mandi hooked Abraham's arm and said, "Come over by the fire. Let's warm up. I'm cold."

He didn't move. "No. Eugene ain't no fool. He might be playing possum. I'd rather watch him." He eyed Smoke. "Did you pat him down?"

"The only thing he has is his clothing." He opened an old ice chest and grabbed a can of Coke. "No phones or wires. We scanned him for tracking devices too, even the ones that go in the skull. He's cold." He raised the Coke can. "Want one?"

"No."

"Cheese popcorn?"

"Later. The pizza held. I could do for some snack cakes later."

Smoke pointed a gun finger at him and said, "I'll make it so." He headed outside and made some trips back and forth, carrying in the metal briefcases and a few weapons.

Abraham stood in front of Eugene and studied him. The older man's skin was sagging, but he had a firm jaw. He was definitely more fit than the shapeless man he'd encountered in the tunnel cave months before. Abraham rubbed his own jaw as if he were Indiana Jones staring at the golden idol. "You said that you talked to him before? He was awake?"

Sid walked over to him and said, "Yes. He's a real smart aleck too. We didn't push hard because we weren't sure what to ask. We thought we'd wait it out for you."

"Can we wake him?" he asked.

"Of course, but I don't recommend it. For ethical reasons," Sid said. "It's basically torture. He might have a heart attack."

"He might be old, but he can take it. And my time is limited. I might drift off at any moment. I need to interrogate him now."

"Have you ever interrogated someone?" Sid asked.

"No."

Sid glanced at Smoke. "Then you might want to let us handle it. Does he have any fears that you know of?"

Abraham shrugged. Ruger didn't fear anything, but Eugene was a different story. "Spiders, maybe?"

54

Sid held a syringe in her hand and asked, "Are you sure that you want to do this?" She squirted a little juice out of the tip. "Mal warned me that it might be fatal."

"Mal who?" Abraham asked.

"Mal Carlson. A friend of ours. He's a scientist," she replied.

"Do you think that he could help out with my situation?"

"We'll keep him apprised. He's definitely interested. But he and his wife, Asia, are on vacation right now." She approached Eugene, who had been secured to a barn support post, and rolled up his sleeves. "Be glad she's not around. She's bossy."

Abraham gave her a smile. Sid carried herself with a businesslike approach. She obviously had a law-enforcement or military background. Smoke, however, was harder to judge. He stood nearby, eating an apple and wearing a Starslayer T-shirt. Both of them were as fit as a fiddle. They complemented each other well.

"The moment of truth," Sid said.

Abraham nodded.

Sid stuck the needle an inch deep in Eugene's forearm and pressed the plunger.

Eugene's eyes popped open. He convulsed.

"Shoot, we should have put a bit in his mouth," Sid said and caught a towel that Smoke tossed her. She shoved it into Eugene's gaping jaws. "Don't bite your tongue off, old man."

Eugene spasmed for about a minute then finally went limp. His forehead was beaded in sweat as he looked at Sid.

She took the gag out.

Eugene spat, eyed the syringe, and asked, "What did you shoot me with? *Gasoline?*"

"I told you it was harsh." Sid stuck the needle in the post. She moved back and stood by Smoke.

Eugene's eyes slid up toward Abraham. His lips twisted. In a ragged voice, he said, "Oh, it's you." He leaned his head to the side. "The weak one. I can see that Ruger isn't back. Good for me."

Abraham dragged a stool over and sat down in front of Eugene. "It's time that we had a talk. I want to know what's going on, and you aren't going anywhere until I do."

Eugene leered at Mandi and Sid and licked his lips. "Pretty women. Very pretty. Ruger always did keep fine company. I must admit, I miss that body of his. The stamina."

Abraham pushed Eugene's head back into the pole. It made a *thunk*. "Nobody cares about your sex life."

Wincing, Eugene said, "I do." He coughed. "I can't talk so well if my mouth is dry. Can I get a drink of something?"

"No," Abraham said. "If you want a drink, you'll have to talk first."

"And if I don't get a drink, I can't talk."

Abraham shoved the man's head back into the pole again. Eugene might appear older and weaker, but he knew better. He'd been Ruger Slade for years. The old man still carried that dangerous edge with him. "Cooperate."

"Ha. You aren't the sort to torture me. I know who you are—a washed-up baseball player. A child of privilege. A drug addict. No, you don't have the stones to get anything out of me." Eugene glanced over at Smoke and Sid. "That's why you have them. Isn't it?"

"No. They are my Uber drivers." He leaned into Eugene's face. "Don't underestimate me. I'm a desperate man. Since I've been Ruger Slade, I've killed hundreds," he exaggerated. "I've even slain two Elders. Do you really think I won't hesitate to put the hurt on you? Your mind might be able to take it, but your body can't." He locked his hands around Eugene's throat and squeezed. "So far as I am concerned, this is the king's business."

Eugene's face started to turn red.

The Henchmen weren't above torture when it came to the king's business. They wouldn't show mercy when it came to completing a task. They were spies, secret agents in a medieval fantasy time. Abraham normally didn't have the stomach for it, but the enemy had put him through enough. Now he needed answers. He let go.

Eugene gasped for air. He coughed and said, "Now I'm really thirsty."

"Tell me what is going on, Eugene. There are portals. Someone controls them. Our world is invading their world. Why?"

Eugene gave him a knowing look and asked, "What makes you think there is an invasion?"

"That's what the other side tells me. I've come across a few other people like us. I dealt with the Shell and the Sect. Someone on that side is working with someone on this side. I want to know who it is and why."

"Hmm…" Eugene said. "You are further along than I could have imagined. Interesting. Can I have a drink?"

"Tell me something first."

"Okay." Eugene sniffed. "There is an invasion. This world into theirs."

Abraham nodded at Mandi.

She fetched a bottle of water out of the old ice chest and slowly walked it over. She twisted the cap off, tilted up his chin, and let Eugene drink. Water dribbled onto his shirt. She wiped it away with her gentle fingers. "Let me wipe that off."

"Feeding me like a child. So pathetic." He couldn't take his eyes off her. "Why don't we take the cuffs off, and we can have a nice chat. I'll tell you what you want," Eugene said to Abraham while looking at her.

"Why the sudden change of heart?"

"I'll tell you why," Eugene said as he took another drink. "No matter what you know and no matter what you do, it won't make a difference. That's why. Pandora's Box has been opened. It can't be closed again."

"Anything that can be done can be undone," Smoke said.

"Is that so? You can undo the damage when a dam's wall breaks? I don't think so. It wipes out all in its wake." Eugene managed another drink. "That is the problem with heroes. They think they can fix anything, but they can't."

55

"Keep talking," Abraham said. Clearly Mandi's presence was having an effect on the man. He liked women. He liked them a lot. "I'm listening."

"I'm listening too," Mandi said in a sweet voice.

"You remind me of the triplets back in Titanuus," Eugene said, with hungry eyes that could devour Mandi whole. "I miss them. They were the perfect mates."

Mandi looked at Abraham and asked, "Do you know these triplets?"

"Oh, he knows them," Eugene said. "There is no way of not knowing them once you are in the same room with them. They are Ruger Slade's servants. Wholehearted ones, I might add."

"I don't know them like *that*," he reassured Mandi.

"Oh yes, he does." Eugene giggled. "Unless he's made of stone, but even Ruger is flesh and blood." He turned his gaze back on Mandi. "My, you are a vision. Will you feed me?"

"I have some leftover pizza and Ring Dings," Smoke offered.

"I'll take anything she touches," Eugene added.

Mandi raised her eyebrows at Abraham, making it clear she

would roll with it. Much like Sticks, she would apparently go to great lengths to complete a mission.

Smoke handed her a box of Ring Dings. With her chest lowered in front of Eugene's face, she slowly fed the pastry to him.

"Mmm. Mmm. Thank you," he said.

Abraham moved back to Smoke and Sid and said under his breath, "Man, this guy is a real perv. I'm not like that. It's no wonder Ruger hates him so."

"Roll with it," Sid said. "Every man has a weakness. You got lucky and found it early."

After Mandi finished feeding Eugene, she sat down beside him and placed a hand on his leg.

Eugene's eyes were filled with glee. "The flesh is weak. Especially mine." He swallowed. "Hey, I'm a sucker for a cheap thrill. So, Abraham, I'm going to try to tell you what is happening in layman's terms. Again, it won't make any difference, the way I see it. And all of you will wind up dead soon enough. They'll find us. Trust me."

"Who?" he asked.

Eugene sighed and said, "That's the harder question to answer. The military. The government. Venture capitalists. I'm a scientist, a researcher at Carnegie Mellon. We had a research grant to study the existence of other dimensions. I can't say who the grant came from. It was top secret but had the stink of government all over it. We call it the Corporation. With the harnessing of nuclear power, we began studies that would affect time and space. The splitting of atoms has a multifaceted destructive purpose.

"The scientific community was abuzz about the ancient star gates scattered all over the world. We created a gate of our own, using nuclear power. In theory, it would create a rift in space. And remember, we didn't come up with this preposterous notion either. We were hired to create it. Needless to say, without any scientific basis to rely on, I had major scientific doubts. Still, we built what we called the Time Tunnel. It's a ten-foot-high doorway framed out of titanium and tungsten. The name is horrible. Professor Maurice coined it, and despite my objections about a doorway that opens another dimension, such as the Dimension Tunnel, Time Tunnel stuck.

"I'm playing nice. Can we remove the bonds?" Eugene asked.

"No." Abraham said.

Mandi patted Eugene's head.

"Fine. You're lucky she is here."

"And to think that you were going to *dispose* of me," Mandi said.

"I was only putting on for the troops. I'd never allow anything bad to happen to you now that I know you. Anyway," Eugene continued, "we turned the Time Tunnel on. It worked. I'm talking, my hair was standing on the top of my head. The raw power… It was, well, amazing. The doorway was black like a sheet of ice. We came out from behind the barrier and looked at the wondrous vision. It began to change. The blackness turned to color. A painting of endless fields formed. All of us saw a new frontier unlike anything we'd seen before. It was a new world.

"The frame of the Time Tunnel started to bow. My team fled. I stuck my hand in the doorway. I felt the warmth of the new world. So real. The frame collapsed as I pulled my hand away. The portal hovered with a life of its own. I looked back at my colleagues, waved, and jumped toward it, but I bounced off the shimmering image. The portal vanished.

"After that, we created one door after the other. The frame could never hold the portal for long. We learned that flesh and blood could not pass through, but inanimate objects could. Our team put everything we had into it. Our donors gave us unlimited resources. But the same result came time and again. The Time Tunnel frame would collapse. The portal would vanish. Then we came to learn about the mysterious disappearance in our highway-system tunnels. The portals we opened were on the loose. People were disappearing. Along with their vehicles.

"I came up with an idea. I volunteered to drive into the tunnel using a vehicle, figuring if I was inside the casing, I could cross. Using a small car, I drove right into the Time Tunnel. That's when I became Ruger Slade. I was in his body, but my body remained here, I came to find out recently. I was comatose the entire time. I hosted a new body."

"It's called a soul swap," Abraham said.

He rose from his chair and paced. Eugene's story sounded believable, but he had to assume lies were twisted in with the truth. He looked at Smoke and Sid. She was whispering in Smoke's ear.

"Eh, you called it a soul swap?" Eugene said. "Where did you come up that? It's profoundly accurate."

"And Elderling named Melris told me," he said.

"An Elderling. Interesting." Eugene shifted in his chair. "Will you please take these off of me? I'm exhausted. And to be honest, I find sharing refreshing. And I have more information, believe me, much more. The Corporation is investing more funding into the Titanuus project. You see, they have been able to pick my brain and more—others that have been through this, as you coin it, soul swap."

Smoke looked at his watch.

"What is it? Sid asked.

"We have company." Smoke took off out of the barn.

56

NOT A MOMENT AFTER SMOKE EXITED THE BARN, THE *WUPPA WUPPA* of an oncoming helicopter could be heard overhead.

"I told you that they would find us," Eugene said. "And I'm not bragging. They find everyone."

Sid put on a black web belt and holstered two automatic Glock pistols. She put on her jacket. "Looks like the interview is over."

Smoke appeared inside the room as the sound of a helicopter soared overhead. "I don't know how they found us."

"Probably the GPS in your vehicle," Eugene suggested. "That gets a lot of people."

"No, I disabled it. Our phones can't be tracked either." Smoke eyed Mandi.

"This is a burner." Mandi held out her phone. "Did that do it?"

"I don't think so." Sid moved over to Eugene and ran her hands over his face and neck. "He must have some other sort of tag on him that we missed."

"Oh, that feels wonderful. Your hands are very warm," Eugene said as he nuzzled her hand with his face. "Don't stop, gorgeous."

"Ew, you really need therapy." Sid patted him down all over. Her hands stopped on his dress shoes. She yanked them off and twisted the heel off one. "Smoke? Did you check his feet?"

"Of course I did," he said.

Sid turned the heel over, and a flat round battery like the one used in a watch fell out. She gave Smoke a disappointed look. "We're compromised."

Smoke shrugged and said, "Bish happens."

Eugene looked at the battery and with a smile said, "I told you."

"Everybody, get to the Hellcat!" Sid ordered. "We can lose 'em in the hills."

"What about Eugene?" Abraham asked.

"He's dead weight. We have to go." Sid grabbed the metal suitcases.

Smoke snatched up more weapons. "Grab and go," he said.

"Bye bye," Eugene said with a devilish grin. "I hope to see you ladies again."

The party broke free of the barn's front door.

A streak of fire raced through the sky with a roar. The fire collided with the Hellcat.

KA-BOOOOOM!

The car turned into an inferno of explosions.

"My Hellcat!" Sid screamed with anguish in her soul.

"My LAW rockets!" Smoke added.

With fire in her voice, Sid said, "Everyone back inside!"

Abraham closed them inside the barn.

"Morning glory!" Sid cursed.

"Looks like we have a fight on our hands," Smoke quipped.

"Ah, you missed me," Eugene said, delighted. "So glad that you are back. I missed you too. I have a feeling that we are all going to become very close. At least those of us that are still living."

"What are we going to do?" Mandi said in a loud, worried

voice. The whirling propellers of a military-grade transport chopper roared overhead.

Abraham put his arm around her waist. "I'll protect you."

"That's a very sweet thing to say," Eugene said, "but it won't do you any good. Those are soldiers out there. If there is one helicopter, I bet two more are near. Probably a score of well-armed men at least. It looks like you have firepower, but it's not as if you have Black Bane." He tensed in his bonds. "It's times like this I wish I was back in Ruger's body. Talk about exhilarating."

Sid took a knee and opened both of the metal briefcases. "I didn't think it would come to this." She pulled out a sleek bodysuit and tossed one each to Abraham and Mandi. "Take off your clothes and put those on."

Abraham held the suit up before his eyes and asked, "Are we going scuba diving?"

"No. It's called a sweetheart suit. Bulletproof." Sid stripped down to her black bra and panties. For a taller woman, she had great natural curves. The muscles in her arms flexed when she pulled her own suit on.

"Hubba hubba," Eugene said. "Teacher, take me back to school."

"Will you shut up?" Sid said.

Mandi stripped down to her bra and panties. Her body left Eugene's tongue hanging out of his mouth. Her curves jiggled when she pulled the tight suit on.

Smoke was nothing but sculpted muscles with scars all over. He was built a lot like Ruger but sleeker.

Abraham, by comparison, had plenty of meat packed over hard, unseen muscle. His belly, though much slimmer, still hung down. He fought to pull the sweetheart suit on. Mandi helped him by tugging fiercely on his sleeves. They zipped each other up.

Sid and Smoke put on their old clothing and boots.

A spring of new energy coursed through Abraham's body. He couldn't help but smile. Mandi gave him a frisky look.

"It's nice, isn't it?" Smoke said.

"I feel like I could run a hundred miles." Abraham's gut still bulged, but not as badly. "Slimming too."

"One of these fools does not belong here," Eugene sang in a familiar *Sesame Street* tune. "One of these fools is not the same. One of these fools is too fat for his suit."

Smoke walked over to Eugene and said, "My wife told you to shut up."

"I'm sorry, I didn't hear her. I was too busy drooling," Eugene fired back.

Smoke pinched the man's neck.

Eugene's eyes closed, and he slumped over.

"What's the plan?" Smoke said.

Sid loaded more extended ammo clips into her gun as Smoke did the same—some of the clips had blue, green, and red tape on them. "Those bastards took my car. We'll take their helicopter." She tossed Abraham and Mandi each a gun. "You know how to shoot, don't you?"

"Right now, I feel like I can do anything," Mandi said. "Can I keep this suit?"

"We'll see, cuz," Sid replied. She opened a small metal bottle and spilled four emerald-green pills into her hand. "Everyone take one."

"They look like vitamin D pills," Mandi said. "What does it do?"

Smoke grinned. "We call them super vitamins. They give you a real boost. They'll heighten your senses and enhance your strength. Keep one handy in case of emergency."

Mandi took a pill in hand.

Abraham backed away. "I don't mix well with pills. I'd rather not."

"We're going to have to scrap," Smoke said. "Can you fight and shoot if you have to?"

"I can handle it."

Smoke nodded. He bent over and grabbed some goggles with round blue lenses from the metal case and tossed them to Abraham. "Good. Then you come with me."

57

ABRAHAM AND THE OTHERS FOLLOWED SMOKE OUT THROUGH SOME loose wall panels in the back. They headed away from the landed chopper and into the woods.

"We'll split up," Sid said. "I'll keep Mandi safe. You and Smoke take care of them." She kissed Smoke. "Be careful."

Mandi gave Abraham a quick kiss. "You too."

The women moved deeper into the woods and vanished in the trees.

Smoke crouched down and eyed the barn. He was like a big cat waiting to pounce.

The goggles Abraham wore did wonders for his night sight. The house and barn looked as though they were sitting illuminated by a blue daytime sun.

"These things are incredible," he mumbled.

The helicopter had landed behind the farmhouse. Its blades were still whirring loudly. Another helicopter flew overhead, slowly hovering over a hundred feet high. Soldiers appeared on the lawn, over a dozen of them snaking through the yard. They surrounded the house and barn. The red lasers from their automatic pistols were on.

"There's a lot of them," Smoke said. He spun his pistols on his fingers. "It's going to be a party. Can you use that weapon?"

Abraham looked at the gun in his hand and said, "Yeah, but I'm a lot better with a sword."

Smoke took a long black-handled hunting knife out of his belt and said, "Take this, Highlander."

Abraham spun it in his free hand. "That'll do. So, are you going to kill these guys?"

"I hate to kill 'em. But those folks are black ops. Off the record. They know what they are in for. My guess is that they are on a capture mission. But if they blast away, take them out before they take you."

"Got it." Abraham eyed his gun. It had a long blue clip in it. "What is the difference in these clips?"

"The blue pierce armor. The red are explosive. The green, well, take them out as a last resort." Smoke nodded at him. "Stay close. Follow my lead. Let's go."

The soldiers entered the house and the barn in small teams while other soldiers stood guard. They used flashlights and turned the beams over the fields. Above, the helicopter activated a spotlight. The huge light scoured the area.

Abraham and Smoke crouched behind a well while the helicopter beam passed over them. They peeked over around opposite sides of the rim. Some men with flashlights were walking the grounds, while others slunk toward the forest. Two soldiers came out of the back of the barn where Abraham's group had come out earlier. The soldiers pointed into the woods, away from the well.

"It's time to find out if they are here to kill us or not," Smoke said. "Wait here."

"What are you going to do?"

"Be ready," Smoke said. He took off at a dead sprint back toward the woods.

The soldiers shouted out. "There's one!"

The helicopter light shined down on Smoke. Smoke stood in the beam with his arms raised and guns waving.

He's crazy!

"Take him out!" one of the commanding soldiers said.

The farmland exploded in a hail of gunfire.

Smoke sprang toward the woods like a deer.

Holy sheetrock! They are trying to kill us!

Abraham had fully expected that the soldiers were trying to capture them. They'd fooled him. They were shooting. He huddled behind the well.

Smoke vanished into the woodland's edge. A squad of four soldiers quickly worked their way up the slope, going after him. They passed the well no more than thirty yards away.

Abraham aimed at the soldiers. His hand was shaking. *I can't shoot those men in the back... can I?*

Smoke raced out of the woods with his guns blazing and the helicopter spotlight right on him. Two soldiers fell. Two more fired back.

More soldiers converged on Smoke.

Abraham started pulling his trigger. The muzzle of the Glock flashed. Men were falling. Others were coming running at him and firing. Before he knew what happened, his clip was empty. *Blazing Saddles!* He discharged the weapon's clip and fumbled to reload another magazine. His ear caught the sound of footsteps crunching over the stiff grasses. He turned around as he stuffed in his clip. A soldier had him dead to rights with a pistol pointed at his chest. The soldier wore a black ball cap. He cracked a wicked smile and opened fire. *Blam. Blam. Blam.*

58

ABRAHAM GROANED AS HIS CHEST CAUGHT FIRE. THE FULL FORCE OF every bullet sent shards of pain exploding through him.

"Say, you ain't bleeding, and you're still breathing," the thuggish soldier said.

Gasping for air, Abraham managed to say, "No. Sorry to disappoint you." As much as his chest hurt, he might as well have been dead.

The soldier shrugged. "I guess it needs to be a head shot then."

Abraham kicked the man in the shin as the gun went off. A bullet whizzed by his ear. He jumped on the soldier and drove his knife into the man's gut. The soldier let out a ragged sigh and died.

With blood on his knuckles, he pulled the blade out and crawled back behind the well. He charged the slide on his weapon and fired at another wave of soldiers coming right at him.

Smoke jumped behind the well and asked, "How's it going?"

"I've been shot three times, but I'm still breathing," Abraham said. "You?'

"I took a couple of rounds. Hurts, don't it?"

"That's putting it mildly."

"You'll get used to it."

"Believe me, I am, but I'd rather not."

The helicopter spotlight shone on both of them.

Hails of gunfire blasted into the water well's stones.

"We need to move!" Abraham said.

"Follow my lead." Smoke rolled across the grass and fired into the soldiers. Two more soldiers dropped. He came to his feet and sprinted right at them. "Eee-yah!"

Abraham took off after the ranging man. He fired at everything moving that wasn't Smoke. One of his shots ripped through one man's chest and knocked down another. *Man, these bullets are nasty.*

They skirmished with the soldiers all over the yard. They battled behind the barn and the house. Soldiers came at them in twos and fours.

The sting of a bullet punched into Abraham's shoulder. He shrugged it off. Even in his old body, his blood was running battle hot.

The helicopter chased them over the yard. Automatic gunfire blasted out from the chopper. The grass spat up behind their fleeing feet.

Smoke dashed up the steps onto the front porch as Abraham followed behind him. Smoke crashed through the front door. Abraham dove through a glass window.

A man tackled Abraham, and a knife cut his cheek. They wrestled over the floor, knocking over light stands and bumping into a china cabinet. The soldier was a large man, strong as an ox. He wrestled like an angry bear.

"I will break you like egg," the soldier said in a thick Russian accent. He busted Abraham in the nose with his forehead.

Abraham's nose caved in, and his eyes watered. Warm blood ran down his chin. He punched his knife at the man and fired a shot.

The soldier grabbed both of his wrists in a viselike grip. He wrenched both weapons free. In a sudden movement, he hip tossed Abraham to the floor. He pinned Abraham down and locked his fingers on his throat.

Abraham whaled away at the man's ribs. The soldier's body armor absorbed the blows. *Who is this freak?*

The soldier put his weight on Abraham's neck. He was bigger than Abraham and built like a defensive lineman. The soldier's crushing grip started to collapse the muscles in his neck.

Nooo!

Abraham grabbed the man's wrists and tried to pry them apart. The soldier applied more force. In Titanuus, Ruger would have made mincemeat out of this guy. Back home, it was different. He was only Abraham Jenkins, an out-of-shape truck driver fighting for his breath.

No! I'm Ruger Slade. I've fought far worse than this!

He let out a loud grunt. He squirmed and thrashed. His body shifted underneath the hulk trying to kill him. He grabbed one of the soldier's ring fingers and peeled it back. He gave it a yank, and the finger bone snapped out of place.

The soldier let out a yelp and punched Abraham in the face.

Abraham twisted out from underneath the man. He sprang back to his feet, gasping for breath.

The soldier charged and rammed Abraham back into the fireplace. Both men went back and forth, whaling on one another.

He hit the soldier in the face as hard as he could. The fighter spat out a tooth, snapped his finger back into place, and kept coming, huffing for breath.

"You haven't been in a long fight in a while, have you?" Abraham asked, his own lungs burning.

The bearish soldier pulled a knife from somewhere behind his back and started slicing at Abraham.

Abraham blocked the deadly cuts with his forearm. The soldier sneaked one slice across his chest. His clothing was slashed, but the sweetheart suit kept his bowels intact. Back and forth, the men battled through the farmhouse's living room. They fell over a couch in a tangle of limbs. Neither man gave. The fight was still on.

Somehow, Abraham found deep reserves that kept him from being pummeled to death. His will and Ruger's will started to become one. He fought like a demon. He liked it.

"I will break you," the soldier said.

"Keep dreaming, Drago."

The soldier feinted in with the knife and slipped a hard punch across Abraham's jaw.

Abraham fell to one knee. His body wobbled as he became woozy. The soldier's punch had been dead on.

The soldier lifted the knife.

Abraham couldn't lift his arms to block. His strength fled him. He was stunned.

The helicopters light shone into the living room, and a loud whirring came from outside.

"Get down, Abraham!" Smoke cried out.

Abraham fell over.

Bullets ripped through the house. Glass shattered. Wood splintered.

The big soldier gaped as bullets cut the man in two. The top of his body fell from the bottom.

Smoke crawled over to Abraham, blood all over his face. "I told you it was going to be a party."

Abraham spotted his gun and grabbed it. He pulled a red clip from his belt and reloaded. As the house was being cut in half, he asked, "Are they firing what I think they are?"

"A Vulcan Gatling gun. You got it." Smoke pulled a big piece of glass out of his hand. "They must think we are predators."

Abraham rose and fired at the chopper. The bullets ripped out of the gun barrel like red tracer rounds. They zipped through the busted windows and into the chopper.

BOOM!

The chopper turned into a ball of flame and peeled away. It crashed hard and loud into the driveway. A pyre of burning metal ensued.

Both men stood.

"Good shot," Smoke said. "I was wondering if you'd remember about the red bullets. Cool, aren't they?"

"Yep," Abraham said. "Man, I'm thirsty."

"It's the suit. It will dehydrate you."

The house groaned and swayed.

"Uh oh," Smoke said.

The second floor of the house collapsed on top of them.

59

BLACKNESS. SUFFOCATING AIR. ABRAHAM TOOK A SHORT BREATH, and something bit into his lungs. "Ugh."

Half of a house had just fallen on top of him. He could still hear muffled gunshots, but he couldn't see a thing. Abraham pushed out from underneath of what felt like a chandelier. His leg was pinned somewhere. "Smoke," he called out dryly.

"I'm here," the voice muttered in the darkness. "Stuck at the moment, but I'm working on it."

"You're not chewing your arm off or something like that, are you?"

"Too early for that."

Wood and paneling popped and cracked.

Old plaster drywall dust was everywhere.

Abraham spat and said, "We sure know how to bring down the house, don't we?"

"You can say that again." Smoke grunted. Something heavy scraped over the floor. "I think I can see light. Can you?"

With one armed pinned against his chest, Abraham wiped dust out of his eyes and blinked. "It's as black as a coal mine. Man, I hope Mandi is okay. I've got to get out of here." He clawed at the roof that had fallen on him, old plaster and wood framing. He didn't have much wiggle room at all but fought against the weight of it. "Guh!"

"Don't blow a gasket over there," Smoke said. "We'll manage."

The sound of footsteps could be heard outside. The gunfire had stopped. People were walking through the collapsed house. They moved on cats' feet, but the stiff boards groaned underneath them.

"They sound light," Smoke said in a hushed voice. "Women?"

Abraham nodded in the darkness.

"Sid!" Smoke said.

"Smoke," a woman responded in a muffled voice. "Where are you?"

The men tapped on their ceiling, calling out.

Above, the women busted away the roof and subflooring.

Abraham pushed his free arm against the ceiling.

Someone was ripping away his prison. He made out the faint outline of fingers.

"Abraham," Mandi said. She was nothing more than a silhouette. She grabbed his shoulders and started to pull him.

"Gah!" he said. "Sorry, but my leg is pinned under the subfloor."

"Where?" Mandi asked. She ran her hands down his body and followed it down to his leg. "Oh, I'm standing on the section that's pinning your leg down. Hold on." She punched through the flooring. "I just need to get a good grip on this beam. I'll lift, and you slide out."

"You're going to lift the house off of me?"

"Yep," Mandi said. "I took one of those pills. I've got pregnant-woman strength right now. Like Octomom or something. Let's go for it."

Mandi huddled over the beam and put her back into it with a grunt. The joists pinning his legs rose. He slipped out from under them and punched his way up to his feet.

Mandi lowered the joists, jumped over to him, and gave him a bear hug that might have broken a lesser man's back.

"Ow! I don't need any more cracked ribs."

"Sorry." She pulled him down by the hair and kissed him fiercely. "You have to try these vitamins. I feel like some kind of superwoman."

"Come on, lovebirds, let's go," Sid said.

The gang of four barreled their way through the upstairs window and climbed down the wraparound porch. The helicopter and Hellcat were burning side by side in the driveway. Dead soldiers were scattered all over the grounds.

"I killed those dudes," Mandi said with fire in her eyes. "I mean, I could see them moving, like they were in slow motion. It was point and shoot. Like I was playing *Duck Hunt* or something." She wrapped her arms around Abraham's. "I've never killed anyone."

"Sorry." Abraham didn't know what else to say as they followed Sid and Smoke to the other helicopter. "At least you're alive."

"Oh, I don't regret it. It was them or me. Better off them. Evil men. I could see it in their eyes. They had it coming."

The helicopter started to take off.

"Wait! What is happening?" Sid asked and ran toward it in a long-legged sprint. She was fast, but Smoke was faster. They both jumped onto the skids of the helicopter as it took off.

"Are they crazy?" Abraham yelled. As the helicopter rose higher, he could make out the face of Eugene Drisk staring out of the copilot's window. The professor was waving.

As it took off, another helicopter dropped out of the sky. Its spotlights illuminated Abraham and Mandi.

Abraham shielded his eyes.

The Vulcan machine gun on the helicopter fired. Red-hot blasts of gunfire erupted out of the chopper.

Mandi pushed Abraham out of the way. "I'll handle this." The wild-eyed woman stood in the path of bullets that chewed up the grass on their way toward her. She squeezed off bullets in rapid succession.

"Get out of the way, Mandi!" He climbed back to his feet. "Run, Mandi! Run!"

The Vulcan bullets made a path right through Mandi.

Abraham screamed, "Nooo!"

60

THE HELICOPTER PITCHED LEFT, AND THE HAIL OF BULLETS WENT with it. It crashed into the trees, blew up, and caught fire.

Abraham rushed over to Mandi, who lay on the ground. The bullets had made massive divots all around her. He picked her up in his arms and cradled her. "Mandi," he said softly as he shook her. "Mandi. Don't die on me."

Mandi's chest rose and fell as she breathed. Not a scratch was on her.

"They missed!" he said with elation. He shook her, but she didn't wake. "What's wrong?"

The last helicopter in the sky flew in an erratic pattern above him. One person fell out of the chopper, and another person fell after the first. They plummeted through the roof of the barn.

Abraham's heart jumped in his throat.

The helicopter lowered, its lights on Abraham.

He stared it down.

The spotlight dimmed.

Sid jumped out of the helicopter and asked, "What are you waiting for? Let's go. Get in!"

She didn't have to tell him twice. With Mandi in his arms, he rushed over to the chopper. Crouched low, he slipped underneath that chopper's blades and climbed inside. "She's out cold."

The helicopter rose upward.

Smoke was sitting in the pilot's seat with a headset on.

Eugene Drisk was slumped over in the copilot's chair.

Sid checked Mandi's pulse. "She's fine." She spoke loudly, the wind in her hair. "Dehydrated. The super vitamins drained her. Sorry about that, but it was the only way that she could keep up with me. And I didn't have to twist her arm to take it."

"Are they addictive?"

"No. But they give you a hangover." Sid tugged off Mandi's bodysuit. "These suits will burn you up if you aren't used to it. Find her a blanket."

Abraham nodded. He rummaged through the military gear and found a green blanket. He wrapped it around Mandi. "We need some water," he said in a loud voice.

"I'll look." Sid took a turn making her way around the cabin.

"Where will we go now?" he asked.

"What?"

"Where are we going?" he repeated more loudly.

Sid shrugged. "I'll get a headset. There's no telling where Smoke will take us. After a night like this, he'll probably land at the nearest diner to get some milkshakes and pancakes." She found some canteens in the cooler and tilted her head. "Are you all right? You don't look so well."

"What's wrong?" he said, "I feel fine."

"You're as pale as Mandi. Peaked." Sid touched his face. "Oh man, you're dehydrated. You need some serious H_2O." She handed him a canteen. "Drink."

He nodded, gave her a faint smile, felt the helicopter start to spin, and passed out.

61

Suffocating smoke burned Abraham's lungs. He woke in a fit of coughing. Every inch of his body felt as if thousands of needles were trying to poke out of it. His eyes burned, and he couldn't see a thing. The only moving in his body came from his hoarse coughing.

The helicopter must have crashed. Where's Mandi?

Flames were all around him. He couldn't see a thing. The wroth heat of the fires started to cook him.

He coughed and hacked as the flames took his breath away. He rolled onto his belly and started to crawl slowly away from the heat, but he didn't have the strength.

I'm going to burn alive!

Wooziness assailed him, and he felt faint again. With his head down, he summoned his reserves and pushed forward. He inched ahead. The flames were so hot that they burnt his toes.

Someone grabbed him by the arms and began pulling him away from the fire. He couldn't make the person out, for he couldn't lift his head to see. The person didn't seem particularly strong.

Mandi? Sid? Get me out of this hot mess!

The flames roared. The fire crackled and popped. Someone let out a bloodcurdling scream. A loud explosion jolted his body.

Whoever was pulling him from the fire was moving slowly and coughing too.

"Hurry up," Abraham groaned in a dry, cracking voice. He kicked with his feet. "Hurry."

The heat felt as if he were lying just inside a fireplace. He was roasted all over. The smell of his singed hair carried into his nose as if his flesh were cooking.

Please don't be hell. I don't want to go to hell. I believe. Lord, I believe!

Abraham's body bounced down over something hard. His eyes were so watery that he couldn't see. The person pulling him grunted and coughed. He went into another fit of coughing as well.

Someone else latched onto his other arm and helped the other drag him farther. The hot flames enveloping his surroundings started to cool. He coughed and sucked in a lungful of breathable air. He gasped in more air as he was dragged farther from the flames.

Thank heavens!

He opened his eyes and wiped the tears away. "Thanks, guys," he managed to croak. "What happened? Did the chopper crash? Where's Mandi?"

"Who's Mandi?" Horace asked. The beefy man helped Abraham into a sitting position. He slapped Abraham on the back and said, "Cough out that smoke. You need to clear it."

"What?" Abraham's head snapped around. A tavern was burning in the streets of Junction City. It was the one he'd been in with Big Apple, Lord Hawk, Kawnee, and the wraith, Fleece. He clutched his head. "Nooo! Black Bane!"

"Be happy that I pulled you out when I did," Shades said. "It was getting hot in there. A few more seconds, and we might not have made it." He slapped Abraham's shoulder. "No need to thank me. As for the sword, well, I figure it had a good run."

62

Black smoke spilled into the streets. Men and women raced from the river with buckets of water, making a chain of people who tossed water onto the burning building.

"You set the tavern on fire, didn't you?" Abraham asked Shades as the flames consumed the tavern like a giant box of matches. "Didn't I tell you not to do that?"

"I don't recall those exact words. I believe that you were speaking generally," Shades said. "Such as, don't burn a building down because you don't like the service. Or the people that are in it. But, in case of a dangerous situation, set the building on fire."

Abraham was only half listening as his mind tried to sort things out. Minutes before, he had been back home, but now, he was in Titanuus. Smoke and Sid were gone. So was Mandi. She was unconscious, but at least she was safe with her cousin. He hoped.

The upper level of the tavern collapsed on the bottom. A new plume of flames and smoke went up. The old dry wood popped and cracked loudly. In a few minutes, nothing would be left.

His back straightened. "Where's Sticks?" He reached up and

grabbed Shades by the collar and pulled the small man down. "You didn't kill her, did you?"

"Of course not," Shades replied. "I'd never harm a lady."

Abraham looked around. A crowd had gathered around the tavern. Most of them were cheering and partying. Abraham saw no sign of Sticks, Big Apple, Lord Hawk, Kawnee, or Fleece. He recalled his last moments with Big Apple. The horned halfling had stated that he controlled Fleece, who turned out to be the Underlord. If that were the case, then Big Apple controlled a lot more than he'd let on. By the looks of it, the horned halfling controlled the Sect and quite possibly Lord Hawk's guild, the Shell. The question was how… and why. Abraham stood up and asked, "Then where is she? Where are the rest of them?"

Shades lifted a finger, paused, and said, "That's a long story."

He pointed toward a group of soldiers gathering around the fire. They were the Gray Guard. The stalwart group of soldiers grabbed the folks nearest the fire and started asking questions. People were pointing in Abraham's direction.

"I think we should move on," Shades said.

"I'm not leaving Black Bane in that pillar of flame. I have to get it!" Abraham said.

"I'll fetch it, Captain." Horace tapped the butt of his spear on the ground. "I'll deal with the Gray Guard too, one soldier to another. I can speak the language."

Abraham gave Horace and the fire a long look and walked away. He followed Shades into the back alleys and took a seat on a box crate with his head down. He coughed and said, "Spit it out, you little pyromaniac."

"Pyromaniac?" Shades glanced upward and rubbed his chin. "That's a term from your world, isn't it? I think I like it."

Abraham slumped against the wall, grimacing. He could barely move. His bones ached, and his muscles were as tight as bowstrings. He accidentally took a deep breath of the alley's stink and said, "Whew! And make it quick. I don't want to sit in this cat box all night. And where the heck did Horace come from?"

Shades casually leaned his head from one shoulder to the other and said, "Let me start at the beginning. You went in the tavern. I went up the stairs and listened at the doors. I had no trouble tracking down Sticks. Commander Cutter is a loud one, if you know what I mean." He winked. "Once I secured her whereabouts, I decided to slip into the tavern. I made my move from the back alley and into the kitchen. Well, I got there soon enough to over-hear your conversation with Big Apple. You had him pinned inside the fireplace, pointing that gun at him. It is called a gun, right?"

Abraham gave a weak nod. He could hardly lift his chin. The spell that Fleece had hit him with sucked the vitality right out of him.

Shades pulled back his sleeves, revealing his bare forearms, and squatted down in front of Abraham. "That thing got its bony fingers on you, and my hair stood on my arms. I froze in my tracks, but your scream got me going again. That wraith is an omnipotent sort. Otherworldly. I was sure you would be undone, because I've never heard a man wail so loudly."

"It wasn't that loud." Abraham didn't remember screaming, but he didn't doubt that he had. Fleece's touch felt as if his soul were being ripped out.

"Oh, it was. I can still hear it ringing in my ears." He pushed down his sleeves. "That's when I did the only thing that I knew to do."

"Start a fire?"

Shades shrugged his eyebrows. "Create a distraction that happened to be a fire. I had to do something that would stop all of the screaming." He covered his ears. "Other than this. I managed to clear the kitchen quick because the cook was drunk and outside smoking. I locked him outside. It didn't take long to get the coals and the chicken grease burning. I flung it on the curtains outside of the kitchen near the seats. No one was paying attention to me—just you and the harrowing sound of sheer torment.

"The smoke began to carry, and one of the girls from the mud hole was the first to notice the flames and shout, 'Fire!' Just when the goons scrambled to put the flames out, you'll never guess who entered through the front door."

"Sticks?"

"No." Shades backhanded Abraham's shoulder. "Melris."

Abraham made a surprised look and said, "He was comatose."

"*Was* being the key word. The purple man's eyes lit up like the stars the moment he set his eyes on the shade's back. The room brightened in a wash of purple as his hands caught fire. The rod he carried came to life like a burning torch. He slammed it into the floor." Shades flicked his fingers out. "Boooom."

63

"Everyone in the room flattened as if they were hit by a sudden gale," Shades said with awe. "They were tossed like a bull had bucked them. The floor underneath my feet heaved. The bar bowed. The glasses and pottery jangled, fell, and broke. I was on my knees, and very little takes me from my feet. By the time I climbed back to my feet, I found myself sitting in the midst of a storm with flashes of purple and black.

"The purple man and the black shade had locked horns. Like sheets in the wind, without a toe touching the floor, they battled through the tavern. Their bodies blasted through the bars. The flames of the fire spread faster. The purple man, well, he had some sort of aura around his body. The wraith couldn't get a grip on him. Purple smote the wraith with his rod. It made the sound of timbers breaking."

Abraham hung on the rogue's every word. He nodded as he visualized the scene.

Shades paced the alley, gesticulating as he continued the story. "They punched through one wall and reentered through another. Spinning like a dust devil of arcane energy, they trashed the tavern floor. Tables and chairs were lifted from the floor and sent crashing into the walls. The wraith let out an angry shriek. His hands filled with black flames. He tried to choke the purple man to death.

"The purple man slipped his clutches. He swung his rod like a club. The two of them whaled on one another with flaming fists. Their robes came alive like a writhing nest of snakes. They tangled, tugged, and I swear by the Elders, they screamed screams of their own. By the time I gathered my bowels, the two of them blasted through the ceiling and carried on through the roof." He punched his hand in the air. "Pow! They were gone.

"I jumped through the wreckage and headed outside. There they were, standing in the streets, hurling bolts of light at each other. The town lit up with a new daylight. The sounds of a storm rolled through the streets. Cries arose from the rooftops. The little ball of muscle charged at the wraith. He was thrusting his finger at it and yelling at the top of his lungs. He said, 'Take us away. Take us away. Now!'" Shades flicked his fingers out. "Poof. They were gone. The wraith and the halfling. Lord Hawk and the fish lady. Even the goons. Vanished into thin air. Melris took off down the street. His burning eyes were searching the sky. I have no idea where he went."

"What about Sticks?"

Shades shrugged. "I think she and Cutter disappeared with them. I rushed back into the fire to save you. Don't worry, she can take care of herself."

Abraham stood up and kicked the crate. "We don't know that." His head started to ache. He wanted to rest, to take a breath, but he couldn't. "What about the other Henchmen? Are they here?"

"I've only seen Horace. Well, him and the purple man." Shades moved to the end of the alley and peeked into the city. "Horace is out there talking to the Gray Guard. It looks like a bunch of drunks have cleared out. They've already rounded up a heap of them. Got them face down in the road, spread-eagle."

Abraham rubbed his neck. He needed a break. Traveling between two worlds was beginning to catch up to him. He trudged over to Shades and saw Horace making small talk with the Gray Guard. "Fetch him."

"Consider it done." Shades departed.

"This is getting old. I'm getting old."

He didn't have any idea how old Ruger was, but he guessed the man was in his mid-thirties. Most of the Henchmen were, if he were to guess. After the shock he'd taken from Fleece, he felt more like seventy.

The tavern was burning, but the flames were dying down. The hungry flames quickly turned the ancient dry wood to ash.

"Black Bane," he muttered. He had enough problems. The last thing he needed was to lose his sword. He needed something he could get a grip on. The heft of Black Bane in his grip gave him a sense of security. Now, it was underneath piles of burning ash. "Better to have some bad luck than have no luck at all. Gloom, despair, and agony on me."

Horace and Shades approached. Horace gave him a stiff nod. "The Gray Guard cooled. They aren't so bad to chat with. They recognize a soldier's soldier. I told them I saw wild mages battling in the sky. Plenty of other folk support the situation." He clawed at his beard. "What now, Captain?"

"Where did Melris come from? He was out. Simon sat on him," he asked.

"He popped up several hours after you departed. I told him where you went and tried to stop him. He insisted on getting you. There wasn't no telling him no." Horace wiped the beading sweat on his forehead. "Why is this place so hot? It's the cool season."

"The others are coming?" Abraham asked.

"Aye, I told them we'd meet at the river. That was Melris's idea.

He said the Little Vein is the fast way to the Wound." Horace cleared his throat. "Any fool knows that. We've seen the maps."

"Did you see Sticks?"

"No. As soon as we entered town, Melris moved like a hound dog right toward the blaze. He's got some sort of intuition. I didn't even see the fire," Horace said. "He lost me in the streets. The man can run like a deer. I can say that much for him."

Abraham wandered into the street with his brow furrowed. "All right. Get some men and some gear. We need to dig my sword out of that burning heap the first chance we get." His palms itched. Losing Sticks terrified him for some reason. "Shades, get with Dominga and Tark. You need to find Sticks."

"Will do." Shades slapped Abraham on the shoulder as he walked by. "You have to believe she can handle herself."

His jaws clenched. "I'll believe it when I see it. Now go!"

64

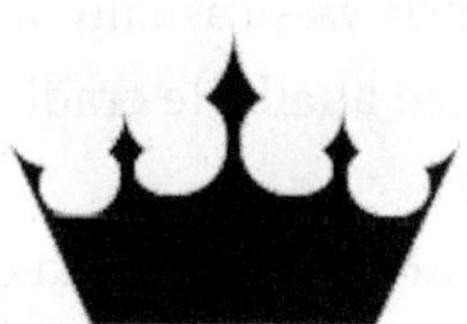

POSING AS VOLUNTEER MEDIEVAL FIREFIGHTERS, A GROUP OF
Henchmen went to work at the burn site. The fire was extinguished. The sun rose. Nothing was left of the tavern except piles
of charred wood and ash.

Horace and Bearclaw were covered in soot as they shoveled
piles of roasted wreckage away. Vern clawed the fallen coals away
with a rake. The Red Tunics lent a hand. Skitts and Zann were on
their hands and knees, digging through the rubble.

Solomon hauled away half-burnt beams and tossed them into a
pile.

Abraham stood over the spot where he thought his sword
might have been. Iris knelt beside him, her eyes closed. She held
her palms downward and mumbled strange chants.

"Anything?" he asked.

Iris didn't reply.

Cudgel wandered over to him, his face beaded with sweat. His
clothing was marred with black soot. "Anything, Captain?"

Abraham shrugged. "No. Keep on digging."

Cudgel flipped his shovel over his hand and said, "I wish we

255

had more Red Tunics to do the digging. I'd like to get some breakfast. And look at me now. I'm all messy."

"You'll live," Abraham said absentmindedly.

He couldn't stop thinking about Sticks. She was in the clutches of Cutter. The thought of her being with Cutter soured his mood.

As Cudgel wiped his bald head with a rag, his eyes popped, and he said, "Look, it's Melris."

Abraham turned. Melris was casually walking down the street as if nothing had happened at all. He cradled his rod of devastation in his arms.

"Where have you been?" Abraham asked angrily.

In his quiet voice, Melris said, "I've been trying to locate the wraith."

"Well, did you find him?"

Melris shook his head. "No. I have no sense of them at all. The wraith is endowed with significant powers."

"The wraith is the Underlord. The halfling controls him," Abraham said. "Did you learn anything about him from your fight?"

Melris hefted his rod onto his shoulder and asked, "Like what?"

"I don't know. Who is the Underlord? What are they doing? Or want?"

"The Underlord is a wraith. He is the living, now undead. His mastery of magic is far-reaching. He sold his mortal life for the power of magic. That is how he acquired abilities. That is why he leads the Sect. He completed their trials and is blessed by the Dark Elders." Melris dusted some wooden splinters from his robes. "I sought him out the moment I had a sense of him. I should have killed him, but he is strong, stronger than I imagined."

With his head rolling, Cudgel asked, "Well, how strong are you, Elderling?"

"I'm trained by the Elders. We are equipped to handle anything in the common world," Melris replied.

Cudgel rolled his eyes.

"What does that even mean?" Abraham asked.

"Yeah, apparently you didn't handle the wraith so well," Cudgel said.

"It means that I am more than flesh and blood. I have Elder magic coursing through my veins."

"Well, I'd like to have some biscuits and gravy running through mine." Cudgel huffed, moved away, and started digging.

Abraham gave Melris a curious glance and said, "What did you mean by the Dark Elders?"

"There are good Elders and bad. The Elders are supposed to keep harmony in the world. They protect the races, but they use them too. Normally, they are inactive. Elderlings like me care for them. When there is a shift in Titanuus, they become restless and active."

"The tide turns. The Elders awaken," Abraham said, quoting a phrase he had heard repeated several times. "Is that what is happening? Is that why you are here?"

"The balance of nature is unbalanced. Titanuus is shaken. We must stop it. We must stop the invasion. That is why I am here."

Abraham wondered who Melris meant by the Elders. *Are they a race of omnipotent beings, like the Greek and Norse gods of mythos? Or am I just crazy?* "I want to find Sticks. Can you help us with that? Or help me find my sword?"

"We need to depart," Melris said. "You should have stayed the course to begin with, but you chose to take a different path. We must follow the king's command and retrieve the stones."

"I'm not going anywhere without Sticks. She's a Henchman. We find her first." He looked down at Melris. "Besides, finding Big Apple and the Underlord is a good thing. We know that one controls the others. We know they stand between us and the truth. If we stop them, the king won't need the stones."

Melris narrowed his eyes and said, "Otherworlder, the king

needs the stones now more than ever. Kingsland, the last bastion of hope, will be destroyed without them. The enemy grows stronger every day. The very Spine of Titanuus tremors."

"If the stones are so important, then why aren't Big Apple and the Underlord going after them?"

"Because they have chosen to side with the invaders. Their faith is in the artifacts that they bring. To them, the magic of Titanuus is part of an antiquated past. They embrace a new future."

"Great, free pizza delivery and thirty-one thousand flavors of ice cream, here we come." Abraham sighed aloud. "Is nothing sacred?"

"Ice cream?" Melris said.

The floorboards beneath Cudgel collapsed, and he let out a surprised shout.

Everyone rushed over to the hole in the floor. A basement lay beneath the tavern. Cudgel was flat on his back.

"Are you well?" Iris said.

"Well enough." Cudgel wormed around. "Nothing is broken. Well, look at what I have here." He lifted up a charred scabbard with a sword in it. The pommel of Black Bane shone.

"Toss it up," Abraham said.

Showing a mouthful of white teeth, Cudgel said, "Finders keepers."

"Get him out of there," Abraham ordered.

Solomon bent over the gap, stretched his long hairy arms down, and grabbed Cudgel, who reached up. The troglin reeled the stout man up as easily as lifting a baby.

"Thanks," Cudgel said. He gave Solomon a pat on the back and handed Abraham the sword. "Here, Captain."

Black Bane's scabbard was crusted over with char and soot. The leather encasing it appeared dry and cracked. Small flecks of charred leather fell off the sheath. Somehow, the flames hadn't entirely consumed it and eaten it away. The sword's grip and pommel were intact but blackened with ashes and char.

Abraham pulled the sword halfway out of the scabbard. The blade shone in the sunlight.

"It's good, eh, Captain?" Horace said.

He nodded. Out of the corner of his eye, Shades, Dominga, and Tark approached. They were accompanied by three men wearing the burgundy tunics over the chain mail of the Black Squadron.

"What's this all about?" Abraham asked as he stared down the Black Squadron members, all of whom had short hair on the top and were shaved on the sides. He looked at Shades. "Well?"

Shades opened his mouth, but a Black Squadron soldier with a full brown beard cut him off. "You are Ruger Slade?"

"Yes," Abraham said.

"Commander Cutter sends a message. He has the woman. Follow me if you want her back. Only you and one witness," the soldier said.

"A witness for what?"

"The duel."

65

Abraham raised an eyebrow and asked, "What sort of duel?"

The brown-bearded soldier looked at his men and chuckled. He spat on the ground and said, "If you don't know what a duel is, then you are dead already."

The other two Black Squadron members chuckled and spat. They eyed the members of the Henchmen who began to gather.

Vern strolled forward with his hand on his sword belt and said, "I'd be happy to duel with any of you Hanchans. You are the worst swords in the world. I'll prove it."

One of the soldiers wandered in Vern's direction. His leader pulled him back by the collar.

"You'll get your chance," the leader said. "Once Cutter finishes off Ruger, we'll dispose of the rest of them. They are wanted men, after all." He fixed his hardened stare on Abraham and spat again. "You and one witness from your Elder-forsaken group. You have Commander Cutter's word that no harm will come to you once it's over. He wants all of your men to hear it for themselves from the lips of your own vermin."

"Commander Cutter sounds very confident in his abilities. But tell me, eh, what is your name?"

"Tomas. Second in command."

"Tomas, second in command, I don't think that you thought this through. What happens when he dies?"

"Well, er, the woman will be returned to you," Tomas said.

"You can't take the word of a Hanchan," Horace warned. "They are all liars."

"And lousy fighters," Vern added.

"It's a trap, Captain," Horace said.

"Time is pressing. If I don't return with you soon, the woman will be killed," Tomas said. "You should come with me immediately. You and one man. Command your company to stay behind. All of them. If so much as a one of them shows, the woman's throat will be cut."

Abraham turned and faced his command and said, "Everyone stay put except for Horace. He'll come with me." He saw the disappointed expressions on their faces and winked even though he felt like crap. "I'll make it quick. Come on, Horace."

Tomas and his men led them back into the city, leaving the Henchmen behind. Horace strutted with his chest out and spear in hand. "You should let me fight him, Captain. I can take Cutter. I'll kill him."

There was nothing Abraham would rather do than take Horace up on the offer. He was empty. His bones ached, and his muscles throbbed. Fleece had really done a number on him, and he hadn't recovered. He was drained. Normally, Ruger's body was up for any fight. At the moment, his body could barely walk, but he didn't show it.

The road led them to the exterior of one of the giant stacks. The top of its chimney, hundreds of feet in the air, spewed out clouds of gray smoke. A suffocating warmth emanated from the great pillar. An open doorway led inside the stack.

Tomas led the way. Abraham and Horace walked between them and the other two men. A stone stairwell led in a tight downward spiral with burning torches hung on the wall. After a thirty-foot descent, they entered a grand circular chamber underneath the stack. Torches lined the walls. Ash piles were everywhere. The suffocating warmth increased. The great stones above them pulsated with an orange heartbeat glow of their own.

"Welcome to the Waste," Tomas said. He navigated through the piles of ash on the dusty floor toward the other side of the chamber. "Commander Cutter awaits."

On the other side of the room, Cutter stood with his men, over a score of them. Cutter, the biggest of them all, sat on a large wooden chair built into a wooden podium like a throne. His bastard sword lay across his lap. He rubbed a finger underneath his lip as he eyed Abraham.

"Where is the woman?" Abraham asked.

Cutter took a deep breath through his nose. Without looking, he hitched his thumb toward his men in the back. Two men came forward with Sticks locked in their arms. One of them was wearing her bandolier of knives.

Abraham's blood ran hot the moment his eyes found hers.

66

———

Sticks's right eye was swollen shut. Her cat makeup had smeared on her face, and she had a split lip. A rope was tied around her neck, raw with burn marks. She sagged in the soldiers' arms. She lifted her chin and glanced at Abraham through her one good eye.

"What did you do to her?" Abraham shouted.

"I didn't do anything," Cutter said. "She tried to escape. We had to subdue her. She fights like a wildcat, that one. Took one of my men out. That's grounds for killing her." He tapped his fingers on the blade of his sword. "Be thankful that she is still alive."

Abraham wanted nothing more than to split the man in half. The problem was he wasn't sure he could do it. Even speaking took effort. He decided to delay. *Keep him talking.* "I'm here. Let her go. There is nowhere for me to go, and I never run from a fight."

"Never? Ha! When we crossed paths in Hancha, you avoided it then," Cutter said.

"No, you backed down. I was being merciful to you and your men. We killed Arcayis the Underlord that day. We'll kill the rest of your brood too. Big Apple, Fleece, Lord Hawk… all of them are going down."

"The only one going down today is you. As for them, they have their visions, and I have mine." Cutter rose from his chair and stepped down off his podium. "Mine is to be known as the greatest swordsman in the world. I'll settle for that."

"More like the greatest lackey. Big Apple has you twisted around his finger. He is only using you for his gain."

"Says King Hector's fool, who wears the King's Brand. You are the one that is a slave, not I." Cutter rested his sword on his shoulder. He gripped the hilt of his sword in two hands. "Enough chatter. It's time to duel. I've been waiting a lifetime for this."

"Your lifetime is over," Horace stated.

Cutter eyed Horace and said, "We'll see, spear chucker." Sweat ran down from the corner of his eyebrow. "Let's discuss the terms of the duel. Death. Mercy. Yield."

"Why not make it to the death?" Abraham asked as he pulled his sword free from its deteriorating scabbard.

"I want you to beg for mercy. I want you to yield from fear," Cutter said as he narrowed his eyes on Abraham. "I want all of my men to see it. Your men to see it. For death is the easy way out. Even though, most likely, I will kill you."

"And when I kill you, your men will stand down? Sticks, Horace, and I go free."

Cutter raised one hand and said, "You have my word as the Commander of the Black Squadron. Tomas will see it through."

Tomas nodded.

Cutter moved by Abraham and Horace. He made his way past the head-high ash piles toward the center of the chamber, where no piles sat. A thirty-foot-wide ring of black stone lay in the floor, partially covered in ash. He stepped to the middle.

Abraham moved inside the ring.

The Black Squadron members stepped onto the black line,

enclosing the swordsmen in the middle. Horace stood among those men, arms crossed with the butt of his spear on the floor.

On the opposite side of the ring from Horace stood Sticks, her knees wobbling and her chin sagging into her chest.

Abraham faced off with Cutter, ten feet between them. He rested Black Bane on his shoulder. "I want more than our freedom after I win."

"Oh, and what might that be?" Cutter said.

"I want to know what Big Apple and Lord Hawk are planning. I want to know where they went to."

"We are not their handmaidens. We are soldiers of Hancha. That is who we serve."

"I know better than that."

Cutter shrugged his mountainous shoulders. He was a huge man, much like the current Guardian Commander, Pratt. He waved a hand. "Fine, I'll agree, but only because it won't come to that. Are you finished delaying, Slade the Blade? I'm ready to fight. I've been planning this day for all of my life."

Abraham nodded and sized Cutter up as he did so. Cutter tended to put his weight on his left foot. His arms were long, and his bastard sword had a couple more inches than Black Bane. No doubt the swordsman would use his length as his strength. The question was how quick he was with his steel.

Abraham had yet to see the man fight. But he reminded Abraham of the large pirate, Flamebeard, who was a reputed swordsman and whom Abraham had cut down with a few strokes. The problem was Abraham didn't feel anything. He was flat. Seeing Sticks gave him fire, but he soon cooled. His body ached. He remembered having to pitch a game when he had the flu. That was how he felt now. Sick. Tired. Drained.

He glanced at Sticks. She gave him a dull stare. He turned to Horace, who gave him a nod.

Cutter spread his feet out and got into a sword-fighting stance.

He held his sword in two hands, low, and in the plow guard position. He set his gaze on Abraham. His nostrils started to flare. "Are you ready for your final duel, Ruger Slade?"

Abraham got into the same ox guard position and faced the bigger and longer man. The leather on Black Bane's handle squeezed in his gripping hands. He locked eyes on Cutter, gave him a nod, and said, "Death before failure."

67

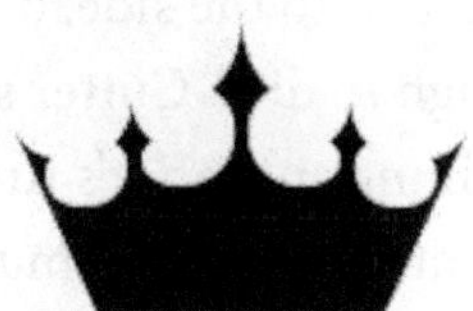

Cutter lunged.

Ruger parried.

Steel kissed steel with a clang.

The Black Squadron let out a wild cry.

"Kill him, Commander!" they chanted. "Spill his bowels on the deck!"

Abraham backpedaled and parried. Cutter's hard flashing strikes jolted his arms and up into his shoulders. He was in a fight —a fight for his life. Cutter was good. Very good.

"You're an excellent defender!" Cutter said as he lunged forward, his sword licking at Abraham's eyes. "But do you know how to fight?"

Abraham kept his lips sealed and breathed through the nose. He had to focus. One miscalculation might cost him his life. He circled away from Cutter's strikes and parried with the tip of his sword.

"Ha! You are weak, Ruger Slade. I always knew it!" Cutter put more shoulder into his swings. His bastard sword crashed into Black Bane with resounding effect. "Swing, man! Swing!"

Cutter's men let out raucous cries and jeers. Their leader was wearing down the greatest swordsman in the world.

Abraham parried with taxed limbs. He backpedaled from the fierce strikes. Fending off the expert swordsman took everything he had. His arms burned. He could see the moves coming before they happened, but his body could barely react to them. Fleece had really drained him. It was worse than he'd thought. *Come on, Ruger. You have to do this!* He jumped to the side, out of Cutter's reach.

"Stand still long enough to die!" Cutter said as he poked his sword forward like a striking snake. "It's time to put an end to you. You are an embarrassment. I expected a much better fight than this."

"And I expected better conversation," Abraham fired back. He countered a strike with a swing of his own. Metal crashed together.

Cutter blocked then unleashed a fatal swing at Abraham's neck.

Abraham crouched underneath the decapitating swing.

Cutter kicked him in the chest.

He fell on his backside. The soldiers let out victorious cries as Abraham scrambled away.

Cutter's sword bit into the stone, making sparks and just missing Abraham by inches.

Abraham swatted wildly at the bastard sword. He fought from his backside. He turned loose a desperate chop that forced Cutter backward. Abraham popped up to his feet. He braced his feet for Cutter's next charge. It didn't happen.

With his eyes fastened on Abraham, Cutter paced. He wiped a forearm across his mouth. "One swing. A weak one at that. I must tell you I am disappointed. Unless you are playing games with me. Is that the case? Hmm… a bit of possum."

With his head hung low, Abraham said, "No. You are far better than I expected."

"Kill him, Captain!" Horace said. "Quit toying with the bastard wielder!"

Abraham thought for certain that Ruger's vitality would have kicked in by then, but it hadn't happened. His chest heaved. Cutter was barely breathing heavily. Abraham licked his lips. He felt like a cat fighting against a wolf. He didn't have it.

He lifted his sword. "Let's finish this."

"Good! I want to hear you beg for mercy." Cutter came at him with his sword cocked back in the wrath guard position. He turned loose a swing with wroth force.

Abraham brought his sword up to block.

Clang!

Black Bane almost tore free from his grip. He staggered sideways.

Cutter pressed. He kept swinging, trying to chop Ruger Slade down like a tree.

It took everything Abraham had to bring his sword back up in time. He was losing. In seconds, it would be over with.

"Abraham! Fight!" Sticks shouted.

Something about the woman's words tapped the recesses of his mind. Abraham reached down deep and summoned his reserves, praying the tank wasn't empty. He braced himself for another blow. He took the full force of Cutter's swing on the edge of his sword. Steel scraped against steel. They locked up their crossguards.

Chest to chest, the men glared at one another. Cutter leaned down on him with eyes full of fury.

Abraham pushed back and said, "You ain't so tough. Is that all that you got?"

"No!" Cutter said. He gave a mighty shove that pushed Abraham into backpedaling. He flipped his sword around his body. "This is!" He charged.

The wild cries of the Black Guard renewed. Their loud voices echoed throughout the chamber.

Fight. Sticks's words echoed in his mind. *Fight!* His blood churned. He stared down Cutter and said, "You might be good, but you aren't no Conan."

"Who?" Cutter asked. He shrugged with a scowl and attacked. "Who cares!"

Abraham waited for Cutter to make his move. The bigger man rushed him with his sword in the high point position and lunged. Abraham turned his hip into his parry and batted the man aside. The fighters battled back and forth. Their swords clashed with the sharp ring of steel. Putting everything he had into his swings, Abraham attacked.

Within moments, both men were frothing at the mouth. Like two heavyweight fighters, they pounded at each other blow for blow. The swords rattled in their hilts. They struck like snakes. Neither man gave ground as they shuffled back and forth.

Ruger's body came to life. Abraham felt hot blood flowing through him again. Black Bane warmed in his hands. He got it going. He anticipated Cutter's moves. His body responded in kind. He pressed the attack.

Cutter parried and backpedaled.

Abraham came at the man in a storm of steel. Clutching his sword in both hands, he started beating down Cutter's sword. "What's the matter? Are you tired of fighting?"

"Never!" Cutter bull-rushed Abraham sword first.

Their blades collided together and locked up.

"I'll beat you!" Cutter shouted.

Abraham looked up into the man's face and said, "No, you won't!" He shoved the larger man backward.

Cutter stumbled in the midst of backpedaling.

Abraham rushed the man and swung low. He took Cutter's right leg off at the knee.

Cutter screamed as he toppled to the ground like a tree. "Nooo!"

Abraham stood over Cutter, sword in hand, and said, "It's over. Tell me what I want."

Cutter's eyebrows knitted together, and he said, "Never. Black Squadron, kill them! Kill them all!"

68

───────

HORACE GORED TWO SOLDIERS AT ONCE WITH HIS SPEAR. IT
happened the instant the enemies whisked their swords out of
their scabbards.

Abraham caught the action out of the corner of his eyes as he
moved toward Sticks. Two soldiers pulled out daggers to plunge
into her gut. They weren't quick enough. Sticks appeared to be
magically free. Small knives were in both of her hands. She
stabbed both men in the neck. She snatched up her bandolier from
the dying man's body and dropped it over her shoulders. She took
the rope from her neck and slung it aside. She winked her one
good eye at Abraham and said, "You're too late to come to my
rescue."

Two attackers wielding short swords flanked Sticks. She
ducked underneath a swing and stabbed the man in the belly. Her
second attacker had the drop on her. His sword was raised and
was coming down on her head.

Abraham closed the distance in two giant strides and took the
man's head from his shoulders with one swipe of his sword. Blood

gushed from the neck as the dead man fell over. His head rolled over to Cutter.

Cutter picked the head up and threw it at Abraham. "May the Elders curse you!"

Horace rushed into a pile of ash and stirred it up with his spear.

"Good idea!" Abraham knew they were outnumbered ten to one, and taking them all on at once would be risky. "Dust it up, Sticks! Split up!"

Sticks dashed through a pile of ash, which exploded into a cloud of smoke. The soldiers chasing her slowed.

Abraham did the same thing. He jumped into the ashes and started kicking and swinging. In moments, he lost sight of his enemies, and they lost sight of him. They fumbled and muttered angrily in the dusty murk. Focusing on the creaking of leather rubbing against skin, Abraham found his mark. He thrust into the chest of a coughing man.

The dead man's final last word sputtered out. "Gah!"

More alarmed shouts followed.

Men groaned and cried out.

The Henchmen struck like thieves in the night. The Black Squadron were seasoned soldiers, but they were taken off guard by this attack. Their warped cries and death throes filled the room.

"Shut your holes, you fools! Shut up and think!" Commander Cutter shouted. "Be silent! Use your ears and listen! That is what they are doing to you! Idiots!"

More bodies fell in one notable thud after the other.

Abraham moved like a ghost. He sank Black Bane deep into at least ten men.

Blood mixed with ash. The floor became sticky with dust and gore. The battle raged on until the final enemy soldier fell silent.

The Black Squadron were no match for the Henchmen.

The dust settled.

Abraham, Horace, and Sticks surrounded Commander Cutter.

All of them were splattered with blood and covered in ash. They looked as though they'd climbed out of an incinerator.

Cutter had made a tourniquet by using his belt on his right thigh above the knee. Seated on the floor, he gripped his sword in both hands. "Come on, I'm still a fighting man!"

With a hard swipe of his sword, Abraham knocked Cutter's sword right out of his fingers. He gazed at the man's bloody stump. The dismembered leg lay nearby. "Yes, and you should keep on fighting. After all, it's only a minor flesh wound." He stuck the tip of his sword underneath Cutter's chin. "Don't make this difficult. Tell me where Big Apple is and what his plans are."

Cutter looked him dead in the eye and said, "No."

"You gave your word."

"To who? You? I gave my word to my men." Cutter scanned the room. "You killed all of them! Even Tomas! My finest man!"

"As I recall, you told them to kill us. What choice did we have?"

"You could have died," Cutter said with a shamed face. He spat. "You should have died. I was beating you. Only your sword makes you better. I should have made you trade the blade and made it an even fight."

"That didn't work in the tournament of swords, and it wouldn't have worked here." Abraham smacked the man's cheek with the flat of his blood-and-dust-caked sword. "Tell me, where are they?"

"What's the difference? You're going to kill me anyway," Cutter let out a ragged sigh. "Kill me. Without this leg, I have nothing to live for."

"Tell me where Big Apple is and what he is doing, and we'll stitch you up. We have a mystic," he offered.

"Can you put back the rest of them too?" Cutter surveyed the dead. "By the Elders, you slaughtered them. My men were better trained than that. I know it."

"Your men stink, and so do you," Horace said. "Let the dog die, Captain. He doesn't deserve any better. He's an enemy soldier that assaults the king. Our king! He deserves what is coming to him."

Abraham could see the desperation in Cutter's defeated eyes. "Sticks, notify the others. Bring Iris and Melris to me."

Sticks departed.

"Start talking, Cutter. Don't let this battle that you lost be the end of you. I can see that you don't want this to end. Isn't being able to fight again worth it?"

Cutter made a painful grimace. "Heh. You put my leg on, and you promise to fight me again with neutral swords."

Abraham glanced over his shoulder at Horace's disapproving frown, shrugged, and said, "Fair enough. Spill it."

"Spill what?" Cutter said.

"Tell me what you know about Big Apple. What are his plans? Where does he hide? All that you know."

"I will tell you this. Big Apple is not worried about you or the stones that you seek because he says you will never find them all. It is a waste of time. The Elders have them." Cutter spat again. "He only cares about controlling the otherworlders and what they can bring. He wants those strange weapons. King Hector cannot stand against them. He wants the King's Steel. The people on the other side want it."

"People on the other side of what?"

"The portal. I've seen them once. Fleece can open them. Sometimes, those artifacts fall out. Most of it is worthless junk, Big Apple says." Cutter turned green, and he yakked on the floor. "Ugh… losing your leg makes you feel awful."

Abraham's eyes brightened. If Big Apple could control the portals through Fleece, then the horned halfling could possibly figure out a way home. "But where is he?"

"Big Apple likes to travel, but he is not so far to find. He will hide among the Shell and the Sect. They have posts in every city on Titanuus. Someone always knows something." He poked his finger at Abraham. "That is where he is trying to build a permanent tunnel to the other world. They have a lair in the Spine. He sends workers to build there. They have been doing it for years. He says it will make gateways that will take them everywhere."

Abraham wasn't convinced that Cutter knew what he was talking about. Sweat beaded the man's clammy face, and he'd lost a lot of blood. He doubted Iris could put his leg back on, but they could stop the loss of blood, and the man could keep on living.

Cutter's eyelids fluttered.

Abraham tapped his face. "Where is Big Apple now? Tell me."

"He's says he's going back to the lair…" Cutter passed out.

He shook the man, asking, "Where is it? Where is it?"

Cutter was out cold.

69

ABRAHAM AND THE HENCHMEN TRAVELED BY BOAT UP THE LITTLE
Vein river toward the Wound. Melris insisted that they get back on
course. Abraham didn't put up much of an argument. They were
under the king's orders, and he wasn't about to dare a side journey
into the Spine searching for Big Apple. He was exhausted. He
might have gotten enough fire back to beat Cutter, but he still
wasn't himself. His body was drained.

The wind filled the white sails of the galleon the company rode
on. All of them were on the main deck of the big river boat. The
sun shone in the sky. Making it to the Wound would take at least a
few days.

Horace and Iris had a group gathered around them. They were
clucking on about the battle with the Black Squadron. Iris wasn't
there, but she, with the help of Melris, had put Commander
Cutter's leg back on. They just put it on backward.

Abraham called Horace out on the cruel gesture.

In his defense, Horace said, "You only said to put it on, not how
to put it on, Captain. He didn't deserve better either. We should
have killed him. That snake will only strike again. He's a Hanchan.

Let me be an example of what happens when you cross the King's Henchmen."

"That's my call, not yours," Abraham said. "Perhaps I'll leave someone else in charge next time."

He had left Horace in disgust. Tormenting people wasn't his way, but perhaps Horace was right. Cutter should have died. He was evil and wouldn't bat an eye over killing somebody. He'd broken his word too. Payback had come, an eye for an eye and a tooth for a tooth.

He sat on the railing, watching the tree line as they sailed past. The winds rustled his matted hair. As refreshing as it had been, he still felt like crap. A shadow fell over his shoulder. Solomon joined him.

"Do you feel like talking?" asked the former hippie turned troglin.

"Do I look like I feel like talking?" he asked.

"You look like you'd rather be dead."

"Heh, you got that right." Abraham looked back at his company. "Let's head to the bow and have some privacy. We have a lot to talk about."

Solomon raised his eyebrows, started walking, and said, "I hope it's good news."

"Yeah, well, I've been to Pittsburgh." Abraham settled himself on the ship's bow and filled Solomon in on all the details of meeting up with Mandi, his encounter with Eugene Drisk, and Sid and John Smoke.

Solomon was all ears and hung on every word. "That's quite a story. More like a modern-day fairy tale." He rubbed his face with one big paw of a hand. "I envy you. I'd do anything to see home again. I wonder who I swapped souls with?"

"My guess is that we will find those answers in that secret Facility 117. I think they are there. At least, that is what Eugene Drisk alluded too." With his hand on the lines, he said, "I really think we are getting closer to figuring this out. The parties are working at it on both ends. They are bound to figure it out."

Solomon closed his eyes, shook his head, and said, "I really need to wrap my head around this. It sounds like an acid trip. Go back to the part about people wanting to come to this world. I don't understand that. Why would anyone want to come here?" He raised his voice. "They don't even have air conditioning!"

Abraham let out a weak chuckle. With the wind in his face, he said, "I know, this is as good as it gets. I think there are a lot of miserable souls in our world that think they would be better off in this world. They are using the portals to move their souls from one body to another. I believe that they believe that they can create a new paradise."

"What are they trying to do, create a permanent Woodstock? I was there, you know, and I had my fun, but man, I can't do that every day. Troglin or not." Solomon toyed with the end of a coil of rope lying by his side. He swung the short end like a lasso. "Do you really think we are getting closer to figuring all of this out? You don't still think it's a dream, do you?"

"Nah. I know that all of this is out of the norm, but anything can happen once we put our minds to it. That's the scary thing about us. But unlike you, I don't think that Titanuus is so bad. I kinda like it."

"Well, you aren't a troglin. Perhaps I'd like it better if I was only me." Solomon curled the rope over his neck and shoulders. "But I enjoy the modern-day pleasantries."

"Back home has changed a lot since you were there. We have portable phones the size of an index card that you can do all kinds of things on."

"It sounds like something from *Star Trek*."

"It's more advanced in some ways, but we haven't conquered space travel."

"We haven't colonized the moon?"

"No, we haven't even been back. A lot of people don't even believe that we were there to begin with. They think the government lied to us. There's a bunch of videos on YouTube about it."

"YouTube?"

Abraham cracked a smile. "It's another thing from the internet. Ah man, when we get you back, you might freak out. I tell you, I got tired of all of the commotion back home. I think that's why I like the simplicity of this world." He cast his gaze toward the mountains on the distant horizon. "It's quiet. It's peaceful. Natural. Back home is a mess."

"Even so, I'd like to see it. I have family that I miss." Looking sad, Solomon turned his head away. "They probably have me locked up like some sort of animal back home. I'm probably foaming at the mouth right now."

Abraham felt strongly that Facility 117 might be the place where otherworlders like Solomon or the troglin whom he now hosted might be kept. The building had a cold creepiness that had seeped into his bones when he was there. He thought about Dr. Jack Lassiter. *That man seemed to be behind it all. I need to get my hands wrapped around that man's throat and squeeze the truth out of him.*

"Keep your chin up, Solomon," he said. "You have to have hope. I can't say for sure, but my gut tells me there is a reason why I am here."

Solomon turned his head slightly and said, "Really, and what might that be?"

"I think I'm supposed to close the portals. I think that is why I go back from this body to that one. I have to work both sides. I don't know why it's me, but so far, I'm the only one that can do it. Does that sound like a crazy theory?"

"No. I've never had faith in a lot of things, but I have faith in you, Abraham. I hope that you can lead me back to my promised land."

As he rubbed the back of his head, Abraham said, "Oh man, that's deep."

Solomon lay down and rested his big troglin head on the coil of rope. He closed his eyes and said, "I've spent enough time in this wilderness. Take me home."

70

Days later, the Henchmen disembarked from the riverboat. They sold their horses and wagon in Junction City and traveled on foot. Melris led the way through the harsh terrain, rocky and full of sparse shrubbery. Nothing creeped or crawled over the bitter land leading toward the Wound. The farther they traveled, the more barren it became in the rugged outback climate.

Per usual, Dominga and Tark scouted ahead.

Abraham walked with Horace, Sticks, and Melris.

Bearclaw and Vern trailed behind them, followed by Iris, Shades, and Cudgel, then Solomon and the Red Tunics, Skitts and Zann, with Apollo and Prospero bringing up the rear. All of them carried heavy packs on their shoulders, along with quivers of bolts and crossbows.

Sticks switched her assault rifle from one shoulder to another. The swelling in her face was down, and her bruised eye was half open.

All of them were sweating like pigs in the intense heat of day, except for Melris. His soft skin appeared as cool as a cucumber.

Step by step, the company moved up one rocky rise after

another. The ground shifted underfoot. Broken bits of black shale were everywhere. They walked from morning until night and set up camp underneath a crag that shadowed them from the moonlight.

No tents were set, but campfires were made. Strips of dried beef and bread called sun cakes were quietly consumed.

Horace scheduled the watch. Everyone else rolled out their bedrolls and hunkered down for the night.

Abraham stared into the fire. Sticks, Horace, and Melris were with him.

He wet his thirst with a long drink of water, handed it over to Sticks, and said, "Melris, we haven't talked much about the Wound. What should we be expecting?"

"You should expect that not all of us will make it," Melris replied coolly. His spacey eyes were fixed on the flames. "It is a place of death. It rots with decay. It leads into the very bowels of Titanuus. Vermin still feast on his innards to this day."

Abraham picked up a handful of dirt, let it cascade through his fingers, and said, "Are you telling me that there is flesh and bones beneath this rock?"

"Absolutely. Much of it is petrified, but there is still succulent marrow deep inside his bones." Melris gave Abraham a long look. "It would be very beneficial if you could summon your dragon. We will need the assistance."

Abraham leaned forward and said, "My dragon? You mean Simon, who almost killed you?"

"Yes."

"I can't summon him. He just came. And you attacked him."

"That was a misunderstanding on my part," Melris replied. "I didn't realize that you had acquired such a powerful ally. We will need it, for the dangers are great inside the Wound."

"And how do you know that the stones are even in there?"

"I don't."

Abraham's jaw hung open.

Horace made a throaty gasp.

Sticks scraped her knife over a round stone.

"Are you telling me that I'm going to risk my Henchmen pursuing a bunch of magic stones that might not even be there?" He dusted off his hands. "I don't think so."

"You don't have a choice. It is the king's orders," Melris said in his strangely youthful, cryptic manner. "The fate of the entire world lies in the hands of a few men. You should feel honored."

"I'll tell you how I feel. I feel stupid." He kicked the dirt, shook his head, and said, "I'm going to bed." He pinched the bridge of his nose and squinted his eyes. "Where's the Tylenol?" He stormed off.

71

ABRAHAM HAD HAD A RESTLESS SLEEP ON THE HARD GROUND.
Sleeping in a breastplate only made it worse. Typically, he had his tent set up and enjoyed the soft pleasures within. One of those pleasures was Sticks. She would curl up in his arms, and he would sleep like a baby. He'd slept alone the past night even though she'd slept nearby. She was up and gone now. He trailed behind the others, yawning.

On a good note, his headache was gone. He trudged along in the back with the Red Tunics, Apollo and Prospero. They didn't say much, and he didn't feel like talking. He'd hoped when he went to sleep the previous night that he would wake up back home. He wanted to be with Mandi and make sure she was okay. He also didn't like the fact that Melris had said some of his Henchmen would die.

"Summon my dragon," he muttered. "He's not even a dragon. What am I supposed to do, whistle?"

Apollo gave him a funny look. Prospero strutted on, eyes forward, arms swinging. Both of the older, durable men wore their crossed swords over their backs. They must have been the oldest in the group. They had tufts of gray in their ginger-brown hair.

Skitts cast a sheepish look over his shoulder at Abraham. The stalwart young man carried a pack fit for three men on his shoulders. His brother Zann carried the same.

Both brothers were likeable in their own ways. *I don't want to see them die. I don't want any one of them to die.*

According to Prince Lewis, over one hundred Henchmen had died over the past several years. Most of that was thanks to Raschel, the assassin. Eugene Drisk had played a hand in that too, as did Lewis and Leodor. Eugene had treated the Henchmen like sacrificial lambs to save himself, a cowardly thing to do.

That's what soldiers do. They die for their country and what they believe in. It's the same with our veterans back home. All gave some—some gave all.

"Pardon me asking, Captain," Apollo said in his scratchy voice, "but why are you lingering with us? You should be in the front, leading. Are you squabbling with Sticks? I can see that, the dry tart that she is."

"No. There comes a point when you start dreading the mission. Facing the unknown. Don't you get tired of it?" he asked.

"I don't have a choice." Apollo winked at Abraham. "You don't either. I don't think about it. I move forward. It's the only way to end whatever it is that we are ending. I'll see it through until they run me through."

"Tell me more about the old me, the real Ruger. You knew him a long time?" he asked.

Apollo nodded. "I'd been a Guardian for a long time before Ruger came. I wasn't cut out for leadership. I was good for following orders, though. I'm a natural with a sword too, though not as quick as I used to be. A hair slower but"—he tapped his noggin—"quicker up here. Ruger is a natural leader. The best.

Fearless. Determined. He's a rock. You fill his boots well. You'd fit them better if you didn't doubt. He never doubted. He just did."

The older warrior's scratchy words lit a fire underneath Abraham. He pulled his shoulders back and said, "Thanks for the chat."

"Any time. If it's any consolation, you're a lot more fun than the old Ruger. He's all business. You're fun."

Abraham nodded. He caught up to Skitts and Zann, who walked with shovels in hand, and said, "Good morning, men. Are you ready to face death today?"

"Feels like my back has tasted death already," Zann groaned. The pack he carried was half as big as him. "It's burning like it's in the netherworld."

Abraham slapped Zann's oversized pack. "Good. Feeling means you're breathing. Shout if you need a break."

The broadly built Skitts said, "I can walk with my pack all day." He shot a glare at his brother. "We won't need a break. Death before failure."

"Yeah, my death is going to be your failure. Because you're going to be carrying my pack." Zann spat. "You can't carry the both of them."

Abraham chuckled and moved on. Something about Apollo's words had gotten a light shining in him. He made his way toward the front of the ranks. He made light conversation with Iris, Cudgel, Bearclaw, Vern, and Solomon. He even cracked a few locker-room jokes that drew forth some chortling laughter. He kept the routine up for hours.

Finally, he made his way back up to Sticks, Horace, and Melris. They all gave him concerned looks.

Horace said, "Do you fare well, Captain?"

Abraham patted his sword grip and said, "I never felt better. Why?"

"Because you are acting crazy," Sticks said flatly.

"Maybe? There's no maybe about it." He looked at her with wild eyes. "I am crazy."

72

THE SUN SET IN THE WEST, BEHIND THE GREAT MOUNTAINS OF THE Spine. The Spine's shadows swallowed the valley's. North of the Henchmen's position, miles away, were pinnacles of rock, mashed together in a leagues-long wall. Tiny flocks of birds swooped in and out of the rocky crevices and nestled in the high nooks and shelving. The wall was a foreboding monument weathered and tested by time.

"Welcome to the Wound," Melris said.

The Henchmen stood on a rocky hill, gazing side by side at the great wonder of the wall around the Wound. It stood over seventy feet high and was nothing short of captivating. The wall was steep at the base, angling up at a sheer but climbable pitch. Tower pillars of rock merged together around the top. At the base of the walls were clay huts with straw roofs that appeared tiny from the distance.

Abraham wet his parched lips with a drink from his water skin and asked, "Why does it have a wall around it? I thought it would be a gaping hole, like a canyon."

"Those are the scars and scabs of the wound. It is crusted over by time. There is a canyon on the other side of the wall. A deep one." Melris started forward. "Come. The journey begins."

Abraham caught Melris by a shoulder and asked, "What about the people in those huts? Aren't they the Wild Men from the Wound? They are quite vicious." Abraham recollected his encounter with the savage men, who prowled like a wild pack of dogs. He'd battled them in the Tournament of Swords at Pirate's Harbor, and they'd nearly killed him. "I don't think they will allow us to waltz through their… well, territory."

"True," Melris replied quietly. "We will have to do our best to avoid them."

"And if we don't?" Abraham asked.

"We will have to fight them and kill them."

Abraham scanned the small village outside the wall. Hundreds of huts were scattered along the wall's threshold. A pit formed in his stomach.

Horace practically stood on Abraham's toes and said, "I'd wager those savages stuff a family of ten to twenty in those huts." He laid a heavy hand on Abraham's shoulder. "We can kill them."

"No, we aren't going to kill anybody if we don't have to. Melris, it's time that you earned your salt on this mission. If there is a way of avoiding them, then you do that."

Melris shrugged his thin, pale eyebrows and said, "I can manage a diversion, but it is best that I save my magic. Have you summoned your dragon?"

"He's not a dragon. He's a Fenix."

"I think he's a dragon," Shades chimed in.

"He's dragon spawn. He might not look like a dragon, but he is still a dragon." Melris started walking east and held a finger up. "We are downwind. That should help. Summon your dragon."

Dominga and Tark approached and gave Abraham impatient

looks. Dominga was drumming her fingers on her hips. Tark's smoky eyes were wide.

Abraham nodded.

Dominga and Tark took off down the slope, running like a pair of deer. They ran silently through the dry bush and vanished over the next rise.

"Don't worry about it. I can help if he can't," Iris said. The mystic was twitching her fingers, the nails glowing with rosy light. "I'll be able to conceal our location if need be, but we need to stay close together." She gave him a funny look. "We've done this before, you know."

"Of course we have," he said as he followed after Melris, who was on the move.

The Henchmen ran missions that took them in and out of many dangerous places. They were used to it. They were prepared. He should have known better.

He looked back at the company and said, "Transformers… Let's roll."

Dusk settled as the company started their miles-long trek toward the Wound. Tark and Dominga led the tight-knit group into a very steep and wide dry gulch that snaked its way toward the wall. The gulch was thirty feet deep and over twenty feet wide. Dry bushes and old branches and logs filled the lengthy washout. A tiny stream of water, only a few inches wide, trickled through the winding channel.

Dominga raised a fist and stopped. Tark moved along the top of the gulch, keeping his eyes toward the villages on the west side. He came to a stop as well. His eyes were big as he pointed down and ahead.

Abraham couldn't see past the next bend. On cat's feet, he caught up with Dominga, who was peeking around a mud-covered boulder. She pointed also.

A large group of Wild Men were hunched over a pool of water. Using their big hands like cups, they drank, washed, and splashed one another.

Blazing Saddles!

Abraham eyeballed a score of the wiry men, built like gorillas and moving about like dogs. They had bestial faces, flat noses, huge nostrils, and pale skin covered in a thin layer of hair. They grunted and barked at one another. He motioned toward Iris.

Iris crept forward with a sheepish look on her face and followed Abraham's stare. Her eyes grew. Without actually saying a word aloud, she said, "I have an idea. It will take a few minutes."

"What?" he mouthed back.

She flicked her fingers out and said, "Don't worry." She nodded at Horace and tiptoed toward him to whisper in the bearded man's ear.

Horace motioned to Cudgel, Bearclaw, and Vern. The three men huddled around Iris. She vanished among their big bodies.

Abraham perked his ears. He could barely make out the sound of her arcane mutterings, which were muffled by the men. He sought out the faces of the rest of the group and held out a hand so they would hold.

Solomon, Apollo, Prospero, and the Red Tunics froze in their positions.

Abraham locked eyes with Tark at the top of the gulch. The ebony warrior glistened with sweat. His athletic body hunkered down in the rocks.

Tark nodded at Abraham.

Abraham nodded back.

The loose rocks underneath Tark's foot gave way. Small stones tumbled down into the gulch.

The heads of the Wild Men of the Wound popped up. They sniffed and snorted loudly. Their big eyes peered about. Two of them scurried up the gulch and made a beeline for Tark.

Abraham lost sight of the Wild Men scrambling silently up the hill.

A crossbow fired. *Clatch-zip!*

A Wild Man howled.

Holy sheetrock!

73

A loud barking sound arose from the savages. "Haroot! Haroot! Haroot! Haroot!"

"Captain, here!" Iris tossed something to Abraham.

He snatched it out of the air. It looked like a potato that had been dug out of the ground. Abraham gave Iris a blank look and shrugged. "What do I do with it?"

"Throw it at those mongrels and hold your nose," she said. "It's a stench bomb."

He stepped around the bend in the gulch. The Wild Men were beating their chests and howling. They started to climb up the gulch after Tark.

"Hey, dog face!" Abraham shouted.

The dog-faced savages froze. Their ears bent behind their heads. They turned their beady hound eyes on Abraham. He took aim and lofted a perfect throw into the center of the pack.

"Fetch!"

The Wild Men watched the potatolike projectile land in their midst and explode in a cloud of inky steam. The stench cloud enveloped all the apish men and continued to fill the gulch. The

Wild Men's eyes puffed up like balloons. They coughed, hacked, and yelped. On all fours, the whimpering savages scrambled up the wall of the gulch and out.

"A stench bomb?" Abraham said.

Just as he finished, Tark raced down the side of the gulch. He had a crossbow in one hand and his sword in another. Wet blood dripped from his blade.

"How many did you get?" Abraham asked.

"Three," Tark said. "The good news is spreading fast. Listen."

A strange barking carried across the plains. "Haroot! Haroot! Haroot!" Some of the voices were distant. The others were farther away. The Wild Men were communicating.

"So much for going into the Wound unannounced," Abraham said. He watched the heads of the Wild Men peeking over the top of the gulch and down at them. "We need to get to the wall… now."

"Into the stench! They won't come near it. That's why I cast it." Iris pinched her nose and took him by the hand. "Where we go, the stink goes."

Abraham drifted into the stinking cloud while still holding hands with Iris. He immediately started to retch but somehow held it back. The sour skunk stink burned his nostrils and gagged his throat. His eyes watered.

This is horrid. Sewer gas isn't this bad. He had a vision of Cousin Randy emptying his mobile home in the movie *Christmas Vacation.* He gagged. *I can't do this.*

The Henchmen churned ahead, racing down the gulch and holding their breath. Wherever Iris went, the cloud went.

Abraham released her hand and increased his stride. He had to get clear of the foulness. He'd rather fight one hundred Wild Men than spend another second in the putrid, stomach-turning smell. He lengthened his stride and moved ahead of the company. With the wind whistling by his ears, he moved out of the midst and gasped for fresh air.

Sticks burst free behind him, followed by Dominga and Tark. Pinching her nose, Dominga said, "Worst plan ever!"

Tark pointed ahead. "The wall!"

Just over one hundred yards away loomed the naturally formed wall. A wide set of rough-hewn steps carved out of the rock zigzagged upward. Hulking forms of men bulging with muscles were nested on their stairs. They howled and beat their chests wildly.

Abraham pulled his sword free of its scabbard. "I don't care. I'm killing them."

The Henchmen and the stench cloud gathered at the bottom of the steps. The Wild Men pelted them with rocks.

Solomon burst ahead, climbing the rock wall like a monkey. "I can't take the stink any longer! Gangway!" His big paws and feet raced up the wall. A rock hit him full in the chest. He shrugged it off, bore down on a Wild Man, grabbed his head of hair, and flung him off the wall.

One by one, the Henchmen emerged from the stinking cloud. They coughed and hacked their way up the stairs as the cloud hovered beneath them.

Standing on the rim of the gulch, the Wild Men continued to hurl fist-sized rocks at them. A few of them flung crude spears. One such spear zinged toward Shades's head. He snatched it out of the air, flipped it around, and flung it back. It impaled a Wild Man in the chest.

"Bull's-eyes!" he yelled.

"It's *bull's-eye!*" Bearclaw said. The wild-haired man snatched up a hunk of stone and hurled it back. He missed the attacker he was aiming for, who ducked underneath the rock. The rock hit the Wild Man behind him in the crotch. "That's a bull's-eye!"

Abraham led the charge up the steps. The Wild Men hidden in the rocks came at him from both sides and above. He ducked flying rocks, caught one in the chest, and sliced off clutching hands and fingers.

Horace forced himself up to Abraham's position and gored a jumping Wild Man in the heart with his spear. He used the attacker's momentum to fling him farther down the hillside. "Kill them all, Captain! Kill them all!"

Step by step, the Henchmen slowly battled their way up the zigzagging steps. Above them, the Wild Men's ranks were thinning. Below them, the group let out throaty howls. They slavered, hurled, and hooted. Fewer than a score of them were left. The stink cloud kept them at bay, but it was dissipating.

From the highest position, Solomon bashed a Wild Man's head into the rocks and pushed the attacker aside. With a gaze outward, he said, "Abraham!" and pointed east toward the villages. "Someone's going to crash our party!"

Abraham chopped off a man's head and whipped his head around. Scores of Wild Men were running on two feet and others on all fours, racing toward the gulch. They left a trail of galloping dust behind them. For men, they moved at alarming speed. They would arrive within the minute.

"Let's get a move on!" Abraham yelled.

Without warning, the cluster of Wild Men gathered at the rim of the gulch burst through the fading stench cloud. They bounded up the twisting stairs like a wild pack of dogs.

Skitts and Zann fired their crossbows into the oncoming swarm then backed behind Apollo and Prospero to reload. Apollo and Prospero's swords glinted in the day's fading light and came down in lightning-quick chops. The brutes' thick skulls were no match for the razor-sharp steel, which split their heads open like melons.

Cudgel bounded down the steps. He swung his mighty mace into the ribs of a blood-hungry attacker. A loud crack of ribs busting was followed by the elated battle cry of the smoky-eyed warrior. "Taste my thunder!"

The Henchmen skirmished in heated battle along the stairwell. The Wild Men kept coming, fearless and savage. They fought with their huge fists, sharp fingernails, and rocks.

Vern caught a fist in the face a split second before he cut a man's belly open. His second weapon hand, filled with a dagger, gouged out a neck.

Bearclaw's double-bladed axe rose and fell, gore dripping from both sides.

The Wild Men of the Wound were falling, but they weren't falling fast enough.

"Faster!" Abrahams said. "Fight faster!"

"You heard the Captain. Kill them faster!" Horace bellowed.

The Wild Man horde closed the gap. Like the last sands of an hourglass, the void was filled with muscular bodies, heaving and howling, running with ferocious hunger. With blood in their eyes, the attackers surged across the gulch and up the stairs.

Abraham took a final quick glance above. At the top of the wall, fifty feet away, was a gap that could be defended. He needed to get his men there now. Waving his sword, he said, "Take the high ground! Take the high ground now!"

Twenty feet below him, the Henchmen at the bottom of the ranks were fighting their guts out. The new swarm of Wild Men came up the rocky precipice like an angry tidal wave. The knot of surging bodies consumed them. The Henchmen started to fall.

Sticks was near Abraham when she gasped.

Horace started charging down the stairs.

Iris flung hornets of fire from her fingertips.

Melris stood quietly among the chaos, observing. He made his way toward the top and passed Abraham.

Abraham grabbed him by the robes and yelled, "What are you doing? Get down there and fight those things!"

"I need to save my energy. I'll meet you at the top." Melris slipped Abraham's grasp as if he were a ghost. "You can handle it."

Momentarily slack-jawed, Abraham said to Sticks and Shades, "Go with him!"

"What are you going to do?" Sticks asked. "We can't beat all of them."

Abraham looked upon the tide of hulks overrunning his men. His heart pounded like a mallet in his chest. His blood rushed in his ears. He set his volcanic gaze on the enemy and shouted at the top of his lungs, "Henchmen!" He jumped onto the side of the steep mountain wall, ran down the slant, and dove sword first into the churning fray. "Cut loose the chaos!"

74

Abraham plunged into the fray. Carnage. The Wild Men flung themselves fearlessly at the Henchmen. The Henchmen hewed them down with precision.

The Wild Men weren't the skilled fighters that the Henchmen were. They lost limbs but kept coming.

"Wall them off! Wall them off!" Abraham shouted. Black Bane became a living weapon in his hand. Stab. Thrust. *Glitch.*

The Henchmen in shirts of chain-mail armor formed a shell around the lesser-armed men. Iris was in the middle of the knot, flinging wild fiery hornets into the sky. Dominga helped the Red Tunics load crossbows and fired from close range.

The bodies started to pile up. The Henchmen rose valiantly on the bodies of the slain.

Abraham whisked out a dagger and launched a two-handed attack. He twisted his dagger in a hound-hulk's belly. Black Bane split open the face of another.

The relentless Wild Men collapsed on them. They hurled their big bodies into the Henchmen's rigid ranks. The sheer weight of numbers began to overwhelm them.

A Wild Man caught hold of Skitts by the hair and yanked him out of the ranks.

Vern chopped the Wild Man's arm off at the elbow, freeing Skitts.

With a crossbow bolt, Dominga shot a Wild Man in the face, who was about to clobber Vern in the head with a rock.

"Thanks, gorgeous," Vern said with a wink.

Horace started half chanting and half singing, "Kill them. Kill them all. Kill them. Kill them all." He sang it in rhythm as he thrust his sword into one hard body after the other. "Kill them. Kill them all!"

The sea of the enemy continued to rise. Abraham couldn't see an end to it. The harder they fought, the more Wild Men kept coming. He whittled down two more men to bloody stumps when a wave of savages tackled him.

The Wild Men had him on the ground. One bit his leg, and the other locked his fingers around his neck and started beating his head into the ground.

Abraham wriggled against their fierce clutches. The enemy had him pinned down, beating, biting, and choking him. *Must! Get! Free!* A hard kick slammed into his face from a third attacker that jumped into the melee.

A red dot appeared on the kicking attacker's head. Suddenly, the back of his skull blew open. As the dead body stumbled backward and fell, another bullet turned the head of the man choking Abraham into a canoe. He sat up instantly and rammed his dagger into the earhole of the Wild Man biting his legs. He rolled to his feet and glanced up the stairs.

Sticks was nestled in the rocks, aiming her assault rifle at the battle raging below. The glow of a laser dot gleamed on the black rifle. The muzzle of the weapon flashed. Bullets tore through the enemies' skulls. One Wild Man fell right after the other.

The Henchmen surged and hacked back the attackers.

A loud barking could be heard over the clamor of battle.

"Haaaroooot! Haaaroooot!"

The Wild Men scurried back out of striking distance.

Sticks stopped firing.

The Wild Men started up in a chorus of their chant barks. "Haroot! Haroot! Haroot! Haroot!"

Down in the gulch, a giant imposing figure made his way through the winding channel. He was a Wild Man, walking on his feet and knuckles, standing eight feet tall at the shoulder. He had a beastly face, bulging biceps, and corded neck muscles. A furry loincloth dressed his hips. He came up through the ranks with his massive head tilted and moving with a primordial gait.

"Haroot! Haroot! Haroot! Haroot! Haroot!" the smaller Wild Men chanted.

A red dot appeared on the giant's head.

Sticks locked her sights on the huge man.

Abraham looked up at her and said, "Do it!"

A crack of gunfire echoed over the valley.

The giant Wild Man's head snapped slightly back.

The chanting stopped.

Blood trickled down the giant Wild Man's forehead and over the bridge of his nose. He wiped the fresh blood on his lengthy fingers. He tasted the blood. Shrugging his hairy black unibrow, the monstrous man said in a throaty voice, "My blood tastes good, but your blood is much sweeter."

Sticks put the laser dot on the giant's eyeball.

The giant blocked the beam with his hand. "Don't be foolish. I am Haroot. Your powerful sling bullet cannot harm me. My skin is steel, my bones granite." He lowered his hand and stared right at the laser. "Try me."

A bullet blasted into Haroot's eyeball. Juice spat out. The white of his eye cracked with red.

Haroot tossed his head back and laughed. He rose to his full ten feet in height. He scanned the Henchmen, who were huddled together on the steps. "Which one of you wants to fight me?" He pointed at Solomon. "How about you, hairy one? I have not eaten a troglin in a long time."

Solomon crouched behind an outcropping of rock and said, "I'll wait and see how you fare against the others."

"I'll fight you!" Horace stormed forward. "I've killed giants before, and I'll kill them again, you big-eared fool!"

"Ah, a fat rodent. I like it." Haroot rubbed his jutting chin. He opened his mouth, revealing rows of slavering canine teeth. "Come, fight me, beat me, and you'll be free to pass into the Wound."

"Hold off, Horace." Abraham made his way down the steps and stood alongside the beefy man. "You won't fight him. You'll fight me. I win, you leave, but I'll give you a choice. You can let us pass now, or you will very well die. I've never lost a fight."

"Ho ho. You are a flea. I am a god. We are the guardians of the pass. No one has entered in my lifetime, and no one shall enter now." He wiped the saliva dripping from his jaws. "I assure you. I am Haroot. I am never wrong. My skin cannot be destroyed." The blood on his head started to dry. The skin over the bullet wound healed to a small bump. His red eye cleared. "But your skin…" He leaned forward. "I will peel it like a grape."

Abraham flipped his sword around. "We'll see about that." He lifted his sword over his head into the high guard stance. "Let's have at it, then."

Haroot nodded. "Good. I hunger." He turned his shoulders away and instantly unleashed a backhanded swing.

Abraham jumped backward and chopped off the knuckles of Haroot's fist.

The snarling giant lowered his brawny shoulders and charged like a dog.

Standing his ground, Abraham delivered a deep chop into the

meat of Haroot's neck and shoulder. Haroot let out an ear-busting howl as he trampled over Abraham.

The two men rolled through the dust in a tangle of muscular limbs.

"You hurt Haroot!" the giant said. "You will pay!" He snapped at Abraham's ear. "I will eat your head."

Abraham twisted out from underneath the much larger man and sprinted back to his feet.

Haroot chased him down and slammed him into the gulch's winding wall. The men locked up.

With a dagger in his hand, he started punching holes between Haroot's ribs. The giant's efforts to crush Abraham didn't slow.

"You might hurt me, but you cannot kill me!" Haroot continued to slam Abraham into the wall.

Fighting to keep his grip on his sword and dagger, he head-butted Haroot in the nose. Bright spots exploded in his eyes.

Haroot coughed a wicked laugh.

Horace called out, "Good fighting, Captain."

The giant put Abraham in a headlock with one arm and started beating him in the chest with his other fist. "Now you die! Soon I eat!"

Haroot's powerful punches rattled Abraham's bones. His jaws clacked together. Only the King's Armor saved his bones from being broken into a dozen pieces. The recesses of his mind were calling out to him. Ruger's body mixed with his mind, shouting, "Fight, Abraham! Fight!" He reached down into his reserves and summoned Ruger's great natural strength. In a desperate lunge, he wedged his dagger inside Haroot's mouth.

Haroot's mouth clenched. His eyes crossed. He released Abraham from his crushing grip and staggered back. He reached inside his mouth, pulled the dagger out, and flicked it away. He spat blood. "You fight dirty."

With his eyebrows knitting together, Abraham gripped Black

Bane in both hands and said, "You haven't seen nothing yet." He instantly visualized what he needed to do to the giant fearsome warrior. He'd found his second wind. Blood coursed through his veins like fire. "Let's dance, hairy pants."

Haroot charged.

Abraham sidestepped and chopped an outstretched hand off at the wrist. He dashed behind Haroot and cut the tendons behind his knees.

The giant dropped.

Abraham twisted his hips into the final swing. Black Bane sliced Haroot's head clean from his shoulders. Warm blood spat. The massive man toppled over.

The chanting of the Wild Men fell silent.

Abraham picked up Haroot's head by the hair and held it high for all to see. "Haroot this!" He spiked the head in the dirt with all his might. "Yaaah!"

The Wild Men from the Wound cleared out on all fours, whimpering like wounded wolves all the way home.

75

CATCHING HIS BREATH AS HE HEADED UP THE STAIRS, ABRAHAM SAID,
"Get a head count."

"Good fight, Captain," Horace said as he wiped off the gore on
the tip on his spear, on one of the dead. "What do you call the
move you did?"

"When I cut his head off?"

"No, when you bounced his skull off the rocks."

"Ah, that's called a 'spike.' Something from my world," he said,
scanning the piles of the dead.

Heaps of Wild Men with rent flesh lay scattered everywhere.
Abraham marveled that they had fought off so many muscular
men at once. But the Henchmen were good, very good—the best
who endured. Still, he searched for the Red Tunics. They had been
the first to fall underneath the wave of bruising bodies. He didn't
see them or Apollo and Prospero. His spine tingled.

Vern and Cudgel were lifting bodies out of the way and
slinging them aside.

"I found some!" Cudgel shouted brightly.

Skitts and Zann climbed out of the bloody pile. Caked in blood, they both sucked for breath, cuts and scrapes all over them.

Zann spat a finger out of his mouth. "That's nasty."

Abraham put a hand on Skitts's shoulder. "Are you well?"

"Never better." Skitts's eyes were wide. His crossbow trembled in his hand. "Sorry I fell, Captain. It won't happen again."

"Yes, it will. Just make sure that you get back up again."

Skitts nodded.

"Ruger, up here!" someone yelled.

Tark and Bearclaw were lifting Apollo out of a pile of dead Wild Men. Hunks of flesh hung from his armor. A nasty gash was still bleeding on his forehead.

The woozy Apollo asked, "Where's Prospero?"

All the Henchmen were accounted for except for Prospero. The company rummaged through dozens of the dead. Above, flocks of buzzards with black wings and white bellies began to circle.

Abraham's hand needled his palm. He couldn't bear the thought of losing anybody. It made him sick. It made him think of Buddy Parker, his wife Jenny, and his son, Jake. He'd been so busy he'd hardly given them a thought.

Solomon waded through the aboveground graveyard. He plucked bodies up in his mighty hands and tossed them aside. "Shush!" he said.

The company quieted but brought weapons to bear.

Abraham crept toward Solomon and bent an ear. A muffled snoring sound was coming from underneath the heap. He gave Solomon a curious look.

The troglin dropped his long arms down into the pile and started lifting away bodies. Inside a dugout of the dead, a battered and bloody Prospero snored loudly. He had a peaceful look on his face as if he were dreaming.

Solomon shook his head and said, "We found Prospero. It appears he had a better time than the rest of us."

The Henchmen roared with throaty laughter.

Abraham led the way up to the top of the stairs, where he met Sticks and Shades at the top. "Good shooting," he told her. He glanced at the magazine clips fastened to her web belt. "You didn't use them all, did you?"

"No."

He glanced at Shades. "Where's Melris?"

"Inside the gap, waiting on you… or us, rather," Shades said.

Two stone pillars created a doorway that led into the black space. The pillars were carved out of the natural rock and showed an assortment of monstrous faces. Abraham stepped up to the gap. A chill wind of stagnant air hit him like a slap in the face. He gave the Henchmen a nod and entered.

Melris was standing on a wide shelf of dirt, cradling his rod of devastation in his arms. His violet eyes had a soft glow, fixed on the black abyss looming below them.

Abraham moved out toward the ledge by the Elderling. The Wound was a humongous oval-shaped crater. Its depths were fathomless and as black as coal. A chill wind like an icy breath from an unknown source tore briskly at Melris's robes. Abraham could make out a narrow pathway that led down into the depths.

He looked at Melris. "Do you still think the stones are down there?"

"Yes," the Elderling said softly. "I can sense it."

Abraham lifted his brows, turned, and faced his party. "This is it. Everybody get patched up and eat something." He looked over the rim. "I don't think we're going to find any fast food down there." He sheathed his sword, moved up to Sticks, and grabbed the water skin she offered. "Thanks."

She nodded. "How do you feel?"

"Like I just killed a hairy hound giant. Why?"

"Your pupils are big."

"That's because it's pretty dark in…" Abraham's legs buckled. His view of Horace and Sticks swayed, and he collapsed into darkness.

76

EPILOGUE

Lightning coursed through Abraham's veins. He jumped out of his skin. His eyes popped open. Bright lights hanging above him shone in his eyes. His arms and legs were strapped to a medical table. He squinted. The surrounding room was black. A man wearing an all-white set of scrubs approached.

"You!" Abraham said.

The hard-eyed, curly-haired psychiatrist, Jack Lassiter, smoked a cigar. The two beefy orderlies, Otis, an older black man, and Haymaker, a big dumb-looking older man, walked behind Dr. Jack.

"You!"

"Well, look who's back." Dr. Jack leaned over Abraham's table and blew smoke into his face. "Is that you, Mr. Jenkins? Tell me, whatcha been dreaming?"

FROM THE AUTHOR AND THE NEXT BOOK IN THE SERIES

Thanks for reading *The King's Conjurer*. Man, I hope this was a wild ride for you, because that was my intent. I had a lot of fun on this one, and I want to fill you in on a few things.

I introduced a couple of other characters from Back Home: Mandi's cousin Sid and her husband John Smoke. These two characters are from my urban fantasy series, the Supernatural Bounty Hunter Files. If you are interested, you can read more about them here. LINK.

As I've stated before, I love crossing my book series together. It's a blast bringing in some cameos from characters whom you might have already read about. Smoke and Sid are some of my best.

Be sure to reach out and let me know what you think.

Book #5, *The King's Enemies*, should be released in late March 2019. Amazon Link to Buy!

Please leave a review on Book 4. They are a huge help to me! Here is a link.

*I'd love it if you would subscribe to my mailing list: www. craighalloran.com.

*Follow me on BookBub at https://www.bookbub.com/ authors/craig-halloran.

*On Facebook, you can find me at The Darkslayer Report or Craig Halloran.

*Twitter, Twitter, Twitter. I am there, too: www. twitter.com/CraigHalloran.

*And of course, you can always e-mail me at craig@thedark-slayer.com.

See my full book list below!

Please leave a review. They are a huge help for me!

OTHER BOOKS AND AUTHOR INFO

Craig Halloran resides with his family outside his hometown of Charleston, West Virginia. When he isn't entertaining mankind, he is seeking adventure, working out, or watching sports. To learn more about him, go to www.thedarkslayer.com.

Check out all of my great stories …

Free Books

The Darkslayer: Brutal Beginnings

Nath Dragon—The Quest for the Thunderstone

The Red Citadel and the Sorcerer's Power

The Henchmen Chronicles

The King's Henchmen

The King's Assassin

The King's Prisoner

The King's Conjurer

The King's Enemies

The Odyssey of Nath Dragon Series (New Series) (Prequel to Chronicles of Dragon)

Exiled

Enslaved

Deadly

Hunted

Strife

<u>The Chronicles of Dragon Series 1 (10 Books)</u>

The Hero, the Sword, and the Dragons (Book 1)

Dragon Bones and Tombstones (Book 2)

Terror at the Temple (Book 3)

Clutch of the Cleric (Book 4)

Hunt for the Hero (Book 5)

Siege at the Settlements (Book 6)

Strife in the Sky (Book 7)

Fight and the Fury (Book 8)

War in the Winds (Book 9)

Finale (Book 10)

Box set 1–5

Box set 6–10

Collector's Edition 1–10

<u>Tail of the Dragon, The Chronicles of Dragon, Series 2 (10 books)</u>

<u>Tail of the Dragon #1</u>

Claws of the Dragon #2

Battle of the Dragon #3

Eyes of the Dragon #4

Flight of the Dragon #5

Trial of the Dragon #6

Judgement of the Dragon #7

Wrath of the Dragon #8

Power of the Dragon #9

Hour of the Dragon #10

Box set 1–5

Box set 6–10

Collector's Edition 1–10

<u>The Darkslayer, Series 1 (6 books)</u>

Wrath of the Royals (Book 1)

Blades in the Night (Book 2)

Underling Revenge (Book 3)

Danger and the Druid (Book 4)

Outrage in the Outlands (Book 5)

Chaos at the Castle (Book 6)

Box set 1–3

Box set 4–6

Omnibus 1–6

<u>The Darkslayer: Bish and Bone, Series 2 (10 books)</u>

Bish and Bone (Book 1)

Black Blood (Book 2)

Red Death (Book 3)

Lethal Liaisons (Book 4)

Torment and Terror (Book 5)

Brigands and Badlands (Book 6)

War in the Wasteland (Book 7)

Slaughter in the Streets (Book 8)

Hunt of the Beast (Book 9)

The Battle for Bone (Book 10)

Box set 1–5

Box set 6–10

Bish and Bone Omnibus (Books 1–10)

<u>CLASH OF HEROES: Nath Dragon meets The Darkslayer miniseries</u>

Book 1

Book 2

Book 3

The Gamma Earth Cycle

Escape from the Dominion

Flight from the Dominion

Prison of the Dominion

The Supernatural Bounty Hunter Files (10 books)

Smoke Rising: Book 1

I Smell Smoke: Book 2

Where There's Smoke: Book 3

Smoke on the Water: Book 4

Smoke and Mirrors: Book 5

Up in Smoke: Book 6

Smoke Signals: Book 7

Holy Smoke: Book 8

Smoke Happens: Book 9

Smoke Out: Book 10

Box set 1–5

Box set 6–10

Collector's Edition 1–10

Zombie Impact Series

Zombie Day Care: Book 1

Zombie Rehab: Book 2

Zombie Warfare: Book 3

Box set: Books 1–3

<u>OTHER WORKS & NOVELLAS</u>

The Scarab's Curse—Sword & Sorcery Novella

The Scarab's Power

<u>The Scarab's Command</u>

The Scarab's Trick

The Scarab's War

www.ingramcontent.com/pod-product-compliance
Lightning Source LLC
Chambersburg PA
CBHW070638310726
48982CB00001B/327